The Redeeming Power of Brain Surgery

A Novel

Paul Flower

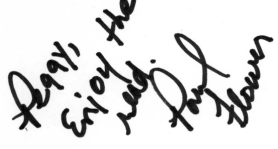

Scribe Publishing Company
Royal Oak, Michigan

The Redeeming Power of Brain Surgery
Published by Scribe Publishing Company
Royal Oak, Michigan
www.scribe-publishing.com

Author photo by Lauren Flower Witt.

ISBN 978-0-9859562-7-1
Library of Congress Control Number: 2013939793

Printed in the U.S.

DEDICATION

To Dad

Chapter One

His son's hand felt like a lie. Lately, to him, everything felt this way. The look of sadness on his wife's face, the burn of a drink in his throat, the whine of a saw in the O.R.; nothing seemed true. Nothing was real anymore. He felt out of balance, too. Even now, the school building, the flag slapping against the heavy fall sky—everything was tipping away from him. It was as though he'd gotten up that morning and screwed on his head carelessly, as though he hadn't threaded it good and tight. While shaving, he'd cut himself, a discrete, semi-intentional knick just under the curve of his chin. He'd stood there like an idiot, eyes feeding the message "blood" to his brain, nerve endings responding with "pain" and the logic center unable to formulate a response.

"Dad? Daddy?"

"Uh? Wha'?"

"Pick up the pace. Chop chop. Move out."

Now, as he snaked through the crush of other parents and children, he had to look down to convince himself the boy was there, attached to the hand, flesh and bone. The red hair, "his mother's hair" everyone called it, was sliced by a crisp white part; his head bounced in beat with his sneakered feet. The child was so painfully real he couldn't be a lie.

It amazed him that his son looked so much like his wife, especially the tiny mouth, the way it was set in a crooked, determined line. He was a kid who liked to have fun, but he could be fierce. Today, the challenge of a new school year, of third grade, had brought out the determined streak. This was good. They would need that streak, he and his mother would.

"Whoa." The tiny hand now was a road sign, white-pink

flesh facing him, commanding him. Far enough. He obeyed. Squatting, arms out for the anticipated embrace, he suddenly wanted to tell everything. Tears swam. His throat thickened. The earth tilted and threatened to send him skittering over its edge. There was the slightest of hugs, the brush of lips on his cheek, then the boy was off, skipping toward the steps as though third grade challenged nothing, caused no fear, as though the world was in perfect balance.

He walked back to his Lincoln Navigator with the exaggerated care of a drunk who didn't want anyone to know his condition. He got behind the wheel and suddenly was no longer in his fifties; he felt sixteen and too small, too skinny and insignificant to handle the giant SUV.

He nosed the vehicle toward home, alternately trembling and gripping the wheel as he merged with the morning traffic. The plan struck him now as odd and silly, the challenges too great. His hands, already red and scaly, itched fiercely. Get a grip, he told himself. Get a grip.

His tired mind—when was the last time he'd really slept well?—jumped from one stone of thought to another. Was everything covered at work? The bills—had he paid them all? Did his wife suspect anything? Yes. No. Absolutely. Of course not. Relax. Relax. He left the expressway at the exit that took him past their church and wondered if the church, too, was a lie. What of the wedding there so many years ago?

Through a stoplight and past a Dunkin' Donuts, his gaze floated around a corner. A flash of inspiration—hit the gas. Let the tires slide and the back-end arc around. Let physics have its way until the big vehicle broke free from the grip of gravity and danced head over end, coming to a stop with him bleeding and mercifully, gratefully dead inside.

No. He had something to do. Had he figured the angles right? Gotten the plan tight enough?

A horn jabbed through his reverie. He had drifted into the turn lane of the five-lane street. He jerked the wheel and cut across traffic into the right lane. Tires screeched, horns screamed. A black Toyota streaked past on his left, the driver's fist, middle finger erect, thrust out the window.

Rage, sharp and bitter, bubbled in his throat. He hesitated, then jammed his foot on the accelerator, cut the wheel hard, and sent the Navigator careening into the left lane.

A staccato barrage of profanity pounded the inside of his skull. He bit his tongue to keep the words in. His heart hammered and a familiar, dizzying pressure filled his ears. The SUV roared ahead, past one car, past a semi, then another car, quickly closing the gap on the speeding Toyota. He couldn't see the car's driver but he could imagine him, some stupid, simple-minded schmuck, eyes locked on the rear-view mirror as the lumbering Lincoln grew larger, larger, larger. The instant before he would slam into the smaller vehicle, he jabbed his brake and turned again to the left. There was a squeal of tires and more horns bleating behind him; the semi rig's air horn bellowed angrily past. Ramrod straight, eyes fixed ahead on the now-slow-moving car disappearing tentatively around a curve, he brought the Navigator to a shuddering stop in the center lane. He tensed and waited for the resounding WHUMP of a crash from behind. None came. Face flushed and eyes gleaming, suddenly rejuvenated, he accelerated quickly then eased the Navigator back into the flow of traffic—no looking back.

❖❖❖❖

He parked the Navigator in the garage next to the Mercedes and stopped to scratch the dog's head before heading into the house. The run-in with the Toyota had helped. He felt a little of the old self-assuredness returning. What he had to do was suddenly in focus. That the plan was silly or impractical no longer bothered him. He disarmed the security system, hung his keys on a peg, slipped out of his loafers and put them side-by-side next to the running shoes on the mat by the door. For a moment, he contemplated getting into his running gear and knocking out a quick four-miler. That really would help clear his head. A glance at his watch told him no, no way. He crossed to the kitchen sink. From the cupboard above it, he took a half-empty bottle of bourbon and a shot glass. He held the bottle at eye level and felt a pang of regret. When had he bought it, just last week? For some stupid reason, the thought made him want to drink more. He poured, drank, poured again, then placed the glass on the counter, replaced the bottle, and closed the cupboard door. He looked out the window over the sink. Through the trees, he caught a glimpse of his nearest neighbor, who appeared to be washing his Ferrari in the driveway. The young, athletic-looking OB-GYN had just moved in the week before. He wondered why the guy was home in the middle of a cold, gray day and why he was washing the damn Ferrari. He had the urge to punch him.

He picked up the glass and stared at the raw skin of his left hand, poured some of the booze over it, then, wincing, switched the glass and poured the rest over the other. Tears welled as the alcohol inflamed the raw nerves. The amber liquid ran off the ugly skin and formed a muddy puddle in the sink. Trembling, he rinsed the glass. He opened the dishwasher, pulled out the top rack, placed the glass upside down on a rubber-coated spike, and closed the door. The fire on his skin quivered and flared. His eyes burned. He was tempted to rinse his hands. Instead, he slowly rinsed the sink, then wiped it and the granite countertop with a paper towel.

He threw away the paper towel, bumped a hip against the kitchen door and walked quickly across the dining room, through an arch and into the living room. He picked up the remote on a coffee table and jabbed the power button for satellite radio. "Hair of the Dog" by Nazareth; he thumbed the volume button until the beat throbbed through the house.

In the second floor bathroom, he crossed to the sink, flipped up the faucet and angled it to the left. He let it get hot, so hot it hurt just to think about it, then pulled up the stopper lever. The water began to fill the basin, steam rising from it in a soft cloud that was both menacing and comforting.

He immersed both hands, bathing the skin in a new fire. He forced himself to keep them there, his eyes clamped shut, for ten seconds, then fifteen, then twenty. The time clicked through his brain.

Thirty seconds.

Thirty-five.

Finally, he could take it no longer. He flung his hands out of the water and whirled, searching wildly. There. He grabbed the monogrammed hand towel from its hanger. A groan escaped and he bit his lip, swallowing a scream. Through tears, he could see the skin was angry, scarlet. He stood for a moment, staring at the hands, which were now swathed in the towel. The music, dampened by the door, seeped through the pain. His phone vibrated against his thigh. Before he could stop himself, he freed a hand, pulled the phone out of his pant's pocket, swiped the device on, and held the phone to his ear.

"Hello?"

His own voice sounded odd, strangled. He cleared his throat.

There was a second of silence, then, "Jesse?"

"Yeah."

"Oh, hi. I thought you'd have the phone turned off. I was going to leave you a voicemail."

Why was she calling? Why now? What should he say? "Hello, this is Jesse Tieter, sorry I'm not available?" To his image in the mirror, he shook his head. There was nothing to say.

Jesse ran a hand through his hair, noticed that his eyes had deep circles beneath them. The circles only seemed to accent his long, skinny nose.

After all the years of lying, the fact that she was his wife and didn't know—couldn't know—gnawed at him. He loved her. He always had. But what he was going to do—what he had done—well, that said he never had loved her, didn't it? Didn't it undo everything? he asked the image in the mirror.

Didn't matter, the image said. It's too late. Put a fork in it. In what? In your marriage, in your life, pick one. Heck, pick both. Those circles under your eyes make you look like death, which is appropriate, don't you think? The strong chin (with the stupid shaving cut), the carefully maintained physique, what is it all worth now? *Nichts, mein Herr.* Kiss it. Good-bye.

Jesse nodded in agreement. What he'd done in his marriage was nothing; who he'd been long ago, well, that made everything else moot. The old Him, the long-ago Him, why, that was the real Him, the Him she didn't know. Their relationship was based on a lie. So anything else he did didn't matter.

He frowned. The feeling of being out of balance returned. His image seemed crooked and blurred. His lips were thin and pale and dry looking. Where was the lip balm? He used to be good about buying her flowers and leaving a card for her that said he loved her. But now he wasn't even good at keeping his lips moist.

"Did you get him off to school okay?"

"Yeah. Yes. Fine. It went fine," Jesse said, swallowing, blinking, trying to maintain his equilibrium. "Do I need a haircut?"

"What?"

"A haircut? Think I need one?"

"Why do you ask that now?"

"Just wondering. I was wondering if I could use a haircut. I mean is that such a big question?" His image, shaggy haired, waved and quivered.

"Well, you always think you need one before I do."

"Not an answer."

"What do you want me to say?"

"What you think. For once."

"Since when did you care what I thought?"

"Since now. I just asked if I needed haircut." The image was focused now. Clear. Angry looking, frowning.

"If it would help your mood, then get one when you get there."

"What do you mean by that?"

"Nothing I guess, other than you've just been awfully cranky lately," she said. "After all these years, you'd think I'd get used to your moods."

"Like you never have them." Jesse sneered at himself.

"What?"

"Moods."

"Moods? Not like you. Sometimes I wish I could figure out what was in that head of yours."

Jesse was suddenly wary of her. His brain felt like a ball of dirty string. It was unraveling, the unraveled portion frayed and tired, the rest of the ball bouncing down some dark steps, down into shadows and blackness.

"Did I get you in the middle of packing?"

"Umm, yes. Yes, you did." He dropped the towel to the floor, opened a drawer of the vanity, fumbled for the tube of hydrocortisone cream. Phone propped between shoulder and ear, he begin rubbing the salve on the back of his hand. "I'm kind of in a hurry."

"I told you, you should have packed last night."

"Thanks for the advice now. I needed that."

"Jesse, come on. I'm just picking on you a little."

"And isn't that fun."

"Well, it used to be. You used to occasionally actually joke around. Or have you forgotten what that's like?"

"I haven't forgotten," he sighed. "I haven't forgotten anything."

"Then… I don't know. Relax. We never used to fight like this."

"So it's all my fault."

"What is?"

"It's my fault we fight."

"I didn't say that."

"Just implied it."

Anger, like a snake, uncoiled in his gut and slithered

through his chest. "Ever think about the pressure I'm under? Ever?"

"Don't start on building that house or working over there. That was all your idea. I said I'd back you on it, but don't start complaining now. Besides," she softened her tone. "The house is done and you don't have to worry about it. You can just go over there, do your visitation, a few procedures, relax at night all by your little lonesome in our darling second home and come home when you're done. Just know we'll miss you while you're gone."

He couldn't respond to that.

"I love you," she whispered.

Again, he couldn't respond.

"Jesse?"

"I'm right here."

"I was going to say that, well," she paused. "Maybe you do have a lot on your mind, a lot inside that brain of yours. And maybe that's the problem."

The snake was gone. But there was a buzzing, the stirring of flies, of millions of them, in his head. "Maybe what's the problem?"

"Maybe you don't need to just keep all of it inside. Maybe it wouldn't be a bad idea to share some of it with someone. Maybe there are people who actually care."

"Starting with that again? Care about what?"

"About you. About whatever it is," she said. "Whatever it is that's bothering you."

He tried to open his mouth. The flies were making it difficult to speak. They were humming, millions of them, humming and humming in his head.

"So now you're going to play that game?"

"What…" He swallowed. "…game?"

"The game where you act like nothing's wrong. That one. The one where you act like, 'Oh, poor me' every waking minute, like we're supposed to either feel sorry for you or just get out of your way because you're so nasty, and then you're all, 'Oh, don't worry, nothing's wrong.'"

"Look. Look. Stop... stop being such a... stop trying so hard," he said. "Let it be." The flies were now an ugly black sound, throbbing in his back, between his shoulder blades, making it hard to breathe. "Let it go."

Her voice, usually strong, quivered with emotion. "Jesse, what's going on?"

He switched the phone to the other shoulder and closed his eyes. For the second time in an hour, he really wanted to spill it, the whole story.

"Is it that girl? Andrea, was it? You know, you did everything you could with her. That wasn't your fault. You know that."

A sigh, ragged and weary, shuddered through his chest and the flies broke free, scattering. A watery shadow—his mom's face?—stuttered through his memory. Trembling, he began rubbing the cream into the other hand. "Look. I... I... I really have to get moving. The guy at the hospital over there is expecting me by one o'clock their time. The Ryan's going to be a mess. I'll be lucky to be in Indiana by noon. Heck, they probably have me in surgery tomorrow at dawn."

"So that's it? That's all I get? Just, 'Bye, gotta go'?"

Jesse put the cap on the tube of cream.

She sighed. "I just wanted to tell you to have a nice trip and I'll see you in a week. Guess I should have skipped it." The phone went dead.

Jesse returned the phone to his pocket and dropped the cream in the drawer. He held the gaze of his image in the mirror. "Buck up," he growled. "Buck. Up." Gretchen and Rev. Conkle at church had been trying to get him to loosen the hold on his feelings. Screw that.

In their bedroom, he unsnapped the suitcase and laid it open on the bed. He took out his phone again, scrolled down the touchscreen and found the list he'd created the week before. He studied it for a moment, then opened a drawer of his dresser. One by one, he removed and refolded all of the items before stacking them neatly, squarely in the suitcase, deleting each item on the list before moving to the next drawer. When the dresser was empty, it was on to the closet. Two garment bags were already unzipped and hanging, waiting. These he filled with the same meticulous speed, smoothing each shirt or tie or sport coat before stowing it.

Packing took fifty minutes, about what he figured. He even remembered to include the shoes he'd left by the door. After that, it was a matter of loading his things in the Mercedes. He was on the road by 10:30 a.m. He didn't leave a note.

Chapter Two

It was the discarded disposable diaper that nearly did him in. Smeared into the wet asphalt next to the Mercedes, it was a pulpy, muddy brown reminder. You've come all the way back, it said. Welcome home, doc. He paused, door open, one tassled loafer poised over the mess, a dark image buzzing through his head. The person who'd dropped this *thing* out of her car, this nothing person, was fat and ugly, someone with a dirty baby on her hip and a baby bottle filled with red Kool Aid in her hand. Right now, no doubt, she was inside the greasy spoon restaurant, feeding her face while the kid squished a french fry in his toothless gums and stuck a dirty finger up his nose.

The scent of the car's leather seats, the warmth of the interior, beckoned. It would be so easy to pull his foot into the car and head back to I-94. Slip into his Neil-Young driving mode. Neil would sing, and Jesse would join in. In an hour, they—he and Neil—would be out of Michigan, gliding through the night, sailing around the bottom of the big lake. In two hours he could be back home.

But if there was anything Jesse Tieter understood, anything he valued, it was an obligation. This one had been around his neck, heavy as stone, for the better part of a lifetime. He had been stupid and wrong to let it hang this long.

The diaper squished under the weight of his first step. Wind-driven drizzle slapped his face. From the restaurant entrance, a tinny loudspeaker played oldies—Fats Domino's "Blueberry Hill" segueing to "R-E-S-P-E-C-T." Aretha.

Jaw set, Jesse Tieter slammed the car door behind him, flipped up his coat's collar, hunched his shoulders, and started around the back of the car.

Paul Flower

To his right, thirty yards away, ran the crumbling two-lane road into town. An old pickup truck slowed, brakes squawking, then shuddered to a stop. The yellow-gold glare of the parking lot lights illuminated the face of the driver: a heavyset black man, his baby face and chubby cheeks cut by shadows. A knife of recognition twisted in Jesse's gut.

The baby-faced driver regarded the oncoming traffic with wide-eyed expectation and a faint smile, as though any one of the vehicles hissing by in the other lane might contain a friend. Simple-minded fool, Jesse thought. Once the last of the traffic had wooshed by, the driver bit his lower lip and palmed the wheel. The truck jounced into the parking lot, the tailgate rattling over a pothole, the headlights washing Jesse. He held his ground, head high, wind blowing his hair, stony-faced, acting as though he'd been left waiting in the elements for far too long. He shot the driver a scowl. The reaction was quick, a flash of wide-eyed surprise, a touch of embarrassment. The guy's passenger turned to glance at Jesse. Her eyes went wide. Good. Good, the voice inside his head—the long-trusted voice—said. Good.

They were early. Even though they'd seen him, they were probably too scared to leave the truck and come inside, at least until the appointed time. The idiots probably would have a smoke or two, something to screw up their courage. Jesse turned and trudged toward the truck stop. He would go in and wait for them, take some time to get his thoughts straight.

The fragrance of greasy food—the bacon and burger and fried onion smells of his mother's kitchen—rushed to greet him as he opened the door. The memories that pooled in his subconscious spilled into his brain, spattering and hissing like grease on a hot griddle.

❖❖❖❖

Jesse numbly, dumbly followed the waitress to a table and took a seat. He stared out the window and, as it had so many times in recent weeks, his mental projector blinked, stuttered, then rolled the film. It was 1967. He was lying in bed, the smells of home and breakfast all around, lying there stewing about The Beatles record and the bike he wanted to buy. And there it was, the truth, solid gold, in the echo of his mother's voice from just a few days before.

"You can solve all our problems," the voice, coming back to him tinny and warbly, said. "You should just kill the man. If you hate him enough, you should. A smart boy like you, a young *man* like you, you could do it like you was on TV. Just pull the trigger, BWAAM!, then go about your business. No one would ever know."

She was right, he'd thought. For once, his mom was absolutely right. As he lay there that hot hot morning, Mom's voice was so real inside his head that it made Jesse Icabone— that was his name back then, Icabone, not Tieter—feel creepy. It was like instead of being downstairs in the kitchen, she'd shrunk herself into a tiny mom, clawed her way up to the room he had to share with his stupid brother, shinnied to the top bunk, and snuggled into his skull so she could tell him this thing. Jesse had felt like that a lot, like Mom had crawled inside his brain. For a second, he was more worried about her being all shrinked up inside him than he was about her being right.

It's not easy being a kid and having your mom in your head, Jesse thought as he lay there. It was not easy at all. Lately she was *always* there. He'd hear her in the sing-songy whisper—the same one she used when they had their special times alone. She'd get him a cookie from the secret hiding place, the place only he and Mom knew about, behind the Bisquick box in the cupboard over the sink. The cookie was most always an Oreo—his favorite. He'd get started on peeling the Oreo apart and she'd hover over him, yakking in that soft sing-song.

"You should do it," she'd say. "Yes, you should. Do it for you and for me." It was scary and weird having her talk to him that way, but it was kind of cool, too, when you thought about

17

it. Geeze, Mom made him feel like a grownup, like Sheriff Matt Dillon in *Gunsmoke* on TV—someone who could just kill a man dead if he had to. Someone who knew it was his job to do and didn't back down.

It was his job to do. He could do it. He should.

She was right. And he was *stupid stupid stupid* for not realizing it until now. He was as stupid as his idiot twin, almost stupider than Dad himself.

The cough of a lawnmower battered the Saturday-morning quiet. To Jesse it sounded like someone had grabbed the thing by the neck and choked it. He twisted and looked through the rusty screen into the backyard two stories below. It was an ugly yard: shaggy grass that needed mowing, broken toys, a clothesline that hung low like a dirty old noodle between two rusty posts. The man was down there somewhere, trying to get the piece-of-junk mower started. Like always, he wasn't having any luck. Everything they owned was junk, and that man couldn't fix any of it. Half the time Mom asked him, Jesse, to try to keep things going. Jesse knew a lot about stuff. Jesse Icabone read books and magazines at the library. He read all the time. He read everything. And he tried to fix stuff the best he could, when he could. Mom said he was the real man of the house. Jesse was *responsible,* just like every good man should be, Mom said. And she was right. He always felt like he needed to solve things. To take care of things. Mom said it was because he was maybe born old. Like he'd been maybe twenty or twenty-five years old when he was a baby.

Something felt heavy in his chest, and Jesse Icabone closed his eyes till it passed. He imagined how other kids lived. Other kids didn't have to take care of stuff. They didn't feel so *responsible.* He forced a sigh from his lungs and felt better. It wasn't his fault, was it? No. It was Dad's fault they didn't have anything nice and that he, Jesse, had to pick up the slack around the house. Mom had told Jesse Icabone that. She was right.

"You down there, addle-brained boy?" He shot the question at the bottom bunk.

The Redeeming Power of Brain Surgery

Just like he'd figured, his brother was gone. He was out in the woods most likely, playing hide-and-seek or something with the stupidest kids around. Jesse used to play games and stuff with Elvis, but that had been a long time ago, back when they were really little. That was before Jesse noticed how weird Elvis was. Elvis was crazy. He was always acting up, getting Mom mad. He was hyper. He was wild. He was *irresponsible*, Mom said. Dad laughed it off. Dad said Elvis just marched to the beat of a different drummer, that's all. Mom said Elvis wasn't completely right. He's a little nuts, is what she said. Mom said Elvis was just like his father, so why should Jesse hang around with him?

At least they weren't identical twins. People said they looked alike but not alike. Mom said if you stared at one and looked half away, your brain might think the one you were staring at was the other one. But then you'd think, no, because they weren't totally *identical.*

Jesse was gifted. He'd gotten all the brains and Elvis, he'd gotten the butt end of the stick. That's what Mom said. She was right.

Mom was right about a lot of things. She said when you lived in a little town people always talked behind your back. Jesse had heard them doing it. Just last week he'd heard some ladies at the grocery store talking. Another time it was some men in the barber shop. He'd heard lots of people talking, talking, talking about Dad and the guys he hung around with—his old army buddies that called themselves the Raiders. Dad had that bad leg from getting shot in the war, but that didn't give him and those no-account Raiders buddies an excuse to hang around the house, sleeping and staring off, sucking on beers and yak yak yakking. That's what people said. Lots of men had come back from Korea all weird and lost, but you didn't hear them giving all those excuses. That war had been over for years, but here they were, going on and on about it, crying over spilled milk.

Dad was crazy, lazy and stupid; that's what people said.

Sometimes he had a job, but most times he didn't. A lot of times he yelled at Mom and him and Elvis, too. He yelled awfully loud, mostly after he'd been drinking good and hard with some of his Raider buddies. Afterwards, he'd do what Mom called "sleep it off." Jesse had seen the man a million zillion times just sleeping on the ratty lawn chair in the yard, Pabst Blue Ribbon cans all over the grass, mouth open like he was catching flies.

Last week, Jesse Icabone had made a big mistake. He'd tried to wake Dad up from the sleeping off, and Dad had come out of it mumbling and lost, his eyes shiny and wild and bloody-looking. Before he knew what was coming, the man's big right hand was on his face, covering his eyes and nose and mouth, the long fingers squeezing, squeezing, a funny sound, like a growling animal coming from the man's throat. It hurt something awful. Jesse couldn't breathe, and the hand had smelled like beer and sweat and something else Jesse thought was just plain bad. Something hot had twisted in Jesse's chest. He had broken free, the heat in his chest rising, rising as he ran. He hadn't stopped, not until he was far away, way back in the woods behind the house. He'd heard his dad's voice, all jaggedy and thick. *I'm sorry,* Dad yelled, *I'm sorry.* But even Dad's voice hadn't called him back.

Now, when he thought of him, Jesse couldn't feel anything but the hot thing.

"I'm sorry, Charlie," Dad had said at breakfast the next morning. Jesse just frowned. Dad sat there at the table, his hair all clean and combed from the bath he'd taken, looking like a little boy that had just got out of bed from being sick. "Sorry, Charlie. I wasn't myself yesterday," he said. "I owe you one, Charlie Tuna."

He'll never amount to nothing. He'll never be good for you. Or us. You should solve it. You're the one who can. The only one. You should do it. And walk away.

She was right.

Yesterday, Jesse had run outside to catch Dad before he

left for work—a dead-end second-shift factory job at this stupid wire factory in town—in his nasty old '59 Ford pickup truck. "Hey, Dad? Can I get a new record? The Beatles, they got a new one out."

The man just laughed and pushed Jesse away, sending him stumbling. "No way we can afford nothing like that, partner," he said as he got in that rustbucket of his. The hot thing had swelled inside Jesse Icabone then.

You should do it, the voice had said. Yes you should. Yes you should.

Dad had driven off, and Mom sat Jesse Icabone down with an Oreo and milk. She told him how mad Dad made her and how much she hated the way they lived.

Mom was right. They lived poor because of him. They had nothing because of him. People talked. Because of him. The house was stinky and ugly. Because of him.

Mom's voice had gone all cool and brittle inside his head. "I even got a idea of how to explain where he's run off to," the voice said. "Not too many people are going to ask. Once you tell one person the story, everyone in town will know it. They'll believe it too, because they'll want to." She laughed softly, way down low in her throat. "People will want to believe he run off and deserted his family. It makes good gossip."

For the first time, Jesse Icabone started thinking through all the angles of killing the man. "What about Elvis? What if he starts asking questions or maybe figures something out?"

"We can take care of your brother," Mom answered with a little snort. "You can take care of him."

She was right. Geeze Marie, Jesse thought. He was the kind of boy who could do it—tell Elvis the same story they told everyone else. He was Jesse Icabone, the smartest kid in town, maybe in all of Van Buren County. And if Elvis asked too many questions, well, Mom would help him take care of Elvis. She would. Wouldn't she?

"You should do it," she said, cupping his face with her icy, knobby-knuckled hands. Jesse frowned and pulled away.

Something about Mom—the way her voice was so sweet but a little *too sweet*—was starting to get on his nerves. She was right, yes. But. Her breath always stunk like bad pickles and cigarettes. She could look a lot nicer if she tried. She was short and skinny, a scarecrow in a dirty blue dress that hung like an old bag on her. Her hair was a dirty reddish color and, like always, messy. Those eyes of hers were like tiny dark marbles bouncing around in a puffy-bag face. Her lips, they were dry and thin, and they twitched sometimes when she was talking. Mom always used lipstick that was red and made her skin look even paler than it was. She ran the lipstick extra-high around her mouth, like she was trying to make her lips seem fatter or something. It ended up just making her look stupid.

She was right. But there was something about her that wasn't. There was something that wasn't right at all.

The spells, Mom's spells, had been happening a lot lately. She'd just sit in a chair in the living room or stay in bed like a big fat slug for what seemed like forever, then all of a sudden she'd come out of it, talking all loud, acting nervous and yelling or jabbering on about this and that. The worst times, when she was really, really in the mood for talking, she'd tell him things he didn't want to know, awful things. One night, when Dad was at work and Elvis was inside watching *Gilligan's Island* on TV, Mom scootched up next to Jesse on the front porch and said in her whisper voice, "'Member when I was gone when you was little?"

He did remember, but only a little bit; it was like a dream to him. She'd left them all alone with Dad, and Dad had to make the meals; mostly, they'd eaten Chef Boyardee ravioli out of the can. That's what Jesse remembered, eating the Chef Boyardee.

"Yes, Mom. I do," Jesse answered carefully, not sure what she was getting at.

"I'd had my fill of—of all this. So I went to live someplace nice for awhile. Went to my sister's in Iowa," Mom said. "She and her husband, your aunt and uncle—probably you don't 'member them since you only seen them but once—they live like people should live. They have a nice place and go to lots of parties and so on. Your Aunt Barb, it was her that talked me into coming back to try and work things out; 'course she got no idea how hard it is. She's got it good."

Jesse was sitting on the porch railing. He felt like jumping down and going inside. Watching *Gilligan's Island* with his dumb brother was sounding like something he wanted to do, after all.

"When we was little, in Chicago, Barb and me, we had everything we wanted: pretty clothes, nice rooms of our own," she went on. "Your grandpa was a good man, a man who worked hard and was real successful. He had a job in a meat-packing plant but was management potential; that's what they told him the year before his heart gave out. He wasn't going to be a packer forever. He was on the fast track, they told him. 'You got management potential,' they said." She spit out the last word, *potential.* "But I grew up stubborn and wild and stupid, you know that?" Mom scootched closer to him. Jesse could smell her breath, could feel it on the side of his face, but he didn't look at her. He stared at her ugly feet in the milky light from the house and the single dirty bulb that hung over the front door. His stomach felt funny.

"We used to come over here for vacations—over to this two-bit-piece-of-Michigan nothing. The summer I turned nineteen, I had to fall in love with the first dumb local yokel that would pay attention to me. He was older than me and a *veteran,* so I thought that made him special. He'd seen the world. Should've known it just made him screwed up. Should say I *thought* I'd fell in love. I really didn't. Never loved him, you understand. Your daddy's never meant nothing to me."

Jesse felt a little sick. Mom turned away, took a deep breath and kept on going, talking like he wasn't there, her voice soft and raspy. "When Daddy said, 'Stay away from that young man,' I just laughed in his face. I got knocked up by your daddy on purpose." She looked down at the dirty wood floor.

"We got married here, and got us this nothing house in the country on account of there was nothing else to do. Suppose it was my punishment, having twins and all. And my daddy had that heart attack right after."

The day after she'd told him that story, Mom'd talked about all the bad Dad did—about him being lazy and *abusive,* she called it. For the first time she talked about the gun she'd hidden and how it was already loaded. She told Jesse how she always relied on him for everything. She relied on him to think for her when she was tired and having a spell. She relied on him to wake up Dad when he was sleeping it off. She relied on him to keep Elvis in line. Now she needed him for this, for taking care of the man. She'd said it in a way that made him feel special. Now Jesse closed his eyes and pictured the gun aimed at Mom. He felt like he was going to puke, so he pictured aiming it at Dad.

She was right.

He could do it. He *should* do it. Nobody would ever know. No one would ever think too-tall Jesse, dumbnut Elvis' twin brother, could kill a man. Jesse could see how dumb they'd look—everybody in town—if he did the killing and got away with it. Stupid, that's how they'd look, standing there at the Dairy Queen and the post office when he walked in, a boy man-killer all normal looking, a perfect little angel. They'd look real real stupid and Mom would look proud.

The more he thought about it, the cooler it seemed that he'd make Mom proud. He couldn't think of a time when she'd been proud of him.

Jesse's face, a long, somber kid-face split by a nose that seemed too big for everything else, twisted into a crooked smile. He stretched, touching the end of the bed with his toes, and ran a hand over his butched-off brown hair. The idea of killing a man suddenly wasn't an idea at all. It was a thing he was honest-to-Pete going to do today, doggone it; something as normal, natural and okay as Honeycomb cereal for breakfast and the sound a baseball card makes when it's clothespinned to the spokes on your bike. It was something he had to do because he was the real man of the house. It was his job. The smile grew bigger as he watched a fly crawling across the crack in the ceiling. He imagined killing the fly and, as he did, he felt something different, something humming in his chest, like electricity was arcing over his heart, moving back and forth from lung to lung. It wasn't a bad feeling at all.

Jesse swiped at the fly and grinned when he felt the thing tickling his palm, trying to get away. He let his fist fall to the mattress and kept it clenched, fighting the urge to crush the fly and the competing urge to let it go. He turned on his side and, with his free hand, flipped on the transistor radio that hung on his bedpost. Larry Lujack in Chicago was talking about the weather being hazy, hot and humid. Lujack started talking up the next song. It was The Beatles' new one, "Strawberry Fields Forever," the record Jesse wanted to buy.

Jesse let the fly go, snapped off the radio and slid off the bed.

Usually, he liked to be careful when he got ready. He had a thing about looking neat. That's what Mom called it: *a thing*. But this morning was different. This morning he had a job to do. He tore off his pajamas, folded them sloppily and threw them in his drawer, telling himself he'd come back later to straighten them. He dressed in a rush, putting on his cut-off blue jeans, an old shirt, socks and PF Flyer tennis shoes. He did take an extra second or two to tuck in the shirt; he hated having it hanging out. Then he glanced at himself in the mirror and grinned. She was right. Heck yeah. She was right.

❊❊❊❊

He usually hated the way the house smelled on muggy days. But that morning, the stink of cigarettes, cat pee and lousy housekeeping had been replaced by the smells of good things: bacon, sausage, eggs and coffee. It was like Dad was already gone; the house and life were better already.

Mom was bent over the kitchen table, her back to him.

Jesse crept up behind her, shuffling quietly across the yellow, cracked linoleum, thinking he was going to yell, "BWAAM!" and scare her.

Mom whirled, her eyes wild, and jabbed a dirty table knife at him. "Haven't I told you what time breakfast is?"

Jesse was already taller than Mom, but somehow she made him feel smaller. "Yes, Mom, you told me. I was just..." His voice came out squeaky.

"Then why'd you sleep through it? You sick? Or you getting lazy like every other man around here?"

"Sorry." The word fell out of his mouth.

"I ain't got all day to wait for you. I'm busy and I have things to take care of, you understand?" She pressed the knife into his nose. Jesse smelled eggs. "You don't get nothing now, you hear me?"

"Yeah, Mom." He didn't care. His stomach was squirming.

"Don't you never, never do that again," she said, some of the edge coming off her voice.

"I won't, Mom. Promise."

Tears glistened on the rims of her eyes. "'Course you won't, baby," she said softly. She started to turn back to the table.

Now, Jesse thought. Make it up to her. "I... I thought about what we've been talking about," he said carefully.

Mom froze, holding a plastic plate smeared with egg yoke.

"I... let's..." He didn't know how to say it.

Mom put down the plate softly, like it was a fresh, unbroken egg. She put the knife on the plate, turned and smiled. "You want to show me what kind of man you are." She stated it softly, nodding her head and expecting him to do the same.

"Yeah," Jesse said hoarsely.

"Oh baby, that's great, baby," Mom said. She put a hand softly to each side of his face. The hands were cold and quivering. "You going to make your mom proud?" Her voice squeaked. The eyes, black pellets, searched his eyes, her brain reaching into his, scouring it, looking for doubt. Jesse felt his knees going to Silly Putty, but he held the gaze—buck up. She let go of him suddenly and hurried from the room. "I'll be right back, honey."

Jesse swallowed hard. His hands felt slimy; he wiped them on his shorts as he wandered to the little window over the sink. From the foyer, he heard the closet door shutting.

His eyes roved among the dirty dishes on the counter. Next to the black-iron frying pan there was a pink plastic bowl with a little milk in the bottom and a couple yellow Sugar Pops stuck to the inside near the rim. The bowl was glued to the plate by a smear of yellow egg yolk. He saw himself as the sheriff again, bringing the man the Sugar Pops and eggs, letting him fill his stomach before he took him out in the street and shot him.

"Here it is," Mom whispered, sending prickles up his back.

Jesse turned. She was just inside the arched entry into the kitchen, holding something behind her back, part of the thing showing above her right shoulder. It looked like two black pipes welded together. He swallowed his disappointment. He'd thought the barrel would be shiny; that the gun would be smaller too—at least like the Winchesters he'd seen on TV. On TV, guys were always using sleek, easy-to-handle Winchesters.

"Well, come on now," Mom said, a pained expression on her face. "If we're going to do it today, we got us a lot of work to do, so we best get started."

Jesse had meant to ease into this thing. But Mom was bringing the clunky gun around from behind her and laying it across his sweating palms. He heard the doors of escape slamming behind him.

Maybe not today, Mom. *Slam.*

Let's think about another gun. *Slam.*

Let's talk through this once more. *Slam.*

What about while he's in bed, sleeping? *Slam.*

Could you give me a second? I have to go to the bathroom. *Slam.*

Slam. Slam. Slam. Slam. Slam.

Paul Flower

He was suddenly above himself, floating, watching this boy, Jesse Icabone, boy-*sheriff*, kneeing the back door open and slipping into the yard, squinting against the glare of the sun, an ugly black-double-barreled gun gripped awkwardly in his hands. Jesse couldn't hear the birds singing or the wind in the trees. There was a humming in his ears, a humming that sounded like angels, something God might like to hear. The hum grew inside him, mixing with the flutter of wings, a million dove wings, he thought, the music of heaven, rising in his chest.

He'd expected to circle around to the front yard and sneak up on the man, but what was this? The idiot was in the backyard, right in front of him, not twenty yards away. He was bent over, his back to the house, fussing with the stupid lawnmower. Had he heard the door? Of course he had, but he wasn't looking. The stupid jerk had no idea what was coming. He couldn't hear the angels singing louder and louder, the doves beating their wings to the music in Jesse's head. He couldn't see the gun, even this huge, stupid gun.

Hurry, *hurry*, Jesse whispered to himself, tears suddenly running in hot rivers down his cheeks. The angels and doves were hurting his head now; they were loud, too *too* loud. He shuffled to within just ten yards—an easy shot at the back of this man, this dumb idiot man. Jesse watched the gun come up, squinted against the pain of the music and the birds, all the stupid birds. Then, without warning, the man shifted his weight and his shaggy-haired head began to turn. No, no, Jesse's thoughts screamed down to the Self in the yard. Don't let him move. Don't.

Jesse turned and let the gun drop behind him. The angels and doves evaporated. He was no longer above himself, watching. He was there, in the backyard, wiping wildly at the tears.

"What's up, par'ner?" The man had turned completely.

Jesse looked to his feet. The dandelions, buckhorn and grass were tall and the gun was behind him; the man couldn't see it clearly, at least Jesse thought he couldn't.

Hurry. *Think fast.* Jesse glanced up, still wiping at his face. "Oh, nothing. Just um... just going hunting with the BB gun. Got something in my eye, though."

About fifty yards away, over the man's shoulder, something—someone?—darted through the woods that bordered the yard. Twigs snapped. The man was putting down his tools and starting to stand. "Want me to help you out, bud—with that eye, I mean?"

Jesse glanced to the man, to his own feet, to the woods. There was something in the man's voice, something that sounded funny. And *who was in the woods?* This was all wrong, all *horribly, terribly* wrong. "Um, ah, no," he said, wiping at the eye. "I got it. I got it out, I think."

The man frowned, his eyes clouding. He opened his mouth, acting like he was going to say something important, paused, seemed to reconsider, then he gave Jesse a tight little smile.

"Suit yourself," the man said, then turned and settled back to work.

Jesse looked to the woods. There was a cough from behind him. Jesse turned. The back door was open a little; Mom stood just inside, her face was hazy and distorted by the screen and the shadows. With a rush of shame, Jesse picked up the gun, swung it to his shoulder and wheeled. *Yes,* he thought, *yes.* The man's back was to him; he was squatting in his tight-fitting jeans, his white T-shirt riding up his skinny back, showing a pale stretch of skin above the belt and just an inch or so of the dirty waistband on his underwear. The stupid, simple idiot didn't have any idea.

Jesse sighted down the barrel at the man at the skin above the underwear. She was right, Jesse thought to himself. *She was right.*

"Jess. Please. Don't. Please no." The voice was so quiet, Jesse could barely believe it had come from the man. *"Please,* bud,

no," he said again, his voice reaching out and squeezing Jesse's heart.

Jesse paused, his fingers frozen on the triggers of the shotgun. The shaggy-haired head turned again. The skinny back, Jesse's target, twisted away. The eyes, the blue-gray eyes that looked so much like Jesse's and Elvis' came around and locked on his. The face, long and narrow with a big hooked nose, was sad and hurt and something else, angry maybe. Jesse had never seen his father like this. No. His father opened his mouth to speak again. Jesse could see the word in his eyes: *Please.*

No.

BWAAM.

Chapter Three

Jesse had been knocked to his back by the kick of the gun.

He struggled to his feet, grimacing against the hollow ache in his shoulder and trying to force the air back in his lungs. For a few seconds, everything was hazy. The events of the morning shuffled through his brain in no predictable order; flashes of images overlapped and careened past one another. Nothing had gone the way he'd figured it would. He closed his eyes, but the world kiltered and swayed, so he opened them again.

"WHHHHY? WHYYYYYYY?" The voice from the woods, half-whisper and half-scream, swirled around the yard on the dirty breeze. Jesse's knees nearly buckled again. It sounded weird—*unreal*—a fake voice from a movie or something, and it quivered down his back like a wiggle of electricity. Jesse took a step as though to leave, to run, get away, but he stopped himself, eyes cloudy, frowning. Wait, he thought, wait. No. Get a grip.

He turned and looked at his father. The face, the pasty-gray face, was so twisted with pain that it punched Jesse's gut. Then the tortured death dance began, and Jesse felt himself go light, airy—empty. It reminded him of the day the week before when he'd watched the robin hatching in the gnarly apple tree at the edge of the woods. He'd shinnied up in the tree and out on this big limb, and there was the nest. The old momma robin had squawked and carried on, but Jesse had sat there, quiet and still, as the beak poked out of the pale blue shell, then the little wet head, and finally the fragile, almost-naked bird.

Watching the bird being born had been too big for words,

really, or for feeling. This was like that, but bigger, awesome, *unreal*. Jesse stood, frozen, as the familiar head kicked against the right front wheel of the Craftsman lawnmower. The cow-boy-booted feet cut muddy scars in the soft green of the yard. The man's skinny hands clawed the air like he was trying to pull up on some magic chin-up bar to get out of the dark, deep pit he was falling into. Jesse took it all in, gawking at the way his father let his life leak away; it spouted out of him like the black-red hole in him was a break in a dam. The blood throbbed onto his white tank top T-shirt, spread down into his jeans then ran onto the ground. The angels returned, humming, humming, humming in a wild, rushing chorus that sounded like fire, musical fire, fire fanned by the wings of a million soaring doves. Jesse, killer, felt something deep and powerful rumbling in his chest, something too big for words. Then, suddenly, his dad stopped gyrating, his mouth slack, his eyes staring past the lawnmower at some point in the sky. The angels, the wings, the fire faded. There was nothing.

The screen door slammed.

Jesse Tieter, M.D., his eyes bluish-gray and empty, stared across the crowded restaurant at the idiot waitress. She'd slammed the cash drawer like she was having a bad day, like someone as backwards and simple knew what a bad day was.

❊❊❊❊

He had come of age in Davenport, the intelligent, intense boy living the lie as his mother had concocted it, living as though his father had deserted the family and he, the bright son, had been shipped away to live with his mother's sister and her husband. The boy who began life as Jesse Icabone from Michigan became Jesse Tieter from Iowa. In high school, he had been quiet, almost withdrawn, a brilliant young man who felt awkward in social situations, who preferred three hours in the library to two hours screwing around with other kids. Focused and hard-working, the valedictorian of his class, he had been distant with his aunt and uncle. He'd cut off most contact with them as soon as he was able to live without their financial support.

Jesse had worked his way through college and med school. During his undergrad years at the University of Iowa, he'd met the perfect girl, someone equally quiet and hard-working who didn't expect much more than that from him. They loved each other in a quiet and reserved way. They'd married the summer after earning their degrees—his, pre-med; hers, elementary ed. Gretchen, pretty and strong-willed, had knocked on doors in Chicago, landing a job teaching Kindergarten at an inner-city school only weeks before his first semester at Northwestern. She waited tables at night. He studied.

His view of their first years together had become distorted. He recalled suppers at midnight—warmed-over pizza illuminated by a candle he'd made in an empty milk carton—and lovemaking on the beanbag chair in front of the black-and-white TV junk-picked from the neighbor's trash. In truth, for Gretchen, their early years had been tense and exhausting. A gifted neurosurgeon, a young and ambitious one, Jesse Tieter, M.D. had in fact focused not on candle-making or lovemaking, but on staking a claim in the medical hierarchy of Chicago. Beanbags and pizza had been a sideshow, career the main event. Jesse was intense and driven, a zealot for his own cause. Not that Gretchen regretted the results. The long study and work shifts had paid off; after completing his education and residency and shunning offers from hospitals across the country, he and a former classmate had formed Neurology Partners of the Great Lakes. The practice was now regarded as one of the Midwest's leaders in technique and treatment.

Jesse and Gretchen had established roots in suburban Evanston, where they'd bought and sold three different homes before settling in their current one, a four-bedroom Tudor Gretchen lusted after and had jokingly called "the house we'll die in." They had gained a small circle of friends and Robbie, their now eight-year-old-redheaded dynamo.

Of the people who knew Jesse—never "Jess," a name he

viewed as only slightly lower in class than Jesse—Tieter, many called themselves acquaintances or colleagues. Few considered him a friend. Gretchen was gentle, kind and well-accepted, although guarded in revealing herself to others. Jesse was an enigma. A brilliant, intense workaholic with a passion for late hours and a lust for perfection. He had a brain for brains, his partner said, but not much time for people. There was something different about him, those who knew him often said. Something missing, something "you just couldn't put your finger on." His wife and son felt this missing thing, but in the nature of families, they had learned to live with it.

In the blackened corners of his memory, the event that marked his life, that defined who he was, flickered like a mostly forgotten black and white home movie. Up until a few months ago, he'd only considered it rarely and half-consciously, seeing it as bluish-white slivers of light streaming between the fingers clamped over his eyes. It scared him as a nightmare might, but then was gone.

Late one night about three months ago, sitting in his recliner sipping a drink and listening to John Lennon, Jesse had been contemplating his life at its middle point. For that night, and several thereafter, he had rooted among the long-guarded memories. As fate would have it, his mom—his real mom—had called. It wasn't unusual that she'd contact him; he'd grown used to the unplanned nocturnal conversations. But this time, they'd veered into the forbidden terrain. She or he had brought up the thing; had spoken the unspeakable for the first time in decades.

Mom, tired and aging, had grown worried. Worried they'd be discovered. Worried that all the years of careful covering-up would be wasted.

Her worry had infected him. Over the days that followed, the confident air of a top-notch doc was replaced by something far less certain. He became indecisive. He began to let tough cases eat at his psyche. An oncologist in South Bend had referred to him a teenager with a stage four *Glioblastoma multiforme*—a viciously fast-growing cancer. Andrea Sparks had been 19 and beautiful. Despite the fact that there was no hope for her, she had looked to Jesse with shining, gracious optimism. His typical reaction would've been to dismiss the case with a clinical analysis confirming the oncologist's worst fears; the way he saw it, the small-town doc just needed someone else to be the bad guy. Instead, Jesse had worked like a demon to help her. For three weeks, he'd pored over text after text, working into the night, e-mailing and calling clinics around the globe. When Andrea had died, he'd gone to his office and wept.

Jesse had hated the feeling of helplessness, the weakness in it.

*****

He fought the urge to go to the bathroom and wash his hands. Gritting his teeth, he shifted in his seat and ran a skinny, long-fingered hand though his hair. He thought again about a haircut. He rubbed the back of one hand with the fingertips of another, trying not to use his nails. Nails sometimes made his skin bleed. He glanced around the truck stop at the flannel-shirt-and-blue-jeans crowd and wondered if his Mercedes was safe in the parking lot. He hoped nobody recognized him or, worse yet, mistook him for his twin.

He just couldn't believe he was here, back home after all these years. He, the great brain surgeon from Chicago, had just finished rendezvousing in the night with a couple of slow-moving, backwoods Michigan morons, hoping they'd handle something he should have handled thirty years ago.

They were gone now. The meeting had been mercifully short.

A fly hopped down from the stainless steel napkin holder and bumbled across the paper placemat, pausing to fidget with its legs in the ring of water left by a glass. Jesse swiped at the fly, clenched his fist and smiled as he felt it tickling his palm. He scratched his reddened knuckles and tightened his fist, squeezing against the tickle until it stopped, then opened his hand and stared at the fly stuck to his skin.

"Stupid, simple-minded insect," he hissed. The waitress slid the coffee he'd ordered onto the table in front of him. Jesse looked up and nodded, held his palm out so she could get a good look at the mess, and gave her a silly little smirk. She shot him a nervous grin and moved on to the next table.

Maybe he'd gone to elementary school with the waitress. Maybe she was one of the buck-toothed morons that had turned his stomach back in second grade. He snorted a laugh, picked the fly off by one bent wing, flicked it on the floor, and rubbed at the gunk on his palm with a napkin. The bathroom and the soap dispenser beckoned again. He swallowed hard and threw the napkin at the little juke box on the table, closing his eyes as he took a deep breath. "Man, that's a lot of blood," he heard his voice say, and he could see it. The blood was spreading out in a crooked circle around his dead dad in the yard, and Mom was slowly stepping around it, her mouth open. The blood was so dark and red and there was so darn much of it. The boy Jesse dropped the gun and stepped back a step, then another. As he fought the urge to run, his tears came harder. He didn't understand this crying. He knew Mom wouldn't like it, but he couldn't hold it back. The tears, the sobs, just came and came and came, pulsing, throbbing out of him.

Get a grip, Jesse told himself. Stop it. Stop it. He clenched his eyes, forced down a swallow and bit his lip hard. You have no time for this, he thought. It's just blood. And he's dead. It's over. It's over.

When he opened his eyes, the waitress was looking at him from the cash register, open-mouthed. Behind her, a busboy was also paralyzed and staring. What had he done? Jesse wiped the tears from his face and nervously glanced around the place. No one else seemed to have heard or seen anything. He shot the waitress and the pimply faced busboy a scowl and shifted in his seat to look out the window.

You're a good man, Jesse told himself. You've made a decent life for yourself. You've helped people. You've saved lives. That counts for something. It has to count for something.

He missed his wife. By now, she and Robbie would be cleaning up after dinner, preparing for the evening ritual of homework and a shower and TV. He would call them later, but he would keep the conversation light.

In the murky glass darkened by the nighttime backdrop and steam from the food and coffee, his reflected face was puffy, the hair mussed and tangled. Jesse turned away to sip the coffee.

The flashbacks from his childhood were coming daily. The grainy mental newsreel was playing over and over in his head like a song. He couldn't get enough of it and he couldn't get away from it. He saw it at night in his dreams, over breakfast with his family, some days even at work during surgery. It rattled him, making him weak, empty and unclean. He'd look into a mirror, a shiny surface, a cup of coffee, and Mom would be there, talking about it. She would be staring into his eyes, reaching in as far as she could go, getting into his brain like she was a surgeon, peeling back his skull so she could see his bad thoughts. She was reminding, reminding, reminding him about what he'd always known—about what he'd done. She was screaming for him to remember the worst part. That Elvis had been there. Elvis had seen everything.

In the truck stop's window, Mom's puffy face was angry and frowning. A cigarette dangled from her mouth. "You're going to let him get away." Her voice was high and nervous. She took the Kool from her twitching lips and sent a shaft of smoke out the right side of her mouth. He could feel her foot tapping the ground in front of him. "You gonna stand there and cry and let him get away?"

"But I shot him, Mom," he heard his boyhood voice say, the boyhood voice coming out jagged and wiggly like a cry-baby's. Jesse coughed and tried to smooth it. "I k... killed him. No... nobody's getting away. I nailed the sucker to the ground.

You saw." Smack. The back of a bony hand stung his cheek. Mom gestured with the Kool toward the woods.

"Him. Your brother. He saw the whole damn thing. Didn't you see him watching from the woods? Didn't you? And now you're standing here crying like a baby while he's getting away—maybe gonna tell someone what he saw."

Jesse swallowed, trying to resist the hot rush of the returning tears. Mom brought her hand up again and he cringed. Softly, she touched his burning cheek with her palm. "Sorry, honey," she said in a whisper, her voice cracking as she talked around the cigarette. "I just forgot myself there in all the excitement." The hand fell away. She took the cigarette out of her mouth and shot another shaft of smoke sideways. "Hurry now and go get your brother. Hurry baby, go." She put a little heat back in her words. "Hurry, you stupid…" Her voice was drowned by the humming of the angels, by the sound of the doves' wings banging around inside his skull. He could kill her. He knew it. He could do it and just walk away; no one would ever know. He looked down at the gun then at his scaly, pink hands. They were shaking as he reached for the coffee cup. Jesse pressed the palms together firmly and squinted, fighting back the tremor. "What good's a brain surgeon with shaking hands?" he growled at himself.

❖❖❖❖

Jesse Icabone, the boy man-killer, searched for the witness, his brother, all alone. Mom helped a little, screaming Elvis' name from the backyard, but she was careful not to follow Jesse. Jesse was glad she didn't, because it wouldn't have been a good idea to leave Dad dead in the yard.

Jesse covered the woods and fields behind the house, crossing the hiking and motorbike trails, rolling under overhangs and poking into thickets. He kept thinking he'd run into somebody—a lot of other kids were usually screwing around in the woods, playing hide-and-seek or war or something; sometimes you'd find older kids in their cars, kissing and necking and stuff. That day, that hot hot hot day after he'd killed his father, the smothering humid air had forced everyone to the beach or the air-conditioned movie theater downtown—somewhere. Through noon and after, Jesse, alone, looked frantically for his jerk brother.

Mid-afternoon he plopped down on a rotting log along a muddy creek bank. His clothes were pasted to him with sweat and his legs were cut and bleeding from the underbrush. He scratched wearily at the mosquito bites on his arms and face and the backs of his calves. It was still hot and muggy but the wind was building and gusty, pushing heavy dark clouds across the sun, turning the day gloomy. In the distance, thunder rolled. The storms that had been brewing earlier were getting their act together and coming this way. Jesse stared at the mud.

"You killed him. I didn't see a thing," the tiny Mom said from inside his brain. "They'll think you did the whole thing on your own; heck, 'cuz you did. I was in the house the whole time."

She was right *again.* He was a killer, Elvis had seen him be a killer, and Mom, she couldn't help him—couldn't lie for him or anything. That's what she'd said, and she was right.

He wanted to go home and clean up the mess then talk to Mom quietly, maybe over an Oreo. He wasn't really mad at her anymore. Mom was moody and sometimes did things that were mean. All they needed to do was talk things over and everything would be okay. After he dealt with Elvis, they'd do that. Then Mom would act a little nicer.

Jesse frowned. The more he thought it through, Mom was right about a lot of stuff. She'd called Dad and Elvis "two peas in a pod," and that was totally true. Dad was so dumb and lazy he'd dropped out of school in tenth grade. Elvis probably wouldn't even make it that far. Elvis and the old man were wimps, too. If a bunch of kids started making fun of him, Elvis laughed right along with them or just hung his head like a dumb dog and walked away. Dad, well, he was always just going to work and coming home and drinking with his buddies and, when he felt guilty, doing what Mom said. It made Jesse sick sometimes to watch.

Jesse stopped himself. He'd been thinking of Dad as being alive. His throat felt thick. He closed his eyes and saw the face—it'd been more like a mask, really, than a face. Where was the man's soul? Was it still there, inside the body in the yard, or had it flown out of him already? Jesse had read about souls and thinking about them now made him sad, sadder than he'd been all day, sadder than maybe ever.

Jesse heard sobbing. At first, he thought maybe he'd started crying again and was so tired that he didn't realize it. He got to his feet slowly, listened, and heard it again; someone else was crying. Jesse jumped the creek, pushed into the woods on the other side and stopped. Above the wind, he heard it once more. Jesse followed the sound, holding his breath and stepping carefully like he was an Indian sneaking up on a settler to scalp him, something he and Elvis had done a zillion times back when they were just little stupid kids, before Mom helped him realize how dumb Elvis was.

He broke through the tree line. Just ahead, above the top of a grassy knoll, rows of pines waved mockingly at him. Mentally, Jesse kicked himself. The pine grove was a hiding place he'd forgotten.

He trudged up the knoll, and stopped to listen at the edge of the grove. The sobbing floated in the air, the breeze snatching it away then bringing it back, teasing him.

Jesse scratched a mosquito bite on his left elbow, then one on his neck. He pulled up the hem of his shirt to wipe away the sweat that was stinging his eyes. The breeze felt good on his exposed, sweaty belly.

The thunder rumbled, louder now, as Jesse ducked into the grove. Planted in perfect, even rows, the trees stretched out in front of him, up over a rise, then angled down and away to the right. The floor of the grove was a thick padding of brown needles. It was a cool and dark place and, because of the needles and the wall of trees, it was quiet. Jesse had always thought it would be a really cool place to read in or maybe even to live in. There was order here; everything was in its place, just the way things should be. The only noise, except for the whistling of the wind through the limbs overhead and the occasional creak of a trunk, was the sobbing; it seemed softer now, too, like you were only allowed to cry quietly in a place like this.

Ahead of him, at the top of the rise, there was a flicker of color sticking out from behind one of the gray-brown trunks. Jesse took a deep breath and tried to calm his thudding heart.

Moving carefully, running from tree to tree, pausing to catch his breath between sprints, he made his way toward his brother's hiding spot. When he was just a few steps away, Jesse stopped, leaned back against a trunk and closed his eyes. He was tired, so stinking tired, and thirsty and hot. He saw his father's face and a knife sliced his heart. He choked back a sob. No. No, the voice in his head said. You don't have time for that. He saw his mom's eyes, smelled the cigarette and heard her say, *"No alibi."*

Jesse tried to focus his busy, tired brain on Elvis. Elvis was easy to hate. Jesse hated him and all the stupid, simple people like him that he had to deal with every day. Geeze, they were everywhere: kids with bad teeth and dirty clothes who thought lighting farts was the most fun thing in the world, waitresses who cracked their gum and talked to him like he was a stupid moron, teachers who always smiled when they gave him a question they thought he couldn't answer.

Jesse wished he had a gun. If he did, he could just shoot his brother and every other idiot he came across.

A gun. The gun. The thought took him back again. His legs were suddenly rubber. BWAAM. The blood. The boots digging. His father's face. All of it bumped through his head like pool balls.

Jesse Icabone bit his lip and snarled at the memories. The voice in his head was firm. "No crying. Get on with it. You can do this. You CAN do THIS!"

Thunder rolled again. The wind followed on its heels, sighing through the grove. Trees swayed and groaned like they were scaredy cats that wanted to tear themselves free and run for cover.

Jesse looked around at the dancing pines, closed one eye and mentally aimed a gun at one. BWAAM, Jesse thought. BWAAM. BWAAM. BWAAM. He mouthed the word as he moved the gun from tree to tree, victim to victim. When he was done, he stared at the sky, his jaw suddenly set, his lips pressed tightly together. Through the swaying green of the pines, he could see blotches of steely gray clouds.

"Hey Elvis, what'cha doing here?" he yelled.

The crying stopped, the thunder rumbled and Jesse felt the cool touch of a raindrop on his face. He stepped around the tree.

Elvis sat on the ground, his back to a pine, his legs pulled up against his chest. His hands were cupped together against his knees like he was holding something made of glass. The knees and legs below his cut-off jeans were scratched and bleeding. Welts on his arms and legs were scratched open and seeping blood too, and his PF Flyers were so muddy, Jesse figured Mom would throw a fit. But his face was the worst. Streaked with dirt, scratches and mosquito bites, Elvis' face was red and blotchy from crying and his expression was something deeper than sad; it looked like someone had come along and kicked his heart right out of him.

"What's wrong, bud?" Jesse asked, squatting and looking into the face that looked like his own: blue-gray eyes, oversized nose, the fuzz of brown hair on his head. Jesse tried to ignore the moron's runny nose and tear-streaked cheeks. "We been looking for you all afternoon. Storm's coming. You look like you lost your best friend."

A clap of thunder rolled under his last sentence, and Elvis shuddered like he'd been slapped. He turned to stare at Jesse and opened his mouth to speak, his hands still cupping something against his knees.

"What'cha got there, bud?" Jesse asked, reaching for the thing.

Elvis gagged on a sob and pulled away.

"Come on bud, we need to get going. You been gone most of the day and Mom will be wondering where we're at. 'You boys don't know enough to come in out of the rain,' she'll be saying." He yammered on like they'd been out for a nice walk together. "She'll be all over us for sure, Elvis."

Jesse reached down and grabbed his brother's dirty arm and jerked him roughly to his feet then let go. Elvis, hands still together, stumbled a few steps and tripped over a log. He fell to his knees, and the thing he'd been holding flopped to the ground.

It was a baby robin.

The bird began to chirp wildly as it tried to hop away. One tiny, weak wing dragged uselessly in the pine needles, slowing it down. Lightning flashed. The sad, broken bird froze. Thunder cracked, and the thing started moving again.

Control your brother, Jesse thought. You can't kill him, because you have no alibi. But you can control him. With two quick strides, Jesse was on the bird. He stomped once, twice, then ground the thing into the soft needles of the pine grove. He felt the soft cartilage breaking under the sole of his tennis shoe. Jesse's stomach rolled and twisted, but he swallowed hard. He set his jaw and turned to his brother.

"Why'd you do that?" Elvis struggled to his feet and rushed at Jesse, his hands balled into fists. "Why?" He was screaming. The wind was growing stronger, moaning through the trees.

Jesse pushed his brother away. "What'd I do? I just helped you stand up. You're the one who tripped," Jesse said, arms outstretched, palms up.

Elvis stood, arms hanging, mouth open.

The rain came, knifing through the trees with the wind. The hair on the back of Jesse's neck bristled.

"I saw everything," Elvis tightened his fists and clamped his eyes shut. "I saw..."

Jesse crossed to his brother and grabbed him by the shirt with one hand. He slammed Elvis against a tree.

"You didn't see a thing, you understand me?" Jesse screamed and twisted Elvis' shirt, holding him fast against the tree. Elvis wriggled, trying to get away and shield his face from the rain.

"Yes I did. I saw. I saw. I saw," he said, voice rising to a howl. He tried to open his eyes against the rain. "I was standing behind the tree. I watched everything. You and..."

Jesse relaxed his grip enough to let Elvis think he could jerk free, then slammed him back against the rough bark. Elvis' mouth opened but no sound came. Jesse pushed his nose to within an inch of his brother's runny nose.

"Look at me," Jesse growled. "Look at me." The crackle of thunder and the flash of lightning were simultaneous. "Look at ME."

Elvis was shaking, twitching, trying to wriggle, his eyes shut. Jesse's heart was an engine, roaring with the storm. The feeling he'd had as the man had died—the powerful rumbling deep inside him—was back. He was man enough to do this, to take care of it. He'd do it and no one would ever know. "LOOK AT ME, YOU ADDLE-BRAINED MORON."

One eye cracked open. Jesse stared into the sliver of blue-gray and spoke in a voice that was low, mean and slithery. "You saw nothing today—not a thing. You understand me? Your daddy left home and he ain't never coming back because he was a lazy, good-for-nothing man, and that's it."

The lightning and thunder ripped in a wild, stuttering dance across the heavens. Elvis froze, his eyes and mouth now wide in a silent scream.

"You..." Elvis croaked out the word and stopped.

"Me?" Jesse grinned and twisted the soaked ball of the shirt a little tighter. It was time for the knock-out punch. "Me nothing. You don't remember a thing about me and if you ever try to remember, if you ever think you saw something that I told you you didn't see..."

Jesse paused again. Elvis' eyes had become cloudy. This was too tough a concept for him. Jesse cleared his throat and thought for a second. "Let's put it this way. You ever tell anybody anything bad about Dad then I can send you to the same place, to the place where he is."

Elvis looked like he'd been punched and Jesse smiled again. "Yeah. Now you get it, don't you, brother?" There was another wicked clap of thunder. Jesse let him go. Elvis slumped to the floor of the pine grove.

"Now you get it," Jesse repeated, kicking him once for good measure.

❈❈❈❈

"Refill?"

Jesse jumped. The waitress was topping off his coffee. "Sure, yeah, whatever," he mumbled, dropping his hands below the table. He thought for a moment, then he sat up. "I mean, thanks."

She poured and then started toward the kitchen, glancing back as she did. She bumped into the busboy. They exchanged glances. The busboy returned to clearing a table, giving Jesse a guarded glance. Jesse flipped the kid the finger. The kid's gaze dropped and he went back to work in earnest.

That the anger rose in him so easily, so matter-of-factly, disturbed him. But, he told himself, this was who he was. This cold-hearted, vicious other Jesse was true. He was real. Fighting him was no longer reasonable.

Jesse wiped a film of sweat from his forehead. The urge to wash his hands, to feel the cleansing rush of the scalding water on his skin, quivered in his stomach and groin. This washing compulsion had intensified over the past several months. The peeling, raw skin forced him to lie to his staff and patients about "skin trouble." Even in the most routine office visit, he had to cover his skin, both as a protection against HIV and to keep anyone from seeing the awful condition of his hands.

His plan was rash and wild and simple and stupid, and he

knew it. Stage one had been building a vacation home here. Stage two had been re-establishing control over Elvis by controlling the people near him. These people had been easy to choose; Mom had told him all about Lavern's and Elvis' stupid buddy, Donnel.

To make it all come together, all he needed were a couple of local hired hands, redneck hoods he'd had to snoop around a few back-alley bars for. This town was full of such creeps.

Jesse imagined his mom sitting in her shadowy room in the nursing home up north. He hadn't gone there in years. But he envisioned her listening to him describe the plan, saw the smile on her face that told him she was pleased with it. "You can really stop worrying," he'd tell her, reaching out and patting her frail hand, sucking her into the conversation. "I'm making everything fine for you, for us, forever." There'd be a fragile smile warming her gray face. She'd be proud of him, happy that he'd done his duty. "I don't want you to ever, ever have to worry again. Not about Elvis. Not about any of this," he'd continue, getting her drunk with the words, with his blinding devotion, before slowly turning the thing around, pulling out the scalpel. "I mean, heck, I always have been good at cleaning up all the shit you spewed into the world." A dirty word, shit, her smile disappearing, the face going cold and hard as he spit it at her. "I mean, that's what it's all about, isn't it? It's all about you," he hissed, the verbal scalpel shining now, in a shaft of sunlight. "It's about you and getting everything tidied up so nobody smells you. Nobody smells the evil sick shit of you." The face, her mean, pruned face, would disappear then, back into the shadows, snapping back to avoid the blade, although he'd keep coming, thrusting it at her. "But it won't work, will it, Mom? It never did and never will, will it?"

"Of course it will. It did. And you watch your tone with me," she'd hiss, her head, all of her, now out of the light, back in the shadowy void of the barren airless room.

He'd laugh then, a dry and heartless cackle. "Sure, I'll watch my tone. You horrible, wretched, sick bitch," he'd say, leaning toward her in the shadows, her wooden chair creaking as the gray face—eyes wide with horror—the long and dirty hair, the smell of her, rocked away from him. "I'll do whatever you want, won't I, Mom? Isn't that the way you've always wanted it? Me, fixing shit—" again, the bad word; she hated her boys to use such words "—for you, just like you fixed shit for me and Elvis. Isn't it? Isn't it?" He could see her in the murky light, rising, stumbling out of the chair, the pale upper arms and stringy neck scare-crowed out of the dirty blue nightgown.

"You stop that," she'd wail. "You stop that kind of talk. You stop." He wouldn't stop. For once in his life, he'd rise, walk to her, stand over her and finish his diatribe as she huddled, fetal-like in the corner. "You got rid of your husband because you wanted this great life. And once he was gone, oh boy, did you live. You lived your life like a hermit, a dirty ugly nothing witch in that big haunted old house, spending all your time tending to stupid Elvis and watching television. You didn't get a better life out of it. Not at all. And now, well look at you now. You're just lying on the beach enjoying the sun, aren't you? These are your golden years. And they've really worked out for you."

"I... you listen here," she'd say, attempting to uncoil, the head turning, maybe that gnarled finger of hers wagging at him in the gloom. "You got no business talking that... why I... I got no golden... but... we had a life..."

"After he was gone, you worked as a clerk in a store, a stupid nothing clerk."

"I had no chance," her voice would rise, growing shrill, almost visible now in Jesse's mind, almost luminous. "I had no chance. I had no time. That stupid brother... "

"You had no chance," he'd say with a snort of indignation, "because you had nothing after he was gone. You had no chance because you're so simple and weak. You had no chance because you were too busy drinking, too busy drinking and doing nothing, nothing really for Elvis, feeling sorry for yourself and doing nothing. And thinking thinking thinking about what you did to us. About what you made us do, me do."

"You stop. You stop right now young man."

"No. You know what? I won't. I won't stop. I won't because you know what the truth is. The truth is, you murdered MY LIFE, and for what? For what? You ended up no better off than before. And I ended up like this. I'm a mess, Mom. A mess, because of you. Because you're a sorry, sick, nothing human being."

"That's not true. That's not…"

"What's not true? How sick you are? Or how about the drinking? The lazy nothing self-pity? Or the fact that you are just as sorry and stupid and worthless as you thought he was?"

"As who?" Her face, he could see it then, he could feel the rage coming off of it in waves.

Jesse broke from the fantasy. Mopping his face with a napkin, he allowed himself a small smile. About two years ago, he'd had someone get in touch with Mom's doctor here in town. Through the intermediary, the local doc had gotten a substantial amount of tax-free income from Jesse, "a silent benefactor in Chicago." In exchange, the doctor had done a complete work-up on Mom, then insisted she was seriously ill, which was pretty close to true. He'd had her admitted to an assisted living facility in Traverse City—a good four-hour drive away. The staff had been told Mrs. Icabone "tended to exhibit bizarre behavior due to a history of depression and side effects from medication;" she was allowed to contact only her son, the doctor. Her mail was closely monitored, too. Nothing left the place that wasn't addressed to Jesse Tieter, M.D.

The *coup dé grace* had been having his mother declared dead. It had been a risky but brilliant move. Again, all it had taken was a lump sum payment to the facility's director. No one, not a single family member or friend, had ever bothered to see if she really was dead. No one had asked for the body. No one had made funeral arrangements. They'd all been so scared of her they'd been relieved she was gone.

As far as Jesse could tell, Elvis, who'd grown up despising his mother, had never questioned her admittance to the hospital or the veil of silence. He never even tried to make contact. Notified of the death, he hadn't even requested the body for burial.

Since then, Mom's health really had deteriorated. Between the booze and the stupid Kools, she had pretty much destroyed herself.

Jesse swallowed hard and stood, still fighting the tremor in his hands. Unconsciously rubbing the back of his hand against a pant leg, he scanned the truck stop for the waitress, then reached for the wind breaker he'd discarded on the seat next to him. He patted his back pocket and fumbled for his wallet. There was no sign of the waitress or the check.

"Well, sorry, honey," Jesse said to himself as he shoved his wallet back in place and started for the door. "Guess that order's on you. I got things to do."

A few strides from the table, he stopped, thought for a moment, then smiled. He walked back, bent over and picked up the dead fly then flicked it on his place mat. "There," he said with a leer. "At least I left a tip."

He turned toward the door, hesitated at a sign that pointed the way to the restrooms. Jesse closed his eyes and breathed deeply. After several seconds he walked into the parking lot and to the safety, and misery, of his car.

Chapter Four

He had grown up in his hometown, living the lie as his mother had concocted it, believing his father had deserted the family. Despite the buzzing in his head that told him something wasn't right, something wasn't true, he'd believed he was an only child.

For his mother, it was one heckuva surprise that Elvis took the lie as gospel. Her plan had worked; her stupid, simple plan. It had been almost too easy. To start with, she'd just gotten rid of any evidence of his brother, burning with the trash whatever Jesse hadn't taken to Iowa. Then she had worked her magic—that's how she saw it, as "working her magic." In late-night talks, and occasional lock-downs in his room—"quiet times" when "he wasn't thinking straight" and needed to "get right"—she slowly worked on Elvis' brain. At night in bed, alone with her thoughts, she'd pictured herself as a doctor, operating, cutting out of his simple brain what he knew about the past, leaving for Elvis just what he needed to remember today. After a month or two, in a move she figured was brilliant, she stopped talking about the other two members of the family. It was like they'd never ever walked the earth. She acted like her stupid husband had gone away and the other boy had never been born. For the boy Elvis, it became a matter of will—his. He could decide to keep them alive in his memory or kill them. Like she'd hoped, he took the easy way out.

As a teenager, school was Elvis' escape. So was free time with his girlfriend and best buddy. To his classmates, he was a laid-back, quiet guy with a weird sense of humor who'd climb the water tower on a dare or skinny dip in Lake Michigan in February, but would never ever speak up in a crowd, especially not in front of an adult. He'd quiver if a teacher so much as raised her voice at him. Not too bright and not too stupid, they called him; he was a simple boy who seemed to have something to prove but didn't have a clue of how to prove it or even what it was. He hated being the center of attention but seemed to crave it. He was weird. In a lovable, goofy kind of way.

He and his girlfriend married the summer after their senior year. She was a determined gal. Wanted a family and a nice house. So she answered an ad in the local paper and landed a job as a clerk at city hall. Already working part-time at the biggest factory in town, Bonner Wire, he was inspired and pressured by his bride's ambition, so he enrolled at a junior college 20 miles away. He hated it—being in classrooms again made him want to puke, he told her; he quit college after a week and went to work full-time at Bonner a month later.

Now, at mid-life, Elvis seemed at peace. You could chalk it up to years of self-control and suppressed emotion. Or you could say he actually had found his place in the world. In truth, he had cut life down to the basics. He made no waves. He hoarded no grudges. He ate balogna when it was served, even if he wanted grilled cheese. He aspired to nothing, even though he knew this attitude irritated his wife to no end. His wife had always wanted a house filled with shiny brass, thick rugs, marble and sunlight. But that was beyond his reach. Why, they'd saved and scrimped just to buy their small ranch: kitchen, living room, a hallway to two bedrooms, and a bathroom; it was your basic tract house some contractor had built with a couple of hammers and a cookie cutter. The house contained no children, another disappointment that ached in her heart. He felt helpless to solve it, although, deep down, Elvis Icabone wished he could.

Elvis rationalized the failures he saw in his life by focusing on his small successes. He had worked his tail off for Bonner Wire, just to put a roof over their heads. A couple of years back, he'd worked his way up to the loopers. These were noisy,

The Redeeming Power of Brain Surgery

dangerous machines that fed copper wire onto spools at high speed, coiling it as they went. The job was tough, demanding and you really had to focus to prevent jam-ups. Jam-ups on the loopers meant the line shut down. A good looper man, especially one who showed he was committed to the company, was hard to find. Now he owned a house and took his wife out to the Phoenix Inn for a chicken dinner once every couple of weeks—not bad, he figured. Not bad at all.

The talk about him in town was a quiet whisper that never died. Almost everyone knew that his dad had deserted Elvis and his mom. There was gossip about a brother or sister leaving. But no one talked about it in front of Elvis. And most people who shared it knew that a part of their story, the good part, the really really important part, was missing.

They said you could feel the missing part in Elvis.

Lavern, his lover and friend and spouse, knew about the missing thing, although she didn't know what it was, exactly—this made the knowing all that much harder. She wanted desperately to fill the hole it left in him.

Today, for him, the thing was humming sadness, grief, meanness, madness and fear, all of it wrapped in confusion. And it was nothing at all. Elvis knew, yet didn't know, that he'd been taught to avoid it, to not *see* it—to forget it. His mother had told him to never ever think about it, so Elvis didn't fully remember that she'd ever mentioned it.

He always had seen Lavern as his savior. Lavern had helped him to think sunny thoughts. Dear, sweet Lavern.

Lately, it wasn't working, the sunny thinking wasn't. It seemed like Lavern's sweetness had soured. And as it had, Elvis' carefully constructed internal wall, the wall that held back the past, had begun to crumble. Lately, when she was in bed and he was alone with his beer and old collection of record albums, Elvis Icabone had felt the past darting around him, hovering, buzzing, annoying him, begging him to pay attention.

Late one night just weeks before, as he slouched in the bean bag listening to John Lennon, Elvis had done something

53

he shouldn't have done. Curious, like a puppy, he'd tip-toed to the edge of the blackness inside him, and he'd tasted something awful—a smell, an odor that was sweet but a little too sweet—rolling off of it. Before he understood what had happened, he was drowning in the past. Flickering, ugly snips of light and sounds, BWAAM, voices and that smell, overpowering and awful and his mom's finger wagging at him and at someone else, someone mean and someone bleeding and a bird, soft and fragile, broken on the ground and a great empty nothing-something hurt. BWAAM.

He'd shut it out.

Since then, he'd felt close, too close, to something about him that he didn't want to know, something best left alone.

❋❋❋❋

What was the word? Phosphor... phosphorescence. That was it. The moonlight on the field was like that, like phosphorescence, to Donnel. Out there in the open field, out beyond the battered hood of his truck, he imagined deer were moving, silent and invisible as ghosts, flitting through the shadows, grazing. In his beer-muddled head, Donnel could see them in the phosphorescence of the moon's glow: deer and other animals scurrying, rooting for food and hunting for each other. He shifted his gaze to Lavern. "So you still want to keep this quiet, huh?" He took a hard swallow from his can and swept a couple empties from the seat between them, aiming them toward a hole in the floor.

"I said I just don't know," Lavern said carefully. There was a tiredness to her voice that worried Donnel. He shifted his big frame into a position facing her. The truck rocked a little.

"Listen lady, maybe you just nodded off and didn't catch what's been happening around here. A couple months ago, this guy shows up at your house in a big ol' Mercedes, looking kind of like your husband, only this guy's all dressed up with his hair cut fancy? Says him and Elvis are twins, they was separated when we all was kids before we even got a chance to know him? That's pretty weird, don't you think? Seems like we woulda knowed he had a brother. And now that we supposedly do, seems like something we might want to ask around about, doesn't it?" Donnel stopped and took a long drink. "Wait, wait," he continued, gesturing with the can. "There's more. This twin brother from hell says he's been raised in Iowa by some aunt and uncle. Only now s'posebly he's a brain doctor from Chicago who's been working part-time at the special new nervo... neurogo..."

"Neurology," Lavern said quietly.

"Yeah, yeah, this new special place where they've been taking brain patients at the hospital the last little while—working back in 'his old hometown' as a 'visiting specialist on a special, small-town project,' he says. Hoo boy, that's one huge mother of a story, you ask me."

Donnel took another quick swig and kept going, on a roll now. "Oh, and here's the cool part. He says something awful happened in the family when we all was younger. We're s'pose to believe that, even though Elvis don't seem to remember none of it. He don't even remember he's got a twin brother. He ... he ... what'cha call it?"

"Repressed the memory."

"That's it. Recessed it. You buy all that?" Donnel snorted at the thought.

"I believe him," Lavern said in a whisper. "I believed him the first time he come to the door; I believed him tonight still."

Donnel thought again about deer. Hunting season was only a couple weeks away. "Why don't no other black dudes hunt 'sides me? Ever wonder that?" He looked at Lavern. She was biting on her lower lip—one pretty, white tooth clutching the pink of her mouth. "You're scared, aren't you?"

"Scared?" She looked out the window. "Scared of what?"

"You're scared of what the brain man, this Jesse Tieter, M.D., said tonight."

She sighed, her breath coming out in a long, shaky rasp. "I don't know," she said.

"He didn't do it and you know it. Elvis didn't shoot nobody as a boy," Donnel said softly, trying to convince her with each word. "Elvis wouldn't hurt a fly. He couldn't hurt a fly. I can't even get the guy mad; I tried before. He just ain't the type."

For several minutes, the only sounds were the old pickup's engine idling and the music low, leaking out of the one battered speaker that worked. With a sigh, Donnel leaned his head back.

"And another thing—what Jesse says about Elvis turning dangerous now that he's middle aged," he continued, "well that's just crap. That's what that is." Donnel tightened his grip on the beer can, then raised it to his lips. He saw Elvis in his head and tried to swallow the vision with the beer. "I got half a mind to tell Elvis everything—see what he remembers."

"You can't Donnel. You can't," Lavern murmured. "He couldn't take it. He'd go nuts if he isn't half there already."

"Well, then, maybe I'm gonna talk to the police."

She hesitated, then: "Donnel, no. No. Don't."

"I know some guys that know some guys that are state cops. State cops would maybe have some records or something of stuff that happened long time ago."

"There aren't any records of this. That's the point."

"Maybe there's records you don't know about. Maybe they got something on this brain doctor-brother dude."

"Please, please don't. It would just make everything, I don't know, all messy."

Donnel thought about it for a second. "Look, we been friends a long time," he said, lowering his voice, choosing each word carefully. "We all love each other, me and you and Elvis, like family you know? But what we ain't told Elvis, keeping him in the dark about this brother thing and all that, well, that's pretty sick. I'm talking serious sick."

"We only just found out ourselves."

"Exactly. But Elvis' got every right to want to be mad. Was me, I'd want to kill us, know what I'm saying? The man's fifty-something years old and he don't know he's got a twin brother, and we ain't telling him. That's sick for sure."

"I just don't think blasting this story all over town's going to do anybody any good."

Donnel stared at her. Lavern's dyed-red hair shone in the green light of the dashboard and her bottom lip stuck out now in a pout. She was a cute little gal; she always had been. A pain kicked his heart. He'd loved her as long as Elvis had, maybe even longer, and she knew it. But Donnel and Elvis'd been buds since they were kids and well... Donnel took a swig. He thought he should shut up, but the beer had really loosened his tongue. "You're getting sweet on him, aren't you?"

"On who?"

"On this twin brother. He been coming over to your house, talking nice to you when no one else is around?"

"I'm not sweet on him. I just..." Lavern stopped herself and looked at the floor.

"Right. You ain't sweet on him and he's not up to nothing, is he?" he continued sarcastically, his voice getting louder. "Tonight, he finally tells us what s'posebly happened—gives us this big old story about what Elvis and his momma done, then he says, Oh, by the way, turns out he, this long lost doctor-brother dude, has a nice new house here. He says there's no sense going to the cops, but you're welcome to move in to his house—even if he's not around—if Elvis turns all violent again and things get rough for you. That's pretty unreal, you ask me. You're going to go along with it? Why is that, Lavern? You like this guy or you afraid of your own husband, the most easy-going dude anybody's ever known?"

"I don't know."

"Wonderful." Donnel drained the last of the beer and tossed it toward the hole in the floor. He took a moment to catch his breath as the can clinked softly on the gravel under the truck. "So I'm s'pose to just haul you away from under Elvis' nose tomorrow, tell him we got a surprise we're planning, just so we can meet Mister Big Shot Doctor at his house. Just so he can show you where the key is and where you can come and hide."

No answer.

Donnel slammed his open palm against the steering wheel. "I got half a mind to put an end to this right here. I got half a mind to, I tell you that," Donnel said.

They sat in silence for a few minutes. Donnel didn't know what she was thinking, and he was pretty sure he didn't want to know. "He's a bad man, honey," he finally said, his voice husky from fatigue and emotion and alcohol. "He's a bad one for sure."

"Take me home, Donnel. I want to go home," she said.

❊❊❊❊

He looked at his watch. It had been forty-five minutes since he'd left the truck stop, thirty minutes since he'd arrived at the house. For a second, he wasn't sure what he'd done with the time.

He clawed at a hand and picked up the cordless phone, hoping the call would divert him from another trip down memory lane. Jesse dialed a number he'd memorized, heard the line connect. As it rang, he stared at his reflection in the kitchen window. He was trying to think of the name of the guy he was calling. It was Larry or Gerry or Barry—Harry, maybe? In his head, the word game jumped to Frankie Vallee and the Four Seasons singing "Sherry."

Jesse waited impatiently for the guy to answer, a dull, aching spot taunting him in the center of his forehead. He wanted desperately to put down the phone, have a couple drinks, maybe smoke some of the dope he'd bought that afternoon—a treat he figured he deserved—then walk upstairs and take a long hot shower. He needed to scrub the nagging filth from his body and go to bed. Turning impatiently from the window, he pulled first his wallet then his keys out of his pockets and tossed them on the kitchen counter. He pinned the phone against his shoulder with his ear and scratched the back of his left hand.

"Yeah?" The voice jumped on the line and Jesse gripped the phone but didn't speak.

"I said, 'Yeah?'" the voice repeated. A hick with an attitude, Jesse thought. He bit his tongue, counting the seconds in his head: one thousand one, one thousand two, one thousand three.

"Anybody there?" the voice asked, the attitude changing from rude to lost.

Jesse smiled and kept counting: one thousand eight, one thousand nine.

"Hello?"

One thousand eleven.

"HELLO?" The guy was sounding really nervous.

"Hello." Jesse said, his tone calm and matter-of-fact.

"Yeah. Um.."

"This the guy? The guy who can ahh… help me?" Jesse said.

"Yeah."

"You in a place you can talk?"

"Of course. Sure. Yeah."

Jesse chuckled. "You think talking like this sounds stupid—like we're in some kind of spy movie?"

"What?"

"Talking like this."

"What?"

"Never mind. You do what I want?"

"Ah, yeah, yeah, sure I did. I mean, I'm gonna. I'm gonna do it."

"What?"

There was a pause. The guy was lost. "What do you mean, what?"

"What are you going to do for me?"

"I… I've got it set up that this guy has some problems, you know, like you wanted."

"You make sure the wife finds out and gets good and

agitated?" Jesse closed his eyes. His head throbbed.

"Oh, she'll find out." The guy snorted a goofy laugh.

"How?"

"Well, I'll have someone call her. I know people who know them."

"No, idiot, I mean how are you going to, ahh, cause problems for him?"

"What's it matter to you how I did it?" The voice had an edge again.

Jesse paused, letting the rudeness echo back at the guy.

"Hello?" The guy said.

"Maybe I have the wrong man," Jesse said.

"Whoa, buddy. Hold on. Hold on. Hold on there," the guy said, now obviously shaken.

Jesse said nothing.

"You still there?"

"Yeah," Jesse finally responded. "I'm here."

"Look. I work with him, right? I mean, actually, he works for me. I've got it all figured out. He'll get framed-up good. You're going to have to trust me a little. Don't worry, man. I mean, you're gonna hear. Lots of people are gonna hear about this."

Jesse was silent again.

"Let's put it this way," the guy went on, searching for words. "My... my friend—the guy that told me about you? Well, he said you was talking five thousand, right?"

"I said *three*—four tops."

"Well," the laugh again, a donkey laugh through his nose. "You're going to want to pay me ten grand now, for what I'm planning."

Jesse couldn't help himself. His interest was piqued. "What is it?"

"Let's just say something real real serious is going to happen to somebody and he's gonna get blamed for that. That work for you?"

Jesse paused to think this through. "You talking about

something violent? He'd have to be accused of something violent."

"Heck yes," the guy answered with enthusiasm. "Violence is no problem."

Jesse felt a quiver in his chest. He closed his eyes and smiled. This was going more smoothly than he'd planned. The phone still clamped to his ear, he clawed at the back of his hand.

"What do you think?" The hick voice was whining a little. "Can you keep tabs on him?"

"Keep tabs on him?"

"Yeah. Afterwards."

"What'cha mean, watch him like?"

Jesse sighed. The pain in his head throbbed. "Yeah, watch him like. Keep an eye on him; let me know where he goes and stuff."

The guy paused. Then, "How much altogether?"

"Four grand."

"Five—what about five? This is huge."

Jesse took a deep breath. "Fine. I'll find someone else."

"Whoa, four's good. I'll keep on him. Or, um, I'll get someone to follow him too. I'll do it all, man."

"Okay, mannnn," Jesse said, mocking him. "And one more thing."

"Yeah."

"Take down my numbers." Jesse recited the house number for him, then his cell phone number. "Only don't call me directly unless he does something really weird that I should know about. Then, and only then, can you call me, you understand me?"

"Got it. How do I get my money?"

"You'll get it. Don't worry," Jesse said with a sigh. "I'm an honest man. You can trust me. If this works out, you'll get your stupid money."

Chapter Five

The boys waited out the storm in the pine grove, Elvis in a ball on the ground and Jesse pacing over him. When the rain and wind finally moved on, Jesse gave Elvis another good kick to the ribs. "C'mon," he said.

They walked back to the house in a crooked single file, Jesse leading, weaving between the trees and underbrush, Elvis trailing by a few yards. Occasionally, Jesse glanced back over his shoulder. He smiled at the sorry-looking mess shuffling behind him.

At the backyard, Jesse stopped, uncertain about breaking through the tree line. He couldn't yet see the entire yard. He imagined the body still there, lying in the wet grass, now soaked by the rain. Elvis didn't wait. He brushed past his twin and broke through the trees. But what was this? He angled not in the direction of the house but toward the road that ran in front of it.

Jesse fought the urge to panic. "Hey," he barked. "Hey, come back here." But Elvis didn't stop. Through the trees, Jesse could see him walking, stalking quickly away from the house. "Hold it right there," he wanted to say. He wanted to run like a crazy man, to grab his brother and stop him, stop him, stop him. But no, Jesse thought. No. He couldn't hold him here. Could he? No. Yes. No. No. No way. That wouldn't work, would it? Jesse remembered the look in Elvis' eyes, the look of fear when they'd been back in the pine grove. "Don't forget what I said, brother," he yelled, trying to sound as tough as Sheriff Matt Dillon. "Don't forget a thing. You do anything stupid and you'll go where he went, you hear?" Through the trees, Jesse saw Elvis stop. "You hear me?"

Elvis continued on. But Jesse decided then that he wouldn't talk. He wouldn't because he was too scared and weak. Yeah, yeah, he might see one of his friends. He might whimper and cry. But he wouldn't spill his guts. No, he wouldn't. He'd been warned. Forget him, Jesse told himself. Forget your brother; you took care of him.

Jesse took a deep breath and started toward the house. He tripped over something and went down hard. Angry, he stumbled to his feet, wildly kicking at the root or rock his foot had found in the weeds. He slipped on the wet footing and nearly went down again. Jesse dropped his hands to his knees and lowered his head. Eyes clenched, he ordered the world to stop spinning. *"Please, no,"* the man's words swam in his head. He could see the face coming around, the eyes turning to look at him. Why had the man done that? *How had he known?* It was like he'd bent over the lawnmower and waited for the slap of the door and the sounds of Jesse getting ready. He had turned, wanting to stop him, then he'd shrugged and gone right back to work. Why fight it? Maybe that's what Dad had thought. Why fight it? *Why?* He couldn't erase the image of his father's eyes. No matter how he tried, no matter how hard he controlled every other stupid thing, he couldn't get rid of the blue-grayness of those eyes. To Jesse, that just wasn't fair.

He bit hard on his lower lip. The tears started and just kept coming. He bit till he tasted blood. With shaking hands, he wiped his eyes and mouth with the hem of his shirt and took a long, good look at the blood on the cloth. Mom would be mad at him for getting blood on his shirt. He wondered how he was going to explain it. He pictured her in the house baking a blueberry pie, humming to herself and waiting for him to come home to clean up the mess in the yard. Jesse shuddered at the thought of the body still lying there with those eyes gazing at the sky. The eyes would be locked open, staring, pleading.

Please, no.

*****

The backyard was empty. There was no body, no Mom or shotgun. Even the lawnmower was gone.

Jesse walked toward the back door, feeling her eyes on him. She wasn't baking a pie, he decided. Most likely, she was just in there, sitting at the kitchen table with a cold Pepsi, an overflowing ashtray and a pack of cigarettes. The radio was playing, tuned to a country radio station. She was tapping her foot and chain-smoking while she twitched and waited.

Without thinking about it, he crossed to the place where the body had been. The grass was matted, wet and dark but the blood was pretty much gone. Mom had either done something to soak it up or the rain had washed it away. Jesse stared at the muddy place where the man's feet had dug into the sod.

The sun broke free from the storm front and sent a shaft of heat through the trees. Jesse sighed and turned from the spot. Around him, the yard was glowing. He studied the half-acre of shaggy grass and weeds carefully, like he was a guy buying property. The peeled-paint and sagging-roofed house squatted uncertainly in the middle of the lot, about fifty yards back from the road. A dirt driveway looped up from the road and ended by the back door. Their old, rusty Ford Country Squire station wagon was parked in the driveway; the car leaned to one side on a flat tire.

Jesse knew it wasn't much, but he believed—he knew—that he could make the place better. He'd make sure the lawn was cut as nicely as those golf courses he'd seen in magazines. He'd get the house painted and have the car fixed. He'd maybe plant some of those little flowering trees in the yard to dress it up a bit. Mom said he had ambition. He'd show her just how much he had.

The sun and the planning made him feel stronger, more in control, more like the man of the house. He started toward the back door, wanting a cold Pepsi and thinking he'd have a nice long chat with Mom. They'd talk about how they'd help each other, about how they were still on the same side, that they had to work together.

She was at him before the door slammed behind him.

"Where you been? I've been watching that clock for the past fifty hours waiting for you. Where you been?" Her voice jabbed from the cool shadows of the kitchen. She was at the table, cigarette smoke drifting in a haze around her head.

"Been looking for Elvis, you knew that," Jesse shot back, trying to set the tone he thought a strong man should take.

Something rocketed out of the haze and smacked the wall to his right. It was Mom's ashtray. It bounced off the water heater, clattered across the counter then fell to the linoleum. Ashes showered him, sticking to his wet skin and clothes.

"You let him get away, didn't you. You let that stupid addle-brained boy see the whole thing, then you let him get away."

"No, Mom..."

Another object came zinging at him. This one caught him in the side of the head. Stunned, Jesse watched it tumble and skid across the floor. It was her lighter. His head stung where it had hit him, but he told himself not to touch the spot.

"You don't lie to me, boy. You left me here to clean up your..." the right words escaped her for a moment. "...that mess you made in the yard. Then you let him get away."

Again, Jesse felt the hate in his chest. He swallowed hard and took a deep breath, then another. Slowly, woodenly, he walked to the ashtray and lighter, picked them up, walked over to Mom, tossed them on the table in front of her, then pulled out his usual chair and sat down.

They stared each other down; Mom, a ragged shadow across the upper half of her face, two fingers holding a cigarette in the air just in front of her freshly lipsticked lips, Jesse like a stone, his hands on the table in front of him. Finally, he spoke in a whisper husky with anger. "I did not let him get away."

"Then where..."

He cut off her question with a wave of his hand. "You don't worry about that."

The black-marble eyes flickered with something he'd never seen before. Respect? Fear? Jesse wasn't sure. Clumsily, he asked the question that was gnawing at him. "What'd you do with, um... with the body?"

The dark eyes gleamed. She took a long drag on the cigarette. "What do you mean, 'What'd you do with it?'"

"Where'd you put him? Where?"

"You didn't see him when you come in?" She smiled now, enjoying the game. "He wasn't out back in the yard like you left him?"

"No Mom, I..." Jesse was trying to maintain his composure, but the fear was back in his voice.

She leaped up from the table, and reached for his hand.

"Come see, baby. Come see," she said, suddenly gleeful.

Mom half-dragged Jesse down the shoulder of the road in the direction of town. He tried to slow her down, but she had a good grip on his hand. All he could do was scramble to keep up.

They jogged and walked hand-in-hand for a mile or even two, maybe. To Jesse, who was already tired and wet and miserable, it seemed like they'd walked forever. Mom didn't slow down until they reached a two-track trail that led off the road into the woods. Here, she stopped, nodded at an official-looking sign that marked it as Fire Lane 32b and gave Jesse a wicked grin.

They walked rapidly down the fire lane, then a side trail that angled off to the right, and continued on until they reached the edge of a clearing. In the middle of the clearing was an old barn that seemed to have frozen in mid-collapse. To their left, a hundred feet away, was the remaining rubble of an old farmhouse. Only one wing of the place still stood; the rest had come down long ago. Small trees and weeds grew in the remains.

"Good hiding place, huh?" Mom said, her voice raspy

and ragged. She coughed, then struggled to clear her throat. "Nobody ever comes out to this place no more."

Jesse wondered how she could be so stupid. Elvis and his buddies explored every inch of the countryside like a bunch of stupid Indians. They loved places like this.

"What'd you do," he said between ragged breaths, "haul him down here in broad daylight and stick him in one of these old buildings?"

"Yep. Used the wheelbarrow; likely broke my back flipping him into the thing," she said proudly. "Covered him up; you'd of thought I was hauling a load of trash."

Jesse was speechless. This was wrong. It was all turning out *so terribly wrong.*

She was off again, jogging toward what was left of the barn. "Come on boy. Come see. Come see," she yelled. She tripped on the uneven ground and stumbled for several steps, regained her balance, then disappeared behind the barn. Frustrated, scared and too tired to argue, Jesse followed. He found her standing in the waist-high weeds by a small, windowless shed that was a tiny version of the barn. The building's roof sagged and there were wide gaps between the dry, gray boards that made up the walls.

"A smokehouse," Mom said, opening the door and motioning for Jesse to come closer. The hinges protested with a groan. "I used to hide out back here years and years ago as a girl. I smoked my first cigarette back by this little place." Another phlegmy cough interrupted her thought. "Smoked it with your daddy. Seemed the best place to bring him now," she added quietly. She stepped to the side. "Go on in, baby. Say hi to the man."

Jesse wanted to run. He wanted to go home and take a bath and get a drink. He was thirsty and dirty. Filthy. The last thing he wanted to do was see the body again. This was all wrong. All so wrong.

"No, no Mom," he stammered and turned to leave. "I don't... I don't have to. I mean, I'm sure you did a good..."

She let go of the door and grabbed him by his skinny upper arm. Her mouth was near his ear, whispering and smelly. "Go in. Go on. You can do it. Go on in there and sing him his favorite song."

Jesse frowned.

"Go on boy. Sing that one song to him." Before he could stop her, she'd guided him inside.

She'd looped a rope around Dad's chest and up under his arms, then over a rafter. She'd hauled him up to hang there like a piece of meat. It swung slowly in the gloom, lit by dusty shafts of sunlight and turned gently by the breeze wheezing through the cracks in the smokehouse walls.

Jesse could barely hear Mom saying something about the body being safe from dogs and animals hanging like that. He avoided the man's eyes. He could picture them up there in the shadows, gray and blue, forever staring into the universe, always saying, *"Please no."*

Tears pooled near Jesse's heart. The feeling of death, the heavy sadness of it, swirled in the smokehouse. The door of the place creaked and clunked against the outer wall. Jesse could smell his Mom's breath; he could feel it on the back of his neck. He should've run, he thought. He should've gone home to take a bath, to get clean.

"You brought him here." He heard the words whisper from his mouth, but didn't feel them.

"Yep. I wrapped him in a bunch of old curtains we had in the basement, then just piled him in the wheelbarrow with some coffee cans filled with dirt to weigh those curtains down. I about broke my back, doing it myself." She started pacing as she rambled, sounding both animated and nervous. "You would've thought I was just pushing some old junk down the road. Of course, the cans kept falling off; that was the hard part—that and finding a place to stuff the curtains. I finally just jammed them into what's left of the farmhouse."

Jesse swallowed a sob. He couldn't believe this. The man couldn't be left here like this. *"Please son. Please no."* His father's voice sang softly in his head.

"What song you want me to sing, Mom?" he heard himself say from far away.

She giggled. "Well, that one he was always humming—you remember. Being in a old smokehouse where your daddy and I use to sneak a smoke, you ought to get it. Don't you get it, boy?"

The body twisted and twirled lazily in the breeze like it was dancing, and Jesse heard the tune seeping into his head, drifting in from maybe last week, the week before—or had it been that morning? Maybe, he thought, he'd heard the man stumbling through the song as he worked on the lawnmower.

"'Smoke Gets in Your Eyes,' right Mom?" Jesse whispered.

"That's it. That's right. That's the song right there. It's that smoking song."

Chapter Six

Donnel's truck rumbled away as slowly as a receding thunderstorm. From her front steps, Lavern watched the rusty hulk, bathed in the hazy-glow of the streetlights, lumber down the street. When it was gone, she sighed and shook her head as if to sift the memories that fluttered like falling ashes in her head. Her eyes roved among the one-story ranches that lined the narrow street of the subdivision. Even in the dark, the houses were plain and disappointing. They all looked the same. Plastic picnic tables and broken toys huddled and half-hid in the shadows of the yards. A light, muted by pink curtains, glowed in a back room at the Tylers' across the street. Their baby had been awfully gassy lately, Deeana Tyler had told her. Lavern imagined Deeana holding the baby as she hop-stepped the way she always did when one of her kids was fussing. Deeana would be cooing and singing as the naked baby head bobbed above her shoulder. Usually, the baby would calm right down when Deeana did that hop-step, at least that's what her husband, Mike, said. Lavern, well, she'd tried the same thing when she'd volunteered to babysit for Deeana and Mike last week; the baby, a beautiful little girl they'd named Cindy after Mike's mom, had just kept squalling.

The smell of it, of baby lotion and the acidic sharpness of wet diaper, lingered. Head lowered, Lavern studied the vapor of her breath against the darkness. Finally, she turned and unlocked the door.

Inside, a single lamp was on, on a living room coffee table. The house was silent and cool. Elvis, she knew, was asleep. Despite the beers and the late hour, Lavern was painfully alert, her nerves alive as bees in a hive. Quietly, she pushed the door shut, took off her coat, opened the closet door and hung the coat on a hanger, pushed that door slowly till it, too, clicked softly shut, then dropped her purse on the coffee table. She shuffled into the kitchen and rooted around in the refrigerator for a few minutes before settling on a jar of Cheeze Whiz. Back in the living room, she plopped on the couch, unscrewed the Cheeze Whiz lid, scooped out a glob of the orange goop and sucked it off her finger. As she wrapped herself in an afghan, Lavern stuck her free hand in the cracks between the couch cushions and pawed for the remote. She found it, pulled it free and pressed the power button. The bluish light from the TV warmed the room. The late, local news was on and Lavern held down the volume button, reducing the anchorwoman's voice to a low murmur. She watched, only half interested, as the anchor started a story on possible layoffs at a couple of companies. When the picture switched to an extremely serious reporter in front of the plant where Elvis worked, an alarm in Lavern's head told her to turn it up, but she ignored it. She was sucking on the Cheeze Whiz and letting her mind drift.

Lately, Elvis' nightmares had come more often. She'd begun to lie awake, waiting for the cadence of his breathing to change and for him to begin the awful slide into his mind. He'd mumble and groan, then twist the blankets and sheets away from her. On the worst nights, the dreams ended with him wet with sweat and sobbing in his sleep. She thought it was weird that you could cry without waking up. Weird.

Lavern sighed. Elvis and Donnel didn't know how much she already knew—how much she remembered. She could still see him running to her—his head swaying left and right with each long, lopey stride. He'd been a skinny, scrawny scarecrow of a boy and he'd come galloping across her yard that day, yelling her name between big gasps for air. She waited for him to reach her, thinking he was going to push her down and start a game of tag or something. "You're it, Laverny-wormy," she'd thought he'd say. Instead, he ran right up to her and threw his arms around her. He let her put her arms around him too; something he'd never let her do even though she'd always wanted to. As she lowered herself to a sitting position on the ground, she realized he was sobbing, and was covered with bits of leaves and dirt. He was sweaty, wet and dirty too, and he smelled awful. For a second or two, she almost hadn't wanted to hold him.

Elvis was just a boy and she was his friend. She wasn't his girlfriend, he'd tell his buddies—just "a girl who happens to be my friend"—but that day, things between them changed.

"What happened? What's wrong?" she asked.

"They... I... g... g... and... he's... he's... " He tried to answer, but all he could do was shake his head and cry.

It felt weird at first, holding a boy curled up like a baby in his mom's belly, but she got used to it. And as she held him, for the first time she loved him. It wasn't a little girl love, but a full-grown one—one that would last forever, like on TV.

"Elvis you got to tell me. You got to tell what happened to you," Lavern said, trying to drag the truth out of him. He didn't speak; he just tightened against her, so she kept him close, sitting there under a tree in her backyard. They stayed that way for what seemed like an hour, Lavern rocking him gently while he sobbed. A lot of the time, Lavern wanted to push him away because he did smell, and it was so hot and sticky and the mosquitoes were awful. But for the first time, she felt like someone in love, or maybe, she thought, she felt like a mom; she'd always wanted to have a baby of her own, not just a doll baby, but a real one to hold and cuddle. As she held Elvis' sweaty head against her chest, she rocked him. "Please, baby, tell me. Tell me what you're talking about," she said. But he just shook his head no.

Lavern shivered as she pulled an afghan off the back of the couch and wrapped it around her. Later that day, long after Elvis had pulled away from her, mumbled "thanks" and run off again, she'd found out that Elvis' father had disappeared. The word had gotten around town pretty quickly; back then, divorce was unusual. A man deserting his family, well, that just never happened.

To Lavern, it seemed like something scary and mysterious had happened to make Mr. Icabone leave. Elvis had made it seem like something *horrible.*

That night, after the disappearance, Lavern had stayed awake and thought about it for hours. Lying in the bed she shared with her sister, Brenda, she'd heard her mom and dad in the next room, talking about the Icabones. Lavern's dad was a big, muscular truck driver with a loud voice and strong opinions about the "morals of the country" and "personal responsibility" and "doing the right thing." She could still hear him going on and on about that "screwed up Icabone family" and "this world's going to hell when you see a man leaving his family" and so on. Lavern's mom, soft-spoken but tough like always, told him to quiet down. Lavern had been afraid then, thinking her parents were missing something, that the story about Elvis' dad leaving had something awful in it.

The next day at church, she'd closed her eyes during congregational prayer time and prayed good and hard for Elvis. She'd prayed his dad would come home soon and that whatever was wrong would get set right so the world, especially Elvis Icabone, wouldn't go to hell.

Over Sunday dinner, Lavern had wanted to talk about what happened. When she was passing the corn to her dad, she opened her mouth and almost brought it up. But Lavern was stopped by another, stronger fear—that her father was looking for an excuse to make her stay away from Elvis.

Then and now, Elvis' family had been a mystery, Lavern thought, scooping another wet fingerful of Cheeze Whiz and slipping it into her mouth. Oh, she'd gotten to know his half-loony mom pretty well, especially after she and Elvis'd been married awhile. But when they were kids, even before his dad had gone away, Elvis had never let anyone visit him at home; no one, not one of the other kids, ever got to see his mom or dad or inside his house. Back then, Lavern was about the only one who'd known for sure that Elvis had a brother, although she'd never met him. The brother liked to be alone and liked to read a lot; Elvis had told her that once not long before his father disappeared. Elvis'd called his brother "a real smart kid who went to a smart kids' program at Brickwood Elementary" instead of their school, Ballard Street Elementary. He'd spit the words out, like his brother was his biggest enemy in the world. When she'd asked him to tell her more, he'd changed the subject. He'd never said anything about being a twin.

Just a week or two after Elvis' father had gone away, Lavern heard the brother was gone too. When she had a chance, when she and Elvis were alone, she'd asked him about it. He'd gotten super angry, something she'd never seen before or since. Elvis shoved her to the ground and held her there, straddling her, his eyes wild and crazy. "Don't you never talk about him or none of that again. Don't you never. You promise," he'd screamed. "You promise right now and forever. You'll never *ever* talk about none of it."

Today, Elvis didn't remember what had happened to his father; he didn't seem to remember his brother at all. It seemed impossible that someone could forget people like that. But, looking back, Lavern realized he'd started denying what had happened right away. In the weeks after his family broke apart, Elvis'd been louder, crazier—had played harder—than he ever had before. He'd acted like he was doing it because something was bothering him, something he wouldn't explain. Now he'd buried the memories so deeply they only came out at night. She, well, she had just let it be. Looking back, she wasn't sure why, but she'd just never brought any of it up. Years had come and gone. The whole strange mess had faded away.

For the rest of the town, well, it was all just a sad old story about a screwed up family; the dad had left, a shadowy, half-remembered brother (or was it a sister?) had moved away, and that moody woman had raised her son in the old house they'd all once shared. Like Lavern, no one else ever spoke to the remaining Icabone boy about his father or sibling; let sleeping dogs lie, they'd figured.

Lavern scowled at the TV. She had tried to get the truth out of Elvis' mother before she died. The nasty old woman had called the house one day; she'd do that maybe once or twice a year, wanting to talk with Elvis. This time, she had gotten Lavern at home—Elvis would just hang up if he answered—and she'd started in on "how easy it is to hide stuff in this town..." and "boys being rewarded for being good and being punished for being bad." It had been a very awkward conversation; Mom Icabone had been acting like there was something she wanted to say. Lavern had pried a little. Apparently, she'd pried too hard, too fast, because Mom had hung up.

Not long after that, Mom had called to tell them she was "being forced by her stupid doctor to live in a nursing home up north." Lavern had wanted to visit Mom before she left; the old woman still lived in the house Elvis had grown up in out on M-140. But, Elvis didn't want to have anything to do with his mother. Lavern couldn't blame him, really. She'd put off going to see Mom and had missed her chance. One day, some other doctor had called and told them Mom'd croaked. Elvis had sighed at the news, made a strange face, and had never talked about it, or her, again. He and Lavern had skipped the funeral. They had never even visited the grave.

The years had piled on top of one another, and Lavern had begun to think she'd never understand what had happened. Then, just as Elvis' dreams had gotten worse, Jesse had shown up.

She pulled the afghan over her head and thought she caught a whiff of Jesse's cologne. He'd sat here, next to her on the couch, and put the whole story together, saving the last part of it for tonight at the truck stop.

Geeze, she thought, biting her Cheeze Whiz-ed finger until the tears flowed. Jesse said Elvis had killed their father. For the first time, Lavern wondered if it was true. Who knew? With that mother, who knew the truth about anything? Did Elvis do it? Did Mom? Did Jesse? So many questions, she thought, sucking a glob of Cheeze Whiz off her thumb and letting it dissolve.

To make matters worse, despite all that she knew or suspected, Lavern had to admit she was attracted to Jesse. The guy was sexy, sweet, rich and... she paused to find the word. Dangerous. He was dangerous in a way she thought was exciting.

Elvis was no brain surgeon, Lavern thought with a little grin. He was pretty slow, if you wanted to put it bluntly. On top of that, he really didn't believe in himself. It was one of the reasons he didn't move up into management at the plant. It was why they couldn't have nice things. It was why they couldn't even afford pre-paid cell phones half the time. It was frustrating. But, Lavern thought, he was gentle, tender, sweet and a little crazy. It was Elvis who had brought home the kitten he now referred to as "her cat"; he'd found it abandoned and had surprised her with it one rainy, fall night. She could remember him walking in the door with the thing stuffed inside his shirt, its whiskered nose poking out between two buttons.

Lavern had promised Elvis she would never talk to anyone about his family. But now she'd betrayed that promise. Not long after Jesse had shown up, one night when she was feeling pretty desperate, she'd talked to a friend at the police department. He put her in touch with a detective at the state police post. She told the detective the story—as much of it as she knew. Since then, she'd kicked herself over and over for bringing the police into it. Evidently, some kind of missing person file still existed on Elvis' dad. Her city cop friend had told her the state cops had now brought in some dude from outside the area to work undercover on this thing.

She'd betrayed Elvis and now she'd sort of lied to Donnel. The police were working on it. Where it would lead, who knew?

She clenched her eyes. "You got to help me find the truth, God. You got to help me know everything that happened. You just got to show me. You got to, you hear me?" she hissed, then stopped herself. That was maybe a little too harsh a prayer, she thought. "Please, God, if you could, it would be cool," she added. There, she thought with a smile, that was better. Amen.

She knew God didn't expect her to sit back and watch. "God helps those who help themselves," they'd chanted in Mr. Melvin McGarr's sixth grade Sunday school class. The words still echoed in her head when she got into trouble like this.

It was hot under the afghan. Lavern flipped it off and looked down at the orange mess of Cheeze Whiz in the jar. Slowly, she started forming an outline of a plan. It helped that they had a lot of friends. It was times like these when it paid to live in a small town; people would come to your aid whenever you needed them.

She could picture Jesse's assistant at the hospital, a neat young woman named Emily. Lavern had met her once when she and Donnel had gone to see Jesse. Emily knew something screwy was going on, but she seemed to be a real sweetheart who, Lavern thought, secretly wished Jesse dead.

Emily would be a good person to talk to first.

Lavern sighed heavily. In her gut, she felt the need to shock Elvis. Getting him to open up and talk would take getting him good and mad or something; her gut told her that. There were other things she needed to think through, but she needed some rest first. She was already dreading the idea of getting up and going to work. She knew that if she didn't get to bed she'd have a hard time answering phones, taking complaints and all the other annoying things that were part of her job. People couldn't fight city hall, but when it came to fighting the department of public works, they had to go through her.

On TV, the news had changed to sports. Some guy with a fat neck was yammering on about the "local high school basketball scene." Lavern flipped off the set, stood unsteadily, and carried the jar into the kitchen, where she dropped it in the wastebasket. After brushing her teeth, she scuffed to the bedroom, put on her pajamas, and eased into bed. She watched Elvis sleeping for a moment, then lightly, tenderly kissed her fingertips and brushed them across his forehead.

The Redeeming Power of Brain Surgery

❈❈❈❈

Elvis rolled away from Lavern and peeked at the digital clock on the bed stand. It was 11:23 p.m. He thought he'd smelled beer and cheese under the toothpaste on her breath. He imagined it was Donnel's beer and Donnel's freaking cheese, and Elvis' stomach turned. He listened to her breathing and thought about all the cold nights they'd cupped together like spoons for warmth. Now they were knives in a drawer, he on his side of the bed, Lavern on her side.

When he was sure she was asleep, Elvis got up and walked into the living room. He flicked on the lights and wandered through the house, touching furniture, the walls, trying to feel, to cut through the numbness in his head.

Her purse was on the couch where she'd thrown it. Elvis picked it up and dumped it out on the couch. Some of the junk, a pen and a half-empty box of white Tic Tacs, slid to the floor. He pawed through the rest of the stuff, letting more of it fall. He thought about taking the loose change—something, anything to make her mad.

A piece of white paper stopped him. It was folded, important looking. Elvis, hands trembling, picked it up and sat on the couch. The pile of Lavern's stuff tumbled, some onto the floor, most into the crack between the cushions.

On the paper, written in ink, in Donnel's fat, funny handwriting: "M-43 East to Dormill. About 6/10 mi. down, left on M-140. Three miles out 140 to Fire lane 32b, right."

He sat and stared at the words for a good, long while. The directions were to some place near his old stomping grounds, out near the old house. He hadn't been there in years. It was their love nest—it had to be. The thought occurred to him as a fact. No doubt came with it. Elvis just knew. Donnel had a place where he and Lavern were going to meet. Elvis scrounged around until he found a stub of a pencil. He scribbled the directions down on a piece of paper from the pad Lavern kept by the phone.

Paul Flower

Elvis carefully put the purse back together. Then he turned off the lights and sat on the couch, staring at the pale streak of streetlight cutting through the crack in the curtains.

Silently, he cussed himself out for being so simple-minded; he hadn't seen what was happening between Lavern and Donnel until a couple months ago. Even then, he hadn't said anything.

"Tonight, you finally caught on, didn't you partner?" he whispered angrily, recalling what he'd seen. When Lavern had said a friend was picking her up "down around the corner," he'd gotten in his car and had driven the other way around the block. He'd watched as Donnel's truck slid to the curb and Lavern got in. He'd followed them to the truck stop, then he'd come home.

What an idiot, Elvis thought—how stupid and spineless. Even now, he couldn't find the strength to confront them.

He sat, twisting it in his head, and thought for the millionth time that he didn't deserve this.

Chapter Seven

Jesse looked down at his PF Flyers. They were so muddy and wet. His legs, well, they were a mess, too. His legs had maybe a zillion mosquito bites on them, some of them he'd scratched open. He felt dirty and exhausted, so he didn't talk to Mom as they started down the road toward home. He trudged like a beaten dog behind her, eyes on the ground.

Mom had been right about a lot of things, but not about the body. The hiding place was lousy and stupid. Jesse was too tired to know what to do about it. Besides, there were so many other details to worry about. Had she remembered to hide the gun? Had she put it back under the stairs? Should she maybe throw it away or bury it somewhere? Did she have all the details about the alibi worked out? Would they both say the same thing when people asked about the man leaving home? And what about the man, was he in heaven? Was he in hell? Or was he restless and wandering and looking for trouble like a spooky ghost?

Jesse scuffed along in the gravel, trying not to blink. If he did blink, and blinked too long, he thought—he knew—the man's eyes would be there pleading with him. *Please no*, they'd say.

Jesse wanted to wash the image away. He wanted to wash himself good, wash every stinking pore until he was clean, until all the dirt was gone. The day had gone muggy again. The air was thick with the smell of rotting leaves and the weight of the unfinished rain. As they neared home, a deer fly buzzed at his sweaty head. Jesse kept walking and flicked at it. The fly retreated for an instant then was on him again. It found his ear. A gagging sound squirted from Jesse's throat as he slapped at it again. He broke into a jog, passing his mom before turning around and running backwards, looking for the fly. It was on him, buzzing at his face then his ears. It found the back of his neck, sat there and bit, a tingly jab that sent tiny fingers of electricity through his scalp.

Jesse, wild-eyed and sobbing, skidded to a stop in the gravel. He slapped the back of his neck, waited, then brought the hand around slowly and stared at his palm.

Empty.

The fly, black and mean, buzzed at his neck, his cheek, his face.

Mom shuffled along, oblivious, mumble-humming "Smoke Gets in Your Eyes."

Jesse turned and ran toward home, his tired mind quivering with an idea: the stupid fly had been sent by God. He didn't know where the idea came from, but he didn't know where the fly had come from either, so yes, yes, God could have sent the fly. Maybe God had even sent the idea that he had sent the fly. Yes. Yes. It was all possible. Jesse knew it. Jesse had been to church. He knew what God was about. To him, to God, nothing was impossible. God could send a fly and could send the idea that he'd sent the fly to the kid being bugged by the fly. Yes. Absolutely. Mom hadn't cared to go to church, but Dad had made Jesse go with Elvis and him. It was one of the few things Mom hadn't argued with Dad about.

"No big deal," she'd said. "Go on, Jesse. Go on. Maybe it'll do you some good," she laughed.

Dad had made Jesse learn about God, and now God was sending a fly, and making him, Jesse, think about the fly because why? Why? At first, Jesse didn't know. He didn't know. He ran harder, crying like a stupid baby, the fly on him, on him, on him, tears and sweat burning in his eyes, his brain in flames, on fire with wild ideas. God had seen the man's soul—it had floated into heaven with a note attached to it—and God, well, he'd sent the fly to punish the person whose name was on the note, the boy who'd killed the man.

The Redeeming Power of Brain Surgery

The fly smelled death on Jesse and wanted to get inside. It wanted to get at whatever had gone bad in Jesse Icabone. It was all so stupid and made no sense. No sense at all. But still, Jesse could imagine that it was absolutely true.

Sweat and tears burned his eyes and he closed them. There they were, his father's eyes, inside his own. Those eyes, sheeze, pleading with him. *Please no. Please no.* "Please no," Jesse screamed the words as he tripped and fell, headlong, onto his weed-riddled yard. He rolled to his back and looked up at the sky. The man's eyes stared down from a retreating thunderhead. Jesse choked. He scrambled to his feet, ran toward the driveway, and followed it around to the back of the house. He wanted something cool to drink and a bath. A good, long, hot bath would make him feel a whole lot better.

❖❖❖❖

Jesse put the martini glass on the edge of the tub and lowered himself into the steaming water. He didn't hear the groan from his chest. He couldn't see the red scratches he'd clawed on his skinny legs. He felt only vaguely the burning relief of the water on the screaming itch of his skin. Eyes closed, he took a long drag on the joint and held the smoke in his lungs for five, ten, fifteen seconds. Now he could see the itch. The itch. The itch. It had spread from his hands to his groin and thighs. He could see it in his mind's eye. It was red and ugly and everywhere. Frankie Valli sang in his head, but the music was lost in the itch.

The alcohol and dope whirled, turning and tilting the room. Time passed. Now his skin was raw from repeated washing, his pajamas, sandpaper. When had he left the tub and come upstairs? He didn't know. He lay in bed trembling, bathed in sweat, and he was a child again; coming around the house toward the backdoor, passing the rear of the rusty station wagon, glancing inside. His stomach lurched. Through a grimy window, Jesse saw Elvis, a boy as dirty and sweaty as he was, sitting behind the steering wheel. Elvis wasn't moving.

One hand was draped over the top of the wheel. All the windows were closed.

Jesse felt sick. He was hot, so very very hot. The journey back from the smokehouse had been so long and so hard. He put his forehead against a shady spot on the side of the station wagon and tried to catch his breath, then wiped his nose with the disgustingly messy shirt and glanced toward the front yard. No sight of Mom. He peered inside the car again. Elvis' hand was limp over the wheel. Now the underside of his wrist was gently rocking it back and forth, like he was going for a Sunday ride. Dad had driven the car that way. Jesse and Elvis would ride up there in the front seat next to him, and the man would steer with the bottom part of his wrist while he hummed dumb songs with the radio. The memory made it hard to breathe.

"Hey, Elvis. What'cha doing in the car?" Jesse croaked at him through the glass. The head didn't move, just the wrist; Elvis rocked it back and forth. Jesse pounded on the window with his fists. "Hey addle-brained boy, don't you know you could die in there?"

Elvis flinched and cocked his head to one side.

That was enough. Jesse took a step and jerked on the handle of the right rear door. It swung open with a groan. Heat and a sick, soggy smell staggered out. Jesse swallowed so he wouldn't puke. "Get out of the stupid car, you addle-brained faggot," he said, but Elvis kept his eyes straight ahead.

Jesse slid into the back seat, pushing through oil cans, pop bottles and other junk to find an open spot. He twisted and looked out through the filthy rear windows. Mom was coming around the house, so Jesse reached out and pulled the door until the latch clicked shut. He didn't want her in on this.

The air inside the car was a thick, sweaty-wool blanket. Jesse, still winded from the walk, felt another quiver of nausea. He swallowed again and tried to soothe his ragged breathing. His head swam a little. Sweat stung his eyes. "Elvis, you okay?" His voice was hoarse.

Elvis, his face flushed and shiny, his one hand still hanging over the wheel, said nothing. Jesse leaned over the seat. On the seat, Elvis' free hand was curled around the battered barrel of the old .22 rifle their dad had bought them. They'd used it only for target practice; Dad had let them, but only when he supervised, and with the understanding that the BB gun was the only gun they could use in the woods. Jesse's throat tightened.

"Where'd you find that old thing?" Jesse's voice came out unexpectedly high pitched and nervous. He wiped a tear of sweat from the tip of his nose.

Jesse glanced from the rifle back to Elvis' face. Elvis bit his lower lip with the corner of one tooth. A tiny trickle of blood seeped around the edge of the tooth.

Jesse felt a sob in his throat. Anger rose like a fist to kill it. Control, he reminded himself. Control yourself. Control him. Mom strolled by the car without seeing a thing, still humming. She went inside the house.

"Hey Elv-man," Jesse said, the quiver in his voice steadying. "Listen, bud, um, listen bud." Jesse cleared his throat. "I don't know what you think you're doing in here, but you best get your butt in the house for supper."

Elvis didn't move.

Jesse slid over the front seat headfirst and his brother lifted the gun out of his way, holding it to his chest, protecting it. Jesse settled awkwardly into a sitting position. He turned and faced his twin, who looked like a stupid statue holding the gun. In the suffocating heat, sweat dripped from Elvis' nose and his face was the color of raw beef. He stared out the windshield, looking proud and stupid.

Jesse's right palm slapped his brother's cheek. Elvis stiffened, but his eyes stayed forward; his mouth remained clenched in a tight, pink line. Jesse punched Elvis' head, bouncing it off the window. Elvis released the ancient gun and doubled up, his hands gripping his head, groaning.

"Trouble with you is, you don't get it," Jesse said. He bent and grabbed the gun by the broken stock. "There's something happened here you're too simple and stupid and addle-brained to ever understand. If you try to understand, you're going to just muck it up. So don't try, you hear me?"

Elvis was still doubled over, his head beating softly against the steering wheel. He started to cry. Jesse got to his knees, back against the passenger's door, and pointed the muzzle of the gun at his brother's head. "Look at me."

Elvis didn't move.

"Look at me," Jesse repeated, his heart thudding against his ribs, the anger spreading through his chest. Elvis faced him, tears mixing with the sweat and dirt on his face. He opened his mouth to speak, but words wouldn't come. Jesse pressed the muzzle of the gun into his brother's forehead and Elvis recoiled. Jesse chased the retreating head with the muzzle, pinning it against the window. Elvis, eyes clenched, squirmed to get away but he had nowhere to go.

"You got to forget all this—all of it. Go on and live your stupid little life and forget it. You hear me? You hear me?" Elvis stopped squirming. He kept his mouth clenched.

"You're digging at something here that's way, way, way too big for you to handle, you understand? I can tell you're digging at it. I can see what you're thinking, you addle-brained idiot, you stupid, jerk-headed moron. You're thinking there's something going on here that you can do something about. Well, you can't. Your daddy's gone and we're all going to miss him. There's nothing you can do about it. You got it?"

Elvis had gone limp, almost lifeless.

"You got it," Jesse repeated quietly, a command more than a question.

Finally, Elvis, still sobbing softly, whispered a small, crooked "yeah."

Jesse waited a full minute, counting the seconds, with Elvis skewered on the barrel of the gun. At last, he spoke, "Look up. Look at me."

For a second, his brother's face reminded Jesse so much

of his father's, he couldn't think. A buzzing filled his ears. He held Elvis' stare for twenty agonizing seconds. Finally, he spoke with a hiss.

"BWAAM."

❊❊❊❊

He jolted awake and sat up in bed. Alone, Dr. Jesse Tieter suddenly felt small and lonely. He got up and walked through the house, turning on lights. In the bathroom, he urinated, then washed his hands for several minutes and dried them carefully, tenderly. In the kitchen, he made another drink and drank it, washed the glass and put it away. He rambled back through the house, turning off the lights. He lay down in bed and stared at the ceiling. Soon, the smell of pork and beans filled his head. He could see himself, young, so young, sitting at the table, poking at his pork and beans and hamburger. That's what they'd had for supper that night. They'd just sat there, the three of them not speaking, poking at their food, acting like the new seating arrangement at the table—the fourth chair empty, the yellow plastic napkin holder sitting where the man's plate and silverware should have been—was perfectly normal.

Finally, Mom gave up on the meal.

"Guess we're all just too hot to eat," she said, then ordered Elvis to the bathtub. He shuffled from the room without a word.

When he'd gone, Jesse expected Mom to say something about the murder; he hoped she'd maybe talk over the story they were going to tell the neighbors and everybody else. They needed an alibi. Instead, she fixed him a glass of iced tea and sent him to the front porch, acting like that was normal, too. It wasn't. Until that night, Dad would've gotten himself a cold beer and gone out to sit on the porch; Mom would've stayed inside to smoke and yell at the boys while they cleared the table and washed the dishes. Just last night, they'd have done that.

Jesse sat outside for a good half hour, taking in the last of the daylight, listening to Mom cleaning up and the screeching of the red-wing black birds and tree frogs. He watched the hot wind play with the tops of the trees and tried not to think about how funny he felt. Something about the way things were going—the quiet meal, the iced tea—bothered him. Things were normal, but way too normal.

Sitting there, he didn't feel at all the way he thought Sheriff Matt Dillon felt at the end of a day. He was beginning to think that killing someone wasn't as simple as it looked. It was pretty complicated when you thought about it. Pretty complicated? Heck, it was like nothing you could imagine. Shooting someone's only the start, he told himself, then you have to handle your mom and the body and your ding-dong brother and those eyes, those *stupid* eyes that are in your head now. How's a kid supposed to handle all that? How? About the time he'd decided to stop trying, Mom called him in to take his bath.

Chapter Eight

The next morning, Elvis could close his eyes and still see the hand-written directions to Donnel's and Lavern's love nest.

As he sat at the kitchen table, her hand brushing his face felt like a lie. He realized that lately, everything had begun to feel this way: the grin on Donnel's face, the taste of beer on his tongue, the hum of the machines at work. Nothing seemed true. Nothing was *real* anymore. He felt out of balance too. The bacon frying on the stove, the cat prowling the dirty dishes on the counter, everything was tipping away from him. It was like he had screwed his head on carelessly, like he'd been too impatient to thread it good and tight. This morning, he'd gotten up early and had stood right here in the kitchen, one of the gas burners turned up on the stove, his tongue held to the flame. He'd done it just for a second or two, crouched over the blue fire like an idiot, one part of his tired brain screaming ow! and the other part not reacting at all. Had that been real?

"Hey baby, baby?"

"Huh?"

"What's wrong with you today, baby? You okay?"

Now, as she moved away from him, he had to look at Lavern to convince himself she was there, attached to the hand, flesh and bone. Real. At the sink now, staring out the window, she seemed sad. Despite himself, he felt a cramp in his chest, the cramp he'd felt when he'd first loved her as a kid. Always a little chubby—more to love, he always told her—she was cute, even drop-dead pretty when she put on the right clothes and makeup to go out or to work.

This morning, turned half-away from him, the sun

sparkled in her eyes, brought out the red in her cheeks, kissed the tip of her tiny nose. She did that thing with her dyed-red hair, the flip over an ear that never completely worked because a few strands of hair always fell forward, and he had to blink. Tears swam. His throat thickened. The earth tilted and acted like it was going to send him skittering over its edge. She was so real it hurt. She couldn't be a lie.

He'd never been what people called "the confrontational type," and the thought of being one made him a little sick to his stomach. So Elvis finished his coffee and brushed a dry kiss across her forehead on the way out the door.

He should've called in sick. There was something about the day that wasn't good, that tasted like stale Cheeze Whiz and skunky beer. But staying home would have meant thinking about her and Donnel and every other thing that popped into his mind lately when he had time on his hands. Besides, he hated lying. And not going to work when you weren't sick, well, what else was that but lying?

So he went. And just the act of driving was almost beyond his ability; his car, an ancient Chrysler Cordoba he'd bought for a box of Craftsman wrenches, felt too big for him. Behind the wheel, he was like a fifteen-year-old taking driver's ed. Driving, he hugged the curbs on every turn and merged only when the car behind him flashed his headlights to move over.

Somehow he ended up in the Bonner Wire parking lot, engine off, staring out the cracked windshield at the long, ugly brick building that had been his daytime home since high school. For a moment, his thoughts drifted from the idea that Lavern was cheating on him with his best friend, to the problems here. Bonner Wire had always been a nice little mom-and-pop operation, but the third generation of the Bonner family, headed up by Randy Bonner, had been ambitious. They'd gone out and spent a lot of money on new equipment and hired a bunch of new sales guys. The upshot of it all was that over the past three years, the plant had been running full-tilt over three shifts, and the Bonner family had gotten fat and sassy and recently up and sold out to some big-ass corporation from Switzerland. The sale had caused quite a lot of talk in town; rumors were flying around about the foreign owners laying off a bunch of the old workers and bringing in people from other plants.

Still behind the wheel, Elvis leaned against the door of the Cordoba and pushed hard to open it, reminding himself that he was way too valuable to be laid off.

Soon, he was at his machine and losing himself in his work.

About eleven o'clock, the new plant manager waddled into Elvis' area. He was a short, fat, bald guy everyone called Mr. Faceless because they couldn't remember where he'd come from or his real name.

About five minutes went by, Mr. Faceless just standing there with his hands on his fat hips before he finally moseyed down the line to where Jerry Plannenberg inspected the finished coils and okayed them for shipping. Jerry was a real jerk who also happened to be Elvis' supervisor. He'd started at the plant six months before Elvis, working on a co-op plan during their senior year in high school. Elvis got nervous seeing Mr. Faceless and Jerry talking; it could only mean bad news. Sure enough, after a few minutes of talk, the plant manager walked over to Elvis and said five awful words.

"Talk to you a minute?"

They went into the employee lunchroom and stood next to the hot drink machine, right where Elvis had gotten his cup of coffee—light sugar, no cream—every morning since forever. Mr. Faceless said something about needing to streamline operations and the damn Japanese being so competitive. That was that.

Jerry Plannenberg walked in right after the worst part, so Elvis tried to act like it didn't hurt. He acted like the conversation was about the coffee machine or a new order of heavy duty wire. Jerry sauntered over to the cold drink machine, his ponytail swaying behind the red baseball cap he always wore, and got himself a Dr Pepper with extra ice, which was the only thing the cold drink machine served; it had broken the year before.

Jerry watched the cup fall, the ice plop and the pop start to drizzle. It seemed like he wasn't listening to what was going on between Elvis and Mr. Faceless, but Elvis knew he was. Jerry waited all the way to the last drizzle, then he scratched his butt, took the cup, turned and glanced at the two of them one last time, and walked out.

"You got to give me a chance," Elvis said to the faceless man, all the fatigue and frustration rising in his voice. "I done this job for years. Nobody here can do what I can, the way I can." His voice rose to a shout and he realized it was wrong as he started doing it, but couldn't help thumping the guy on the chest with his index finger. "I'm the best you got. Swear to Moses I am. You fire me and you might as well close the place down. I'm the best you got. Darn straight I am. You can ask anybody."

"Hey! What you doing, man? Ease off, Elvis." Jerry Plannenberg was standing in the doorway again. He walked toward them, looking concerned. "You okay, Mr. Baylor? You don't look so good." He held out the cup in his hand to the faceless guy. "Want a drink of my pop?"

Elvis was surprised that the guy's name was Baylor. Elvis gave him a look, measuring him for the name, and realized the man's nothing face had gone pasty and gray. Mr. Baylor was breathing hard, and he took the cup with a trembling hand, his eyes buggy and red-rimmed.

"Go ahead, take all you want; I ain't drunk out of it," Jerry said.

Mr. Baylor took a drink, nodded at Jerry and smiled, still panting. Elvis thought about how much he hated Jerry Plannenberg. He was such a suck-up. He'd be all sweet and nice to your face, but he'd poison his grandma if it would get him somewhere. Rumor had it he was a white supremacist, too. The idea of it made Elvis' stomach churn.

The Redeeming Power of Brain Surgery

"You got to watch these guys," Jerry said to Mr. Baylor with a nod toward Elvis. "This one's a real hothead." He scowled at Elvis.

Mr. Baylor shotgunned the rest of the Dr Pepper, made a face, then wadded the cup and threw it wildly at the wastebasket.

"Thing is, Mr. B.," Jerry continued, slipping an arm around the chubby man's shoulder. "If you ain't careful when you lay off a guy like the E-man here, he's liable to start pulling that 'disgruntled employee' crap on you. He's got the mind of a postal worker, if you know what I'm saying." Jerry glanced at Elvis and smirked, then punched Mr. Baylor in the chest. Mr. Baylor let out a ragged gag and recoiled.

"He's liable to make that old ticker of yours act up, Mr. B. Sure, he is." Jerry hit the guy harder, right above the breastbone. Mr. Baylor twisted half away, his mouth wide, his non-face now very red.

"Wa... wa... wait. What you doing, Jerry?" Elvis said, his voice going high.

"I ain't doing nothing," Jerry said, slugging the guy again. "I'm just talking to Mr. Baylor."

Jerry let him go and Mr. Baylor went down on one knee, gasping and clawing and trying to speak. Jerry punched him hard, again, in the back.

"What have you done? Oh my lord—what have you DONE?" Elvis reached for Jerry. "What have you done?"

"What have you done?" Jerry screamed back, mocking him. "Oh my lord, what have you done?"

For Elvis, the room was turning slowly. Mr. Baylor grabbed his left arm and rolled onto his back on the cement floor, one leg hitting a plastic chair that was tucked under a table. The chair skidded a couple feet and teetered over with an ugly sound.

"Sir, sir—you okay?" Elvis' voice was getting louder, but he could barely hear it above the roar in his ears. He knelt by the faceless man. The guy's eyes rolled up into his head and he stopped moving. A trickle of foamy drool oozed from one corner of his mouth. "Sir, oh sir, I'm sorry. I'm so sorry." Elvis swallowed hard, trying to hear. He could feel his own heartbeat, but he had a feeling there was no use to check Mr. Baylor's. He put his hand down on the cold cement to keep from tumbling over. "I'm so sorry," Elvis said again. His voice sounded like a little boy's, all weak and warbly.

❖❖❖❖

"Oh my lord, what have you done?" Sally Dunleavy and a couple other people from the office came running into the lunchroom. Jerry had disappeared.

"I... he..."

"Somebody call an ambulance," Sally yelled. The two people turned and scrambled for the door.

The ambulance came. Elvis wasn't sure if it took seconds or hours. The paramedics spent little time in deciding the man was dead and covering the body with a sheet. Then, before Elvis could digest it all, the cops were talking to him. One of the cops was a fat guy with powdered sugar on the front of his shirt. The other was short, neat and quiet, a note taker. The short one kept his nose pointed at a little notebook, scribbling frantically as the whole thing turned into a big, loud mess, people gabbing and pointing and carrying on.

Someone from the front office mentioned the faceless man had had heart trouble and a bunch of others nodded in agreement. The whole management team had known about the heart, Sally said. "It had been the downside to bringing him onboard," she said. The note-taker cop made a note of it.

Sally also told the cops Elvis was "let go today as part of the downsizing" and Jerry, who'd reappeared, muttered something about "pushing and shoving" and Elvis "being really pissed."

The cops led Elvis away into the management conference room. They sat him down in a big leather chair and, for nearly an hour, they pounded away at "his story." Elvis told the truth, glossing over the part about getting really mad at the faceless man. Every time he started to describe Jerry punching the guy in the chest, the fat cop gave Elvis a quick, ugly stare, threw his arms in the air and began to pace. Elvis couldn't blame him, really. How could a guy, even a tense guy with a bad heart, die from chest punching? Why would Jerry do that, anyway? It made more sense that Elvis had killed the man or at least hurt him enough to make his heart blow out. Even Elvis could see that. Part of Elvis wondered if that was what had happened. Maybe he'd gotten so mad he'd killed the guy and just couldn't remember.

The little cop turned out to be pretty calm. He just kept writing down what Elvis said. When he'd decided they weren't getting any more out of him, he gave Elvis a smile and said, "You ain't planning on going anywhere the next couple of days, are you, Elvis?"

The cop using his first name comforted him a little.

"No," Elvis managed to squeak out.

"Good," the cop said. "Stick around town, okay?"

❖❖❖❖

On the drive home, his emotions ran from sad to worried to sorry to angry. When he stepped through the front door of the house, Lavern's cat, Brad, darted across the floor. Elvis kicked wildly at the stupid animal, narrowly missing him.

He pried off his work shoes without unlacing them and threw them to the left of the door, stormed into the kitchen, got a beer out of the refrigerator, unscrewed the cap, opened the door under the sink, tossed the cap toward the paper bag wastebasket and heard it miss, then closed the door with his foot. He downed the beer in one, long, hungry guzzle and left the empty on the counter.

As Lavern opened the front door, Elvis went into the bathroom and slammed the door. He turned on the water at the sink—just the hot, no cold at all. He let it get good and hot, so hot it hurt just to think about it, then pulled up on the stopper lever. The water began to fill the basin, steam rising from it in a soft cloud that looked scary and comforting at the same time.

Elvis tore off his blue jean shirt; buttons popped and clattered around the room. He stood, skinny arms crossed, staring down at the water, tapping his foot impatiently, waiting. When the sink was full, he cranked off the water, the faucet squeaking in protest, sucked in his breath and pushed his face down into the steaming water. His skin was suddenly bathed in fire. He pushed until his skinny hook of a nose pressed against the chrome drain cover in the bottom of the sink. He stayed there, his eyes clamped shut, for ten seconds, then fifteen. The time clicked through his brain.

Twenty seconds.

Twenty-five.

Face still scrunched against the porcelain and chrome, Elvis stretched one long, stringy arm over his head and snared his Hard Rock Cafe t-shirt; it was hanging from a plastic Abraham Lincoln bust that sat on a plywood shelf he'd made for it. He surfaced with a groan of pain. Flinging a shower of the hot water around the room, he pressed his face into the t-shirt, keeping his eyes shut. His lungs spasmed for air, but Elvis bit down on the shirt and swallowed a scream.

Lavern's fist beat in a mad rythmn through the hollow core door. "You okay in there?"

Elvis almost laughed. Okay? No way, baby. He could hear music from Lavern's iPod—she'd hooked it up to the speaker system he'd bought her last Valentine's Day. The hard-driving song thumped through the door. It was "Hair of the Dog" by Nazareth. The song always reminded Elvis of high school, of the time he and Donnel had driven around half the night looking for Skinky Thomas after Skinky had peed on the tire of Donnel's car. They'd wanted to find Skinky so they could pee on his car's tire, but they'd ended up just having to go to Donnel's house and pee there instead. They'd drunk some beers during the driving around, storing up the pee, listening to WLS AM-89 while they were doing it.

"What'd you do, fall in?" Lavern said.

Elvis dropped the t-shirt, lowered his head and let the shame wash over him. He should say something to her. He should have called Donnel; he could have tried to be confrontational with him. What had he done? At work? What was that? Sheeze, he was gutless and stupid. The loser in him always seemed to come out when things got tough. What had happened at work, well, that was a loser's mess. Wasn't his fault but it was his fault. All of this was.

"Hey. I'm needing you out here." Lavern's slippered foot thudded against the door.

His mom's face floated through his brain and he felt a dull throbbing in his forehead. Elvis squinted. He'd been dreaming about Mom a lot lately, even though he couldn't remember much about the dreams.

"Relax, man," he whispered, but his head pounded; his heart was racing. He closed his eyes and could see his mother wagging her finger at him. Tears welled. Calm down, he told himself. Get a grip, you stupid moron.

Elvis let his gaze wander up to Abraham Lincoln. He'd gotten the white plastic bust from a machine at the Museum of Science and Industry in Chicago. Lincoln was staring dumbly at the opposite wall of the cramped bathroom. An ugly black hole interrupted Abe's forehead, an exit wound that aligned with the entrance wound in the back of Abe's head. Both holes had been melted into the plastic one night when Elvis had a group of guys over to play cards. One of the guys had probably done it. Elvis always figured it was Jubal Brown, he being a white supremacist like Jerry. Jubal had come with someone else that night. Elvis wanted to ask him to leave, to tell him he wasn't welcome here, but he hadn't known how to say it. Besides, Donnel had been out of town that night. Everyone at the house had been white, so it seemed easier to not rock the boat. There was a whole group of jerks like Jubal in town, and Elvis steered clear of them, but that night, well, he'd put up with the guy to keep the peace. Abe had paid the price.

In the living room, Lavern was talking to her pet cocka-tiel, Sherman. Lavern and her pets. Good Lord.

Elvis lowered his eyes from Abe and looked at the mirror. He raised both hands and ran his fingers through his wet hair, making trenches. His face was pink from the water.

"You definitely got a screw loose after what happened today. That woman of yours, she isn't your only problem now, is she?" Elvis said to his reflection, his voice coming out stran-gled. "You're losing your woman, and now you got no job. A man's dead, too. Why's he dead? My god, how messed up is that?" He shook his head.

He liked talking to his image in the mirror, acting like the guy was someone else. Kids had imaginary friends, why couldn't he? It wasn't like he was a nut case or something; it just helped to talk to someone. It calmed him a little to do that right now.

Elvis bent over to pick up the t-shirt and stood slowly, wiping off his arms then rubbing the shirt hard across his stomach and up onto his chest and shoulders. He shook his head, spraying a fresh shower of droplets around the room; Abe got a random shot across the face. Elvis tossed the t-shirt back on the Great Emancipator's plastic head and grabbed one of Lavern's brushes—the pink one with the handle shaped like a poodle—that hung from a crooked row of galvanized screws he'd bored into the wall next to the mirror. Without looking at the mirror again—he really couldn't face himself, not right now—he brushed his hair straight back from his forehead and used one of the poodle's paws to carve a part down the right side. His hand shook a little.

"Relax, relax, relax, relax, relax," he muttered softly. He had a feeling he couldn't relax, not even if someone came along with a gallon jug of whiskey and shot the whiskey and a sedative directly into his brain. For some stupid reason, he thought about the day they'd put Mom in the nursing home. The doctor had called and talked to Lavern. Lavern'd told

The Redeeming Power of Brain Surgery

Elvis, "Your mom's going in a home, doctor's orders." He'd had a sore big toe that day after dropping a box of wire on it at work, so he'd answered, "Fine, we got any Epsom salts?"

He hung the poodle brush back on its screw and caught a flash of himself in the mirror. Elvis stopped and stared at his hair. It was stiff, molded and parted down one side like Ken-doll hair or Abraham-Lincoln-plastic-bust hair. It looked stupid—stupid. He hit the mirror with his right fist, connecting with the fist of his image. The contact sent a jolt of pain up his arm; he'd hit the old scar that ran across the back of his hand. Any time he'd hit that one spot it would jolt him good. The pain felt fine today, he thought as he stared at the mirror. It felt just fine. It was perfect. The pain was. It was just what he needed.

His eyes followed the silvery web spreading outward from where the fists met. Above him, Abraham Lincoln tottered on his plywood shelf.

"Hey, you making a career out of this?" Lavern yelled.

Career? Elvis smiled and thought, oh, Lavern, I don't have a career, not anymore. Don't have a boss either. I lost both of them today and I'm losing you. Elvis choked and tears burned his nose.

He flung open the bathroom door. The knob hit the wall. Abe trembled again then settled back into place with the t-shirt slung over his head.

Elvis took two determined steps into the living room and stopped. Lavern was settling into a cross-legged position on the floor in front of the couch. Behind her, the thick red drapes she loved ("classy," she called them) covered the picture window. To her left, next to the couch, was the cockatiel's cage. Lavern was wearing her usual sweat shirt—this one was a Mickey Mouse one—and stretch pants; her baby face was clenched in an attitude. Her brown eyes glared out from under her dyed-red hair and her tiny, red-lipsticked mouth was set in a hard cold line.

She looked like a frumpy, cotton-clothed, flesh-and-stone

Buddha; her plump hands were out in front of her like she was meditating or pretending she was in *"The Walking Dead."* An overturned bottle of red fingernail polish oozed on the orange shag carpet next to her right thigh.

"Baby, what'd you do to your hand?" she said.

"Nothing. What you doing to the floor?"

"Nothing. Don't go dripping blood on the cat."

Obediently, Elvis stuck his cut hand out in front of him and cupped the other one under it. Brad the cat skittered under a tattered recliner.

"There a reason you were in there half a year?"

"In there?" He said, trying to sound nonchalant. "Ah, I don't know. Just taking my time, I guess."

"Right. You had nothing to do in there for twenty nothing minutes."

"Like *you* got room to be criticizing me."

"What you mean by that?"

"You know what I mean."

No reaction; Lavern just stared off. Something was on her mind. Probably lovin' his favorite best old ex-friend. That. That was on her mind. For sure, that was.

The house was gloomy, candle-lit. Lavern liked it that way. She said it looked elegant. Elvis wondered what the heck elegant was. He cut an arc around her, around the bar that separated the kitchen from the living room, trying not to trip or drip or bang into anything.

"I heard the news, by the by," Lavern said.

Elvis' chest tightened.

"I said, 'I heard the news.'"

"You what?"

"I HEARD THE NEWS. You deaf now or something?"

"You heard."

"Yeah."

"You heard what? What news? What do you mean?"

"You know, the big news. The news news. What everyone's talking about."

Elvis gulped. "Who?"

"Who what?"

"Who told you?"

"Wanda, down at the store."

"Wanda?" Elvis looked out the small, dirty window over the kitchen sink. Their neighbor, a Mexican guy, was duct taping clear plastic to the bashed-out rear window on his old blue Ford. "What exactly was it that Wanda told you?"

"The whole story—everything, start to finish."

Elvis felt the headache pounding in the chamber behind his forehead. He tried to speak but his mouth was sealed by the ache.

"You know what? The way I see it, that man's lucky nobody tried to kill him before," she said.

Elvis shoved his hands under the drippy faucet. He uncupped his good hand, flexed it, and stared at the drops of blood that had puddled in the palm. He thought about how your veins are blue and so was the blood in them, and he wondered how anybody knew it was blue, since it turned red when it hit the air. He wondered if doctors maybe had a way to quick-see blue blood just a second, maybe a heartbeat, before the air and light hit it and turned it red. He'd tried it once, tried seeing it blue. He and Donnel had gone into a dark closet with a flashlight and he'd pricked his finger with a pin. Elvis could still see the shaking white-pink tip of his finger on the edge of pale-yellow flashlight light, a tiny blob of disappointingly bright red blood dancing on the tip of it.

Now, the hand was shaking again. "What, um, do you mean by that—by the man being lucky? You mean like he had it coming?"

"What I mean is, yeah, some people got it coming," she said. "Like 'member that Ardie, Arten, you know, Arden what's-his-name back in high school? He was always doing stuff, like pouring sugar in gas tanks and eggin' houses and all that. He ended up getting his arm broke by the Simko brothers—'member that? They caught him screwing around with the blinker signals on that old Thunderbird they had. People like that, they screw people and they screw people, then BWINKO. Arden had it coming to him. Same thing here, this couldn't have happened to a better guy." She finished with a sigh.

"You think so?" A fly squirmed, buzzing, against the window. Elvis choked on spit. He pictured his mom, her face smiling in the window pane. Then he saw the faceless man squirming in pain on the floor.

"Yeah, I always hated that Jubal Brown, and Wanda tells me the whole stinking town is glad."

"Jubal? Jubal Brown?"

He turned and glanced back at Lavern. She was smiling. "Doesn't sound like you heard," she said.

"No. No I didn't."

"Two black guys caught him spray painting stuff on their car over behind the laundromat this morning. They beat the shinola out of him."

Elvis turned back to the sink with a rush of confusion and relief. His headache ebbed. "Jubal?" he managed to squirt the name out. "He okay?"

"Pretty busted up, Wanda says. Why do you care? You his mommy all a sudden?"

"Well, no, no," he said. "I, you know, just wondered."

"He's going to live I guess."

"Good. Good."

"Know what I think?" Lavern asked with a groan.

Without turning around, Elvis knew she was getting up. She always groaned when she stood. It had something to do with her pelvis; the same condition that had kept them from having kids made her groan like that.

"No. What do you think?"

"I think it's cool that Jubal's going to live. Now, he'll have this thing on his mind all his life. Maybe he'll learn something from it, turn himself around. People do that, you know. They have something bad happen to them, one way or the other, they never shake it. It either turns them all good or bad and mean."

In his head, Elvis' mom was now shaking her bony finger at him and yelling, "You going to remember *this* for the rest of your life..." She'd always said that when she hit him for saying his bad thoughts. He shivered and looked back to the sink, cranked on the water to a trickle. It dripped onto the meaty part of his good hand, up near the thumb. The water hesitated before sliding downhill to mix with the blood. Elvis wondered if he could just freeze there like that. He wondered what would happen if he never moved again. Nobody move, he thought, everyone just stop *doing*, then nobody gets hurt.

"Anything like that ever happen to you?" Lavern's voice was right behind him all of a sudden but Elvis didn't turn. "Ever have something bad happen that stayed with you like that?"

Her question irritated him for some reason he couldn't explain. He focused on a mental picture of Jubal Brown with the shinola kicked out of him. He tried to smile at the image, but the smile was stuck behind his face somewhere.

Lavern sighed. He heard her arms flop at her sides. "I needed to get in here, you know," she said, now from the bathroom. "Stupid nail polish spilled. I needed remover to clean it up. Now I got a mess on my hands. What did you do to the mirror?"

"Sorry," he muttered.

"What is wrong with you? We don't have money to fix broken stuff," Lavern said, her voice loud and back in the room behind him. "Is that how you cut your hand? What is wrong with you?"

"I'll take care of it," he said to his hand.

"No you won't. I always have to do it. You never fix a thing."

Elvis didn't speak. She was right.

She sighed loudly again, then groaned as she squatted. She started scrubbing the floor. "I don't know what's in your head sometimes. Busting mirrors. And you got water in the sink—just left it there."

"Hot water," he said coldly, looking out the window. The Mexican guy was still standing next to the car, a wad of the duct tape stuck to his hand. He looked mad. He was trying to fling the stuff off.

Elvis closed his eyes and tried to work up the courage to talk to her about Donnel, the faceless man and his job. He pictured Lavern getting into Donnel's truck in the rain and the faceless man dying. He saw Jerry smirking at him and Jerry's face becoming Lavern's. He opened his eyes and spoke slowly to the window. "I filled the sink with real hot water," he said with a sigh, "and stuck my head in it. I think I wanted to hurt myself somehow."

The Mexican guy had one wad of the tape stuck to the leg of his jeans. He was working on another, this one stuck to his fingers; it was all twisted up and useless. He looked really mad now. It was getting dark. Soon the guy wouldn't be able to see the duct tape or the bashed out window.

The phone rang. Elvis tore a paper towel from the roll that hung from the yellow plastic holder next to the sink. He pressed the towel to the back of his hand, pulled the towel away and looked. It wasn't much damage, just a small bloody gash out of the ragged ribbon of scar across the back of his hand. The phone rang again. He pressed the towel against the wound and walked back into the living room. Lavern was on her hands and knees, scrubbing the floor. Brad the cat poked a gray paw, tentatively, out from under the recliner, testing the waters. The phone rang again. Brad's paw disappeared. Sherman the cockatiel stretched, fluttered and made the sound he always made when something bad was happening in the house.

Someone pounded on the door. The phone rang again. Lavern wasn't helping. She was scrubbing. Pound. Pound. Pound. The person at the door wasn't giving up.

"Just a minute," Elvis yelled. "Hold your pants on." He

grabbed the phone from the table next to the couch as the front door swung open.

"Hooty hooty hoo, man. Hooty hooty hoo." Donnel strode into the house, past Elvis, pumping his fat fist in the air, making for the refrigerator.

"Hello?" Elvis said into the phone.

"Thought you'd be home by now—hoped it anyway," Donnel said. "Sure could use a barley pop, sure could use one burly barley pop, yessiree sir. Hear about Jubal Brown? That's one white boy won't be talking no trash for awhile."

"Hi Elvis, is ummm... Lavern there?" The voice on the phone was nervous and soft; it sounded like one of Lavern's friends. Elvis couldn't place her.

"Yeah," Elvis said.

"Got the shinola kicked right out of him. People are talking about it all over town," Donnel said.

"I speak to her?"

"Won't be able to talk or eat or nothin' for a month. Wired his jaw shut," Donnel said. "You hear about that?"

"Yes," Elvis said, eyes on Donnel.

"Okay, thanks," the woman answered.

"No. No. Not you."

"What's that Elvis? Elvis, the king. What's that my man, the king of Bonner Wire?"

"Sorry, she's umm... busy right now." Elvis hung up. He walked to the open door, intending to close it. Instead, he stood in the cool fall air, facing outside. A light flicked on in the window of a neighbor's house. A car started. A dog barked. The Mexican guy swore loudly, in Mexican.

Elvis looked back over his shoulder. Lavern had disappeared, probably into the bathroom. There was a dark spot on the floor where she'd made the mess. He breathed deeply and turned back to face outside, thinking the outside air was a welcome break from the polish and remover stink. He pictured himself running down the street, out of the subdivision and away from here, leaving Donnel and Lavern to themselves and this lousy town. Then he remembered what the cop had said about sticking around.

Beer bottles clanked as Donnel swung open the refrigerator. They clanked again as the door swung shut. Pshhtt—that would be Donnel twisting off the cap. Clink—that would be the cap being thrown into the sink. Donnel always threw it there because he knew it made Lavern mad.

"Hey, my man," Donnel said loudly, like he was Elvis' best buddy and not the man who was stealing his woman. "How 'bout closing the barn door? It's getting chilly."

Elvis stepped back inside and swung the door shut behind him. Lavern was back in the room, standing next to Donnel, staring up at him as if she was waiting for him to say something. Donnel looked at Elvis and then stared down at her. There was an awkward, strained moment of nothing and everything. The smell of the remover and polish was sweet and made Elvis a little woozy. Slowly, carefully, Donnel shook his head. Lavern frowned and pouted and gave him a quick, hard nod.

Donnel held her stare long enough to make Elvis feel sick, then his huge shoulders sagged. He and Lavern turned and looked at Elvis. Elvis couldn't breathe. Questions ping-ponged inside his skull.

Donnel had a huge, football-player body—he probably would have been all state in high school, but his grades had gone south their senior year—and a chubby-cheeked, wide-eyed little kid face. His face was very expressive, their Freshman English teacher, Mrs. Carlton, had said. Mrs. Carlton had said it because it was true and because she wanted Donnel to try out for one of the plays she directed. Donnel had never wanted anything to do with the plays. He thought plays were for fruitcakes. Standing there, watching Donnel, Elvis couldn't help but hear Mrs. Carlton's voice. She'd scolded him good for using the word "fruitcakes," and Elvis had agreed with her. Donnel wasn't nice, talking that way.

"Hey, dude," Donnel said nervously, that face expressing,

to Elvis, a world of worry and trouble. "Me and Lavern ah, well, let's just say I got to borrow your old lady just for a little while. We, um, got to run an errand."

Yeah, I bet, Elvis thought. He couldn't believe they were doing this.

"Yeah, baby, we, well, it's a surprise, okay?" Lavern joined in. She touched Donnel's big, meaty, ex-football-guy arm. "C'mon," she said. "Let's go."

Trailing after them like a loyal dog, Elvis found himself again in the doorway. His feet were nailed to the floor by the blood rushing from his heart. For the first time in years, he thought about the three of them back in elementary school. They had sat together with the rest of the class on that big dusty rug in the middle of the room. Mrs. Hillburg had read to them. Donnel always sat close to an edge of the rug. He'd probe around under the rug, one knee and one side of his big butt cocked up in the air, as he stared straight ahead at Mrs. Hillburg. Donnel would nod his head and use that expressive face of his to say, "Oh my, yes, Trusty the tugboat *is* in trouble," and "The little engine *can* do it, I just know he can." All the while, he'd be probing, probing, probing with those sweaty chubby fingers. Lavern'd shake all over, trying to smother a giggle, as Donnel finally pried a dustbunny free. Like Donnel, Lavern was chubby even back then, chubby enough for the back of her pants to be open a little when she sat on the floor like that. Donnel would tuck the ball of dust back there. Then the two of them would look like they were going to explode with laughter, Lavern's face going pink, her brown eyes dancing. She'd have to put her head down so Mrs. Hillburg couldn't see. Her hair, which was dark and shiny—it hadn't been dyed red yet—would fall forward over her face.

Elvis would sit there and try to ignore them. He'd feel jealous, sure, but what could he do about it? Nothing. So he'd sit and watch the light play with Lavern's hair. And he'd try to get close enough to smell her; he loved the way she smelled like watermelon perfume, Zest soap and Butterfinger candy bars. To him, today, she still did smell that way. Or it was a combination of good, fun, happy smells that was pretty close to watermelon perfume, Zest soap and Butterfinger candybars.

There they were, out at the street. Donnel opened the passenger door of his rusty truck. Lavern got in and Donnel slammed the door. Elvis watched as his best buddy crossed around to the driver's side. Donnel stopped and looked at Elvis across the sad excuse for a lawn. To Elvis, Donnel was like a kid on his first date. He was wearing his best flannel shirt, jeans and jean jacket and his breath was pumping out in little white bursts. Lavern was looking straight ahead. Donnel hung his head and then opened the door and got in.

Elvis heard something—a humming—somewhere in his head.

Donnel pumped the gas pedal hard, the way he always did; Elvis heard it thump two times before Donnel hit the ignition. The truck wubble wubble wubbled then found its voice. Elvis stared as his friend jammed the shift lever into gear and lifted off the clutch. The truck nodded once and stalled. Donnel pumped the gas again and cranked the ignition. He ducked down so Elvis could see his face through Lavern's window, waved, and grinned. Suddenly, the truck lurched forward, the rear end shimmying. Donnel gave it the gas. They were gone.

Elvis turned slowly, walked back into the house, closed the door. He leaned against it, breathing hard, feeling his heart slamming doors in his chest. Numbly, he walked to the kitchen counter and picked up Donnel's open beer. He paused, fighting back the urge to put the thing down, run for his car and go after them.

He closed his eyes and started drinking slowly, then picked up speed. He downed the beer, belched, and slammed the empty on the counter. She never liked it when he chugged beer. Elvis belched again, a long low one. She'd hate that too, he figured.

He walked slowly, woodenly, around the bar and into the living room. He fell, face-down, on the couch. It felt like walls were crumbling inside of him. He hadn't cried in forever. But now, again, the tears rushed forward; this time, for the first time, Elvis didn't hold them back. "Oh, Lavern," he mumbled. "Help me baby. Help me."

❊❊❊❊

The old truck bellowed down the road toward town. Behind the wheel, Donnel leaned forward, as though that would get them to the hospital and Jesse faster.

"Is he following us?" Lavern said softly.

Donnel glanced in the rear-view mirror at the empty road behind him. "No—no one back there at all." He shook his head, backed off the gas and settled back in the seat. "What exactly are we doing? We going to keep going along with this Jesse, that it?"

She thought, took a deep breath and said, "Donnel, listen to me." Her voice wobbled. "Something awful did happen when we was little. It happened to his daddy. It was something so bad, he could never tell me about it. I was there, Donnel. Not for what happened. But after. He came to me, Elvis did. He was a mess. But I don't know what happened. You got to believe that," she said. "I never knowed what it was, and I still don't. We don't talk about it. He's either forgot it on purpose or he just don't remember or... I don't know." She bit her lip as a tear rolled down one cheek. Glancing her way, Donnel reached for her shoulder and she brushed his hand away. "There's a chance, just a chance, and I hope I'm wrong, that what Jesse's telling us is true. In that case, well..." Lavern's voice trailed off as she looked out at the passing scenery.

Donnel's voice had an edge. "Look, you know I didn't know his family much. I don't know nothing about his dad or a brother or nothing, but I tell you this, he can't, won't, couldn't, wouldn't, hasn't, will not never no way hurt no one. It's just not in the man. Elvis, he's the King. He's the King of Mellow. He's my man. Always has been. Always will be too, I tell you that."

There was another long silence. Lavern noticed for the first time that Donnel had gotten the old 8-track player working in the truck. One of his Parliament/Funkadelic tapes was playing softly, the funky beat barely audible above the rattle of the truck. She turned it up and allowed herself a small grin.

A cement truck lumbered toward them in the other lane and roared past. Lavern let the noise subside, then turned down the eight-track player. "Jena Lamley, she told me once she saw this thing on *Oprah*. It was about people who were, like, abused as kids. They'd 'repressed' what happened, she said—same thing Jesse called it. Tara Wickers saw this, too. So I did some checking on the Internet. Repression is a real deal, Donnel. Things happen when they're young, and people can't handle it emotionally or whatever, and they just shut it away in a room in their brains. Now a lot of these people all eventually remember. It takes something else—some real strong emotional thing, a crisis or, like, a transition in their, like, lives—to push them back to remembering it."

Donnel chewed on this for a moment. He glanced at her. "So we're gonna screw with the man's mind 'cuz you don't trust him."

"That's not what I'm saying."

"Well, here's what I'm saying. I'm saying let's just ask him what happened."

Lavern sighed. "We can't just *ask* him."

"Yes, we can."

"No, no, Donnel. The people I read about say it's better to give them some sort of nudge and then let him take it from there."

"You sound like the one making shit up now."

"Donnel, he's got to put it together on his own. If we ask him about it, he'll just shut down."

"Oh, so you're an expert on this thing now?"

"No," she said softly. "I just think it makes sense."

"None of this makes sense. None of it."

"Donnel, I know."

The Redeeming Power of Brain Surgery

Donnel stared off down the road. Finally, he grunted. "This just isn't right."

"It isn't. I know. But," Lavern began to cry. "I love him, Donnel."

Eyes still on the road, Donnel reached out a big hand and squeezed Lavern's shoulder. "I know. I know," he said. "I do too."

They both watched the scenery, each chewing the thing over. Finally, Donnel turned up the volume on the eight-track. "See I got the tape to work? *The Clones of Doctor Funkenstein.* It's a classic. Maybe that's what we need. Pipe this into his head and all the ghosts come out his ears. Voodoo, funken-style."

"Pull off the road a second," she said suddenly.

"Why?"

"Just do it," she said, slamming her fist on the dashboard. Donnel braked fast and eased the truck off onto the gravel shoulder.

Lavern sat up, looking through the windshield, a scowl on her face. He followed her gaze across a deep ditch, to the cornfield that bordered the road. The corn had been harvested; only nubs of the stalks remained. "You 'member back in high school or whenever, we used to drag race along here?" Lavern said, her voice low. "One guy, Skinky Thomas I think it was, wiped out..."

"It was a '69 'Cuda. And he walked away—not a scratch."

"Yeah, so you and Elvis did the same thing with that old Chevy Nova. You did it on purpose, just to see if you could take the ditch and not get hurt."

"Yeah, we did it too, did it perfect, except for 'bout getting knocked cold when my head hit the roof." Donnel stopped. "What's that got to do with anything?"

Again, she studied the field. "Just do what I say, baby. This might work. Trust me. Just trust me."

Donnel looked at her and frowned.

"Don't sound like I got much choice," he said.

Chapter Nine

The evening had left a scum in his mouth. But his tooth-brush wasn't to be found. Neither was his mouthwash. Damn it.

Damn.

It.

Jesse slammed the door of the bathroom cupboard. Nothing was where it should be. What was wrong with him? Where was the toilet paper? Couldn't a half-drunk, half-stoned brain doctor take a crap in his own house?

A thin sliver of lucid thought broke through the fog in his head. He hadn't unpacked.

He found the toiletries, brushed his teeth, washed his face, relieved himself, then fell into bed.

❖❖❖❖

He kept floating in and out of what seemed to be dreams. If they were dreams and were not, as he worried, disjointed movies of his life being projected on the ceiling, they were vibrant, high-color dreams, Dolby-enhanced-stereo-sound dreams. He could hear, smell and feel. The water was hot on his skin. In fact, the water was so hot it made him cringe. Jesse had to squint his eyes against the pain as he started scrubbing. He rolled over in bed, and heard, saw, felt himself scrub everything, every part of himself, four times. Scrub, two, three, four, he murmured, scrub, two, three, four. When he was finished, he let the water out, refilled the tub and started again.

He heard the slap slap slap of bare feet running down the hall past the bathroom door to the kitchen. There was a pause, then the sound, muffled, of Elvis, the boy Elvis, throwing up.

Jesse had to swallow hard.

Still in the kitchen, boy Elvis started crying.

Scrub two, three, four.

"You're lucky you made it to the sink, little mister. That'll teach you to get overheated and gulp water like a dog." Mom's voice, high and nasal, echoed down the hallway with the country music from her radio. "Get upstairs now and get in your bed."

Scrub, two, three, four.

"Can I please have one more drink?" Elvis pleaded.

Mom cackled. "What's wrong with you?" Jesse shuddered involuntarily at the sound as she hit Elvis. "You drink enough water to make you upchuck, now you want more?"

"I just want to rinse my mouth out."

She hit him again.

Jesse kept counting as he scoured his skin, trying to ignore the sound of Elvis running from the kitchen, his feet thump, thump, thumping now, growing louder as he passed the bathroom door, rolling like thunder as he hurtled up the stairs over Jesse's head, then fading down the hall to their room. The door slammed.

A faucet squeaked in the kitchen; he heard the water run briefly, then another squeak as Mom turned off the water. On the radio, Conway Twitty sang about some woman who'd done him wrong. Jesse kept on scrubbing, head down, the sequence throbbing inside his head.

He looked up to see Mom peeking through the partially open door. He dropped the wash cloth and soap and slid down into the scummy water, covering himself.

"Don't worry, I can't see nothing.."

Jesse stayed low in the water anyway, his hands still covering his crotch.

"I'm going to be upstairs talking to your brother for awhile. It's time to set him straight on some things. You take your time."

She was gone.

Jesse slid to an upright position, fumbled underwater for the washcloth and soap, and resumed his washing. Scrub, two, three, four.

He could hear Mom yelling at Elvis to let her in, the door of the bedroom opening and closing, then voices, so low you couldn't hear them. Jesse pictured her on the edge of Elvis' bed, talking in a soft sing-song voice.

Scrub, two, three, four.

Scrub, two, three, four.

Scrub, two, three, four.

Jesse lost track of time. The music on the radio and Mom upstairs with Elvis, both were forgotten. His world became the soap, the water and the soothing, cleansing power of the washcloth.

The shadows in the cramped, narrow bathroom grew long yet he kept at it, his mind clear and focused on his chest, then his stomach, his right shoulder and left. From there, he scrubbed steadily downward until he'd reached his knees. He arched his back to get at his butt, then he plopped back down and finished, all the way to his legs, ankles and feet. Then he started over.

His skin became pink, then bright red and sore. Some of the mosquito bites and scratches tore open and bled. Still, the washcloth kept at it, cleansing and cleansing, ignoring the part of him that sensed this was wrong, that he shouldn't be doing it quite this much.

Scrub. Please no. Please no. Please no.

Scrub. Please no. Please no. Please no.

"You fall in in there?"

This time, Mom's face was shadowy. With a sinking feeling, Jesse realized it was getting late. The water had gotten cool, and it was pink from his blood, yet he still didn't feel completely clean.

"It's almost ten o'clock. You better be gettin' on to bed, don't you think?"

Ten o'clock—how could that be? Jesse whirled and looked

out the window. It was dark. He'd been in the tub nearly three hours.

"What'cha done to yourself, boy?" Mom asked, an edge of worry in her voice. She opened the door wider and started to step into the room, squinting at him. A shaft of light from the bulb in the hallway ceiling fell across his chest.

Jesse was suddenly too tired to talk, and he didn't have the strength to hide his body from her. So he sat there, looking down at himself—at the bright red of his arms, chest and stomach above the pinkish gray waterline.

"You 'bout took the skin right off you, didn't you? What you using, some of that Lava soap?"

"No. No Mom. I just washed good, like you always say," he said quietly, his voice far away.

"Oh, baby, does it hurt?" Her voice was soft and right next to him now. She touched his shoulder and Jesse winced. It felt like she'd touched a bad sunburn.

"No," he said, still looking down at the red skin stretched over his ribs. "It doesn't hurt at all. I was just doing what you told—what you said—Mom."

"Looks like you maybe went too far."

"Oh, yeah, maybe."

"Well, you get yourself dried off and dressed, and you can have an ice cream or something before bed."

He looked at her, his mind fumbling with a dark thought he knew he needed to talk about. Finally, it came to him. "What about Elvis? How's he doing? I mean... he going to, um, cooperate?"

Mom smiled. "Sure he is, darlin'. Sure he is." She turned to leave.

"Mom?"

"Yeah."

"What'd you tell him?"

She took a deep breath then let it out slowly. "I told him what we're going to tell everyone else—that his fool daddy took off on us, left his family, and there's nothing we can do but forget him and move on. Told him we'll file one of what they call a missing person's report with the police just in case they ever come across him." She smiled. "But you and me know they never will."

"Oh."

She paused, backlit by the light from the hall. The only sounds were the water dripping into the tub and the kitchen radio playing a song that was just music, no singing. It had lots of fiddle and banjo in it, and Jesse hated fiddle and banjo music. In his exhaustion, the song irritated him, so did Mom's attitude; he wasn't sure she'd done enough to really scare Elvis.

Mom started back toward the kitchen, thought about something, then stopped, leaned back in and smiled. "I also told him if he ever remembered what happened today, you'd kill him."

Jesse felt an icicle slide down his spine.

"Good. Good Mom," he said, smiling nervously.

She again started to leave.

"Mom?" Jesse said, stopping her again.

"Yeah, baby?"

"Can I have chocolate ice cream?"

"Sure you can, baby. Sure you can." The smile she gave him was the sweetest he'd ever seen from her.

❊❊❊❊

An hour, maybe two, later, Jesse sat on the edge of the bed, smoking another joint. There was no end to this night. It was a bleak tunnel of sad possibilities extending infinitely in two directions; squint through it one way and he had a half-moon view of the past, turn the other way and he was blinded by the train light of the future. Looking out the window now, he also felt the guilt and uncertainty hanging over him, threatening to crush him. Screw it, he mumbled. Yeah, he thought, screw it. He wanted to call his mom. He couldn't explain why, except that all roads led back to her. Maybe he wanted to vent at her. Maybe. Yeah. Darn straight. Maybe that was it. Maybe he was ready to let her know what he thought. He ran a raw, red hand through his hair, took another hit, held it in, then exhaled. He licked his fingertips, then squeezed the tip of the joint. When he was sure it was snuffed out, he carefully placed it in the drawer of the bedstand, vowing not to forget it was there. He rolled back into bed. He would call Mom later. Darn straight he would. He would call her and give her a piece of his mind. This thought made him giggle, because he could picture it, the piece of his mind, in his hand. Jesse snickered, doubled up in bed for several seconds, imagining Mom's face darkening as he tried to get her to hold the piece of his mind. Finally he controlled himself, but only after several deep breaths. He dried his eyes, rolled to his side and pulled the covers over his shoulder. Jesse allowed his gaze to run across the ceiling and down to one of the bedroom windows. Elvis, a boy in his PJs, was sitting up in bed, in front of the window, staring at him matter-of-factly.

"You and me, we both know what happened out there. We know, but everybody else thinks he run off," the boy Elvis said.

Elvis picked at his nose for a second, then looked down at his fingertip before wiping it on the sheet. He swung his eyes back to Jesse's. "It's a lie, you know. He didn't run off. I know it's a lie and so do you." Elvis paused. "So does she. Mom, she knows it's a lie too." Elvis' eyes glazed and stared past Jesse, fixing on something just over his right shoulder. "Dad always said lying was the worst thing you could do," Elvis continued, a thin little smile spreading across his face.

Jesse's throat tightened.

Elvis looked at his brother. "I guess we all know that ain't true, right?" He giggled. "I mean, there's worse things than a lie, huh? You and me gotta know that by now. I mean, sometimes the truth's worse, really."

Elvis turned away and pulled the sheet over his head. He curled up. To Jesse, Elvis looked like a sleeping dog lying on the ground after it had snowed; you could tell what was there, you just couldn't see the color or, really, the complete shape, but you knew what the thing was.

For several seconds there wasn't a sound. Jesse swallowed. He was a boy again, a boy whose skin was on fire and whose head was heaving with molten, wild thoughts. His throat felt thick and swollen. So much had changed so quickly. Why, one minute, he'd been up here in this room thinking about strawberry fields and John Lennon and a worthless man. The next minute, it seemed, he'd been a killer looking for a way to cover up what he'd done.

Elvis hadn't told anyone anything. He wouldn't. He wouldn't ever, Jesse thought. Elvis was going to believe the lie. He was going to accept the lie—hide in it. Even as he thought this, Jesse wasn't sure.

The acts of getting out of bed and fumbling around for his clothes, of getting dressed and going down to the kitchen were all part of the same reality, which was a debatable reality at best. It wasn't until he was staring into the cupboard over the kitchen sink that Jesse realized he was awake and adult and in his new house. His head throbbed and he craved something sweet. Part of him wanted another drink, too. The drinking and the pot smoking had left a bitterness, a realization that he had fallen farther than he'd expected to fall. He felt dirty. Dirty and hungry for more.

There was no food to be found. Frustrated, he contemplated going back to bed but imagined the high-octane dreams, his brother's and father's eyes in the dark corner of the room, stalking him. Food, he needed food, not sleep. Somewhere, he thought, a convenience store had to be open. With any luck it would sell booze.

He made the decision to drive into town without making it at all. He was suddenly in the Mercedes, backing out of the driveway. The sounds of birds singing in the trees surprised him, as did the feel of the cool breeze and bright sun of a late spring morning. Was it spring? Wasn't it fall, the middle of the night? No. No, wait. This could be a dream, he heard the little boy saying in his head. He gritted his teeth and took his foot off the gas, allowing the car to crawl. Suddenly, he was the boy again, opening the smokehouse door as he pictured Sheriff Matt Dillon would do it. Out of the smokehouse billowed that awful awful odor. There was a sound, too. It was the hum, the combined buzzing of a million flies, creeping through the gloom in one round, ugly chord.

The head of the corpse was deep enough in shadows that he couldn't see it clearly, but the bottom half of the man was painted in diagonal-sunlit pinstripes from the cracks in the weather-beaten walls. In the pinstripes, he could see the flies. They were a quivering mass that moved restlessly over the man. If he hadn't already known, Jesse wouldn't have been able to tell the flies were on a body. He would've thought the shape underneath them was another kind of meat, a big old country ham maybe.

The flies that weren't on the body were angry black raindrops in the air. Some slapped his neck and face in their rampaging, sending shivers through him.

Jesse remembered that he'd come to finish the job. He told himself that no matter how awful he felt about it, no matter how much he wanted to turn and run away, he had to do it. He pulled the Mercedes to the shoulder of the country road. Trembling, he put the car in park, closed his eyes and felt himself falling back through the years, falling, falling falling to his knees in the smokehouse. He leaned forward slowly until his forehead touched the floor, or was it the steering wheel? To his surprise and disappointment, Jesse began to cry. He was sobbing like a baby and floating above himself, arguing with the man in the car and the boy on the floor.

"Be strong, you stupid moron. Be a man."

Trouble was, the boy-Jesse thought, while standing there in the smokehouse, as cool as killing the man had seemed, the result hadn't been pretty—not pretty at all. He wanted to go back in time, back to before he'd done this thing, and say HA HA, the whole thing was a joke; nobody hurt. He, the boy man-killer, imagined himself as a magician on the Dead Sullivan Show; he saw himself clapping his hands, the dead man springing to his feet, bouncing on his toes, then bowing to the crowd, which loved this little trick he'd played.

Impossible, he thought. The man really was dead, and young boys can't do magic—not big tricks like that anyway.

It had been days since Mom had shown him this awful hiding place—days since he'd become a killer. Now, in the smokehouse, Jesse rose to his feet and forced himself to re-enact the scene he'd already played out in his mind, shaking the man loose, jumping out of the way as the body fell and the flies darted, rolling the shockingly swollen corpse over and sliding the eyelids down, the way he'd seen it done on TV, covering the blue-gray eyes that were still, it seemed, crying out.

He worried that maybe the eyelids wouldn't stay shut. He'd seen a painting of President Lincoln after he'd been laid out in bed, dead; they'd put quarters or something like that over his eyes to keep the lids down. He wished he'd brought a couple of quarters.

The next part was the hardest. Jesse swallowed hard and grabbed the man under the shoulders, in the armpits. It turned his stomach the way the body was swollen and stiff, but how else was he supposed to do this? He walked out of the shed backwards, dragging the body, his own mouth open, his back aching. He slipped and fell once, twice, his mind and heart racing. He recovered and continued, even though his fingers felt dirty and stained where he'd touched the cold skin of the eyelids and where he was touching the man's stiff armpits. Still, Jesse clenched his mouth and closed his eyes, urging himself to be strong.

After a time, he opened his eyes and stared out beyond the windshield of the Mercedes. His hands were knotted to the steering wheel.

He was wet with a cold sweat. He had to be courageous, he told himself. He had to be. Head up, eyes now forward, trying hard not to look down, he felt the weight of the body pulling hard against his fingers, his wrists, threatening to pull his shoulders and elbows from their sockets as he dragged his father deep into the woods. At a clearing, he dropped the body, then went back to the smokehouse and retrieved the shovel he'd brought. He returned to his father's side and took a moment to get his bearings. A large oak tree hung over the clearing. Someone, some kids he figured, had hammered a thick spike in the trunk about head-high to Jesse. He took that as an omen.

He knew not to dig near the tree; his dad had taught him that was where the biggest roots would be. Jesse walked to the spike and stepped off twenty yards or so straight out from it. There were some big flat stones in the grass there. Another omen, he figured.

The soil was sandy, the digging was easy—most of the roots were small enough to hack away with the shovel; for the rest, well, he just dug away the dirt underneath them and kept going. He dug for what seemed like hours. His eyes burned with sweat, but Jesse felt nothing else. He became happily, peacefully numb. When the hole was as deep as he thought he could make it, he dug a little more.

At last, chest heaving, Jesse clambered out of the hole and threw the shovel aside. Grabbing the man by his boots, he dragged the body up over the pile of dirt and then down into the grave.

He climbed out quickly and had the first shovel of dirt ready to throw before he let himself look at the man. Jesse took him in slowly, starting from the legs, then across the now crusty t-shirt, skirting the bloody edge of the wound. From there, his gaze jumped. From a gray face that no longer looked like a man but like maybe a waxy, obese dummy-man, the eyes stared up at him. To Jesse, they seemed sad, sadder than he'd ever remembered them being. It was like the man had stopped pleading and was now just sad over what his son had done.

The heavy shovel slipped in Jesse's sweaty hands. Some of the dirt dribbled onto the man's chest, bounced off his chin and clung to his cheeks. Jesse tightened his grip and, eyes burning again with tears, tossed the rest of the dirt at the man's newly fat face. Without looking again at the eyes, he jammed the spade into the pile of earth, pulled out another load and threw it in the hole. Frantically, he repeated the routine, tears falling.

When he was finished, Jesse stood, shovel in hands, staring at the place he'd buried his father. He thought for a moment, then, working quickly, chest heaving, he dragged the two flat rocks to the mound of dirt and shaped them in a T. He stepped back. It wasn't much, but it was the closest thing to a cross that he could throw together. In his tired brain, he figured anyone who found this might see it as a pet grave and leave it alone, and also that God, maybe, would feel better about him for the cross—about Jesse, for making the effort.

He spent a few minutes scuffing up the freshly dug dirt, then several more minutes bringing old rotted limbs and leaves to the spot and arranging them so they looked natural, like they'd fallen there. Finally, Jesse gritted his teeth and imagined weeds and vines covering the grave, making it seem like the crime had never happened. He told himself to forget this moment, this place, but he realized he never would.

He threw the shovel as hard and far as he could, heard it clang against something in the woods.

Then he was racing away, the Mercedes spewing gravel, jolting onto the blacktop, moving in time, racing, with the tennis-shoed boy-feet in his mind, bulleting down the dark road as though someone else were driving. Something inside him was screaming that he should turn around, that he needed to stop and think—had he disguised the grave somehow?—but something else was telling him to go, move, move, get away.

He barely slowed until he reached Stan's 24-hour Mini-Mart, the sign glowing like a forlorn beacon on the outskirts of town. Jesse hurried inside, walking rapidly, not stopping, not slowing, not until he reached the bathroom, where he washed his fingers and hands, scrubbing them hard, over and over until the skin bled.

As he toweled the hands dry, Jesse felt the cell phone vibrating in his pocket. Gingerly, wincing at the friction against the raw skin, he withdrew it and glanced at the display. He grunted. "Stupid local idiots. I'm not supposed to be on-call tonight." He punched a button, held the phone to his ear. "This is Dr. Tieter. And this better be good."

Chapter Ten

"Put down that tuna fish before I spank your butt." His mom was wagging a knobby finger at him. The dark eyes were daggers, her red hair rumpled, her head cocked to one side like a lead weight was in there. The shrill voice rattled through his head, making it ache. "You'll eat what I tell you to eat—what I make. Tonight, it's beanie weenie casserole so you'll eat beanie weenie casserole and like it; no ifs, ands or buts."

Elvis was seeing her through a camera lens or something, like she was on TV. He tried to look down at the black and white PF Flyers on his feet, but he couldn't see down there.

The tuna fish can flew past his mother's head. Mom ducked. The can hit their dog, a skinny black and white mutt named Hound Dog, then clattered loudly on the blue linoleum. Hound Dog yelped and started chasing his tail. The sound was odd, echo-ey. To Elvis, it was like they were inside an empty fruit jar. He wanted to cover his ears but he couldn't reach them. He couldn't look down either—couldn't see those shoes.

Mom slapped him. Elvis convulsed with sobs. He jerked his head back and she hit him again, hard. His nose throbbed and he turned and ran; he ran away from Hound Dog, the tuna fish and the beanie weenie. He awoke into something far more frightening: the present—what had to be the worst day of his life. He sat up, tried to focus in the semi-darkness. It took him several seconds to decide he'd fallen asleep on the living room floor. Then he remembered falling asleep on the couch. He must've rolled onto the floor without waking up.

He took a swipe at the butt of his jeans, brought his hand back around and stared at it. There was a smear of something red on his fingers. The stuff had dried on his naked back too; he could feel it cracking when he moved. It took several seconds for him to remember Lavern had spilled fingernail polish. She had done a lousy job cleaning up.

Elvis squinted at the clock on the wall; it had gold spires spoking out of it—Lavern told him once the spires were supposed to look like the rays of the sun. Mom had given them the clock as a wedding present; she'd bought it from some junk store. Elvis had always hated that clock. It was eight-thirty. Nearly two hours had passed since Donnel and Lavern had left.

There was a loud crash from the kitchen. Elvis' back contorted in a non-verbal scream. There was a soft thump; it was Brad the cat, he decided, looking for food. Elvis sighed. Stupid cat.

He stared at the candles flickering on the table and thought about how stupid he was. He wondered why he was home alone, why he hadn't followed Donnel and defended his right to Lavern. He wondered how he could have killed a man without even trying. Jerry Plannenberg had something to do with it. As he thought of the faceless man and Jerry, he thought of someone else. But for the life of him, he couldn't figure who the someone else was. The phone interrupted his thought. Elvis struggled to his feet, crossed the room slowly, and grabbed the receiver in the middle of the third ring.

"Hello?"

"Is this the Icabone residence?"

"Yeah, this is Elv..."

"Elvis Icabone?" she finished for him.

"Yes."

"Mr. Icabone, I'm calling from Bally Memorial Hospital and I'm afraid we have some rather bad news."

Elvis could hear his heart again. "Ye..." he said, the word tripping on its way out. "Yes?"

"Sir, are you alone?"

"Yeah, uh-huh, sure."

"Well, um, I'm sorry, maybe we should send someone over, sir. Or do you have a minister, a friend, someone nearby that could come over right now?"

"Why'd I need that?"

"Well, sir, I'm afraid the news is extremely, well... you might want someone with you right now. If you wish, I could send a police officer over; there's one right here with me. Why don't I do that?"

"Why?"

"Well, it would just be best."

"But why? Someone dead?" Elvis said loudly.

There was a long, sterile pause on the line.

"I said, 'Someone dead?'"

"Sir, I really think we should send someone over. See, there's been an accident."

The thought coughed into his head. Hack. It was there. On any other day, Elvis would have ignored it. But today, it was a very reasonable thought. He remembered Donnel's truck shimmying recklessly down the road, Jerry Plannenberg, the ponytail swinging, then someone else, a shadow of someone from long ago tottered across his field of memory. He was chilled; a cold breeze whispered over his naked chest. "My wife, she there?" he asked in a high, tight voice.

"Sir, are you sure you don't have a priest, a minister," the voice continued, sounding polite, sweet and helpful. "Someone we could call?"

Elvis dropped the receiver, walked across the living room, out the open door and down the three steps. He forgot that he was half dressed with dried fingernail polish on his naked back.

Halfway across the lawn, he remembered the stupid candles, stopped, turned and marched back in the house. He blew out each one then walked back through the open doorway, this time slamming the door behind him.

Brad had dashed out into the night ahead of him. He stood in the yard, under a streetlight, watching Elvis, his tail at attention and twitching.

Elvis coaxed the Cordoba to life, flicked on the lights and eased the car, its exhaust rumbling, the suspension creaking, down the street. He left the subdivision and accelerated as he passed the convenience store and drove over the Lemon Creek bridge, past the Compton's grain elevator; it was the trip into town he'd taken a million times before.

From Blue Star Highway he could see, across the empty cornfield, the accident scene on Torchner Road. Elvis made the turn on Torchner, his heart suddenly muddy in his ears. The Cordoba slowed to a stuttering crawl, taking its place in the traffic line. Ahead, streetlights painted the scene. Red police flares sputtered in an arc, funneling drivers away from the right lane to the left. A cop with a red-coned flashlight was directing traffic; as Elvis neared, the cop was holding a hand up to the cars behind him, the ones coming from the other way, and windmilling his other arm and the flashlight—come-on, come-on, come-on—at the cars in front of Elvis. The cars were crawling along, the drivers slowly obeying the cop. A wrecker was waddling down into the ditch along the road toward the old pickup, which lay on its side in the muddy field like a rusty-brown fish bellied out of water.

As Elvis watched, the wrecker came to a stop, a door swung open and one guy dropped out. The guy slammed the door, walked around the back of the wrecker, fished in his jeans pocket for something, got it; the thing flamed up and threw a dancing light on the guy's face as he cupped his hand around it, guiding it to the cigarette already in his mouth.

Elvis felt the Cordoba's greasy steering wheel turn in his hands and felt the car stop on the shoulder. He felt, from far away, his hand rolling down the window. He couldn't feel the cold air; he looked past the gawkers slowing through the accident scene.

The smoker had returned the lighter to his pocket and was directing the driver in backing up to the truck. A family rolled by in a minivan, the father driving, the mother eating an ice cream cone as the kids pawed over each other in the back seat. They looked first at the truck, then, at the last second, they twisted around to stare at Elvis. Finally, the minivan picked up speed and they got on their way, got on with their lives.

The truck was Donnel's, for sure. All lit up by flares and the spotlight from the remaining cop car; Elvis could make out the Cherry Bomb and Harley Davidson stickers in the rear window. There were silvery chrome mud flaps, too, one with the silhouette of a naked girl on it, the other Yosemite Sam.

Elvis watched as both wrecker guys talked it over now, slouching against the side of their rig, dragging on their cigarettes. For an instant, he imagined the whole thing had nothing to do with him. He imagined yelling to them, "Hey, hear about Jubal Brown?" He could picture the two guys as they grinned and spit and said, together, "Yeah, got the shinola beat out of him," then laughing because they hadn't meant to say it at the same time. He could see them throwing their smokes out in the field. He imagined the butts glowing, soft, orange and reassuring against the dark.

Elvis reached under the seat and scrounged around. His trembling fingertips found the plastic bag. He had the joint in his mouth and lit before he even thought about the police car just yards away. He could see the cop behind the wheel, face illuminated by the dashboard light, writing on a clipboard. Didn't look like the cop from work. Didn't look like his partner either, the guy who'd told him to stay in town. Well, screw him, he thought. Screw all of them. Don't leave town, they'd said. Stick around, they'd said. They hadn't said a dang thing about not smoking weed.

A guy in a gray Camaro eased off the road behind him. Elvis took a long hit from the joint and held it as he slid his foot off the brake and eased his car back onto the road. He exhaled. The Cordoba hesitated before chug, chug chugging its way up to speed. He leaned out over the wheel and took another drag. The wind knifed through the open window. He hadn't smoked dope in years. Only back in high school had he screwed around with it a little. This joint, well, he'd found it under a chair the night after the guys had been over at the house playing cards. He'd saved it for some stupid reason. He'd put it in a baggie and stuck it in his car where his soon-to-be-ex-oh-wait-now-who-knew?-dead? wife couldn't find it. He dragged at the thing again, coughing. He could feel it swirling, loosening the nuts on the bolts in his brain. Elvis felt wrong for doing it, wrong and stupid. Wrong and stupid but dang hungry for more.

The car topped out at forty, maybe forty-five; he didn't know for sure, since the speedometer was broken. A couple of cars passed him. Elvis glanced in the rear-view mirror and saw the outline of a vintage Camaro, now back on the road too, a quarter mile behind.

He drove past Zech's Farm Market and past a patch of identical one-story condominiums—a new subdivision someone had plopped in a corner of farmland. The condos ticked him off. Stupid condos. Stupid fucking condo-fucking-miniums. He didn't usually swear. Didn't think that way. But fuck it, he thought.

He thought the pot was smoothing the edges of the pain in his brain. He hoped it was. Yeah, that too. Hoped. Funny word, hope, he thought. Hope. Hope. Hope. He snickered. The pastor talked about hope in church all the time. Hopey hope-ity hope. What did it mean? Hope? Not a dang thing. Hope meant squat. Hope was for losers who didn't get it. Hope was ten pounds of shinola in a five pound bag. That's what hope was. Right now it was. When your lady's maybe cheating and now busted up somehow or worse with your best buddy and you lost your job and people thought you killed some dude with no face, it was. Hope. Screw it. He flicked the last of the joint out the window. Fuck. It.

It was a small hospital, just two, two-story brick wings. He took the turn into the parking lot too hard; the Cordoba shimmied and fishtailed. In a second of stoned thinking, Elvis thought about letting it go, letting the tires slide and the back end come slowly around. He could see it in his head, the old rustbucket breaking loose like a stockcar overcranking a turn at Daytona, the thing dancing head over end, coming to a stop on its top with him maybe bleeding and happily dead inside. Something else, something hard and edgy in his brain, something that seemed new and weird—from the dope maybe?—told him to resist. Elvis squeezed the wheel harder, suddenly angry, steering against the skid, until he'd wrestled the car to a stop. He steadied himself, saw the ambulance, rear-end open and lights flashing in front of the entrance marked Emergency, and guided the Cordoba to a parking space near it.

Out of habit, he pushed his left shoulder against the door as he pulled up on the handle. At first, the door didn't open. Stay, it said. Stay here. Elvis gave it one final, hard nudge and it creaked open, the momentum almost sending him sprawling into the parking lot.

He got out of the car and slammed the door. He took a deep breath and started toward the ambulance. Elvis glanced inside. Empty. He turned and looked through the glass doors to the Emergency Room. There was a reception window and an empty waiting area, both painted with the pulsating lights from the ambulance—red and white and red and white and red and white—like he was at a rock 'n roll show, a concert for The Dead. He felt calm. Calm from the dope. Calm from just knowing, from the feeling in his gut that he already understood what he was about to see.

Elvis stepped on the black rubber mat in front of the double doors. Swish. They opened and the smell of the hospital whisked out. He caught a glimpse of his reflection. He was a sight to behold: naked from the waist up, hair all shaggy and wild. He looked like he'd just lost his wife, his job, his best friend and maybe had killed a man.

An old lady in a pink jacket came through the double doors labeled AUTHORIZED PERSONNEL ONLY. She gave Elvis a funny look. "May I help you..." She paused, not sure what to call him. "Sir?"

"My name's Elvis, um..." He was suddenly nervous.

"Oh, Mr. Icabone?" Her face suddenly matched her jacket. She turned around, retreating to the AUTHORIZED PERSONNEL ONLY area. "Let me get the doctor," she called over her shoulder.

"No. Wait," he blurted out.

She turned slowly, one authorized palm flat against the doors.

"Is my wife dead?"

The old lady bit her lower lip, then again started to push through the doors. "Let me get our neuro... the doctor; you should talk to him."

"No. Wait." Elvis took three long strides and grabbed her by the arm. It was a skinny arm. Skinny and bony.

The lady's head bobbed funny, like he'd smacked her, then she scowled and jerked free. "Let go of me."

"Sorry," Elvis said, a little surprised at himself.

"Your wife and the other gentleman," she looked at him, her voice softening. "I'm sorry, but there were head injuries, severe trauma. Our team here worked very, very hard."

"They didn't make it." Elvis said it flatly, to help her.

Her smile confirmed it; knifing through the fog of the dope and the day, that smile hurt. Oh. Oh. It hurt. His breathing grew heavy and slow. A hoarse-voice whisper of a thought, gruff and low, told him he'd seen this coming and not just on the way here. No. Part of him had known about this for a long time. Hadn't it? Sure. Sure as shootin'. He'd felt a bad moon rising on him for a long time. The hoarse-voice thought in his head told him he deserved it. But even though he'd seen it coming, it was sure hard to have it here, staring at him.

"You're supposed to... I mean, would you like to..." she paused again. "Come with me? I can take you to talk to the doctor who..."

Elvis frowned and pictured Lavern with head injuries and Donnel, half his face bashed in. He imagined Donnel and Lavern kissing in the truck before the truck rolled over.

"No." Elvis felt his own voice floating away.

"But sir. The doctor... he's a specialist from Chicago... he can explain what, why... you should really see the..."

"No," was all Elvis could say. "Not yet, not now."

❖❖❖❖

A soft shower, the kind of rain that made Lavern go all oozy and romantic, had covered the hospital parking lot with a shiny skin.

He was cold. Just before he'd stepped into the miserable night, a nurse had come out and begged him to stay, and when he'd refused she'd offered to find a surgical smock, something, anything, for him to wear. He was sorry he hadn't taken her up on it. When she'd made the offer, Elvis had felt like she was stalling him for some reason. He'd been in a hurry to get out of there. Sorry, no, he'd said. Now his tired brain veered off on another path, imagining how a nurse in that situation would come up with a smock; he pictured her having to poke her head in some operating room and say, "Borrow your smock, doc?" He pictured a surgeon who looked like that guy on the oatmeal commercials, putting down his rib spreader and Styrofoam cup, sloshing a little coffee on the operating table. Elvis pictured another nurse lifting the patient's arm so the pale brown coffee pool could run down the stainless steel and trickle onto the tile floor. The surgeon would wipe his hands on the smock, smearing the blood on it like he was a grease monkey. He'd undo the string at the back of his neck and say, chuckling, "Got a cold one out there?" to the nurse, then he'd hand the smock to her. She'd laugh and nod, like this wasn't the first time she'd had to interrupt him for a cold one.

Something told him to stop, to turn around, go back and find this doctor who had looked at Lavern and Donnel; it was some kind of brain doctor, the nurse had said as he was leaving. He knew he should talk to the guy and ask to see the bodies so he could haul the sheets off them and hug them or say good-bye, but Elvis hated the idea of dead people. Besides, he kept picturing Donnel and Lavern as lovers, sitting close together in that stupid truck, nuzzling each other. He saw, in his head, the faceless man on the floor at work.

This was all too much. Too, too much.

Elvis thought he could hear someone yelling to him from the entrance of the Emergency Room, but he didn't turn around. He reached the car, wrestled the door open, got in and rolled up the window. After starting the engine, he flicked on the lights, slipped the car into gear, eased it around in the parking lot and slammed on the brakes. Wait a second, he thought. Where'm I going?

Home, he answered with a shiver. Go there and get into something warm, like your favorite flannel shirt, the blue and black one. Drink something hot and sort this out.

But going home would be like visiting hell. Elvis couldn't think very clearly, but he knew one thing. He couldn't shower and change clothes and relax with the devil looking over his shoulder.

He couldn't go to the house, not yet anyway—maybe, he thought, not ever again.

Chapter Eleven

The roads were empty at this hour. Good, he thought, steering with his knee. The headlights swooped over the centerline as he fumbled with the cap on the bottle. Steadying the wheel with his scaly left hand, he took a drink, choked and cursed. The whiskey was cheap crap. He sat forward in the seat, searching for his turn; he was desperate to get back to the house, maybe smoke the rest of the joint.

The scene at the hospital, just a few minutes past, had been surreal. His brain was flipping it, playing it over and over, worrying and wondering over it. What the heck were Lavern and her fat black friend up to? Emily? Had she? Yes. Yes. Somehow, she and some of her nurse friends probably had helped them. Maybe. But how? Why?

He rubbed the back of his hand against the stubble on his face. This was going wrong. Horribly, horribly wrong. Calm down. Calm down. Now. Freaking out won't help. Where was the turn to the house? Focus on that. It was up ahead. There? No. Maybe, he thought, he should talk to Mom. Why? Who knew? But sure. Maybe. There, there it was. He hit the brakes and cut hard to the right, bouncing down off the main road onto the gravel lane. He hit the gas and aimed the car toward the driveway, the tall grass in the lane singing an uneven tune on the undercarriage of the car. Maybe Mom, maybe she'd had something to do with this, this stupid, stupid situation. The plan to come back to this stupid town and do all this had been a lousy one to begin with. Had Mom suggested it? Had it been her concept? Maybe she'd fed it to him sometime, somehow and it was all a damn setup.

Everything. Unreal.

He pulled the Mercedes into the garage, killed the engine and flipped on the dome light. After re-reading the note from Lavern, he took out his wallet and stuck it in there, threw the wallet on the passenger's seat, then flipped the light off and slouched in his seat. Calm down, he told himself. Calm. Down.

Back at the beginning, way back, right after the thing, he had tried to convince himself that Elvis would stay quiet forever. Jesse had killed his father on Saturday, and by Wednesday, he was thinking about baseball and the Tigers again; he was listening to Ernie Harwell doing the play-by-play on the transistor radio while his brother tossed and turned in his sleep. But Jesse now had to admit that Elvis—what Elvis knew and the nagging possibility that Mom was underestimating Elvis— had always had been there, eating at his brain, worrying him.

The Friday after the killing, he now recalled, he had felt the threat in his gut, hard, for the first time. He had just jammed a forkful of beef stew in his mouth when he caught the weird blue-gray stare from across the table. A yellow plastic cup slipped from Elvis' hand. During the wild flurry of activity that followed—Elvis whispering, "Sorry, Mom, sorry, Mom" and mopping at the milk with a handful of napkins, Mom knocking over her chair in the rush to slap Elvis across the face and grab a washcloth from the sink—Jesse had stared at Elvis until their eyes met again. The return look, in a face red and tear streaked, told him something new had happened that day, something bad. Jesse hadn't said anything about it till bedtime. He'd waited until Mom had tucked him in and scolded Elvis one last time for spilling the milk. After she'd whispered, "Good night, Jess" at the bedroom door and had gone downstairs to watch TV, he cleared his throat loudly.

"You think you're big stuff, don't you?" Jesse whispered to the crack in the ceiling, breaking the six-day silence between them. "You think you can maybe find a way to work this thing out—you can deal with this—even though I told you there's no stinking way you can."

The Redeeming Power of Brain Surgery

Elvis didn't respond.

"You little, stupid, putrid, nothing piece of sewer meat. You dirty, skinny, addle-brained weasel. You worthless piece of maggot meal." Jesse's whisper rose in the room like steam hissing from a leaky pipe. "Don't make me come down there and beat your skinny little head in. Talk to me."

The bottom bunk was silent.

Jesse rolled to his side and peered over the edge. A shadowy Elvis was curled into a ball, facing his half of the window, looking out into the yard. Jesse could see just part of one side of his face, the part painted with moonlight. The eyes were clenched shut; his cheek all shiny with tears.

"I'm talking to you," Jesse said.

Elvis' shoulders shook like he was cold; he was crying. Jesse waited, counting the seconds to the beat of the thudding pulse in his head. Elvis knotted into a tighter ball. "Talk to me. Tell me what's going on." Jesse spit the words at him.

Elvis curled tighter.

"Now, tell me what happened today. Tell me, right now, you steaming bowl of worthless pus. You dribbling piece of..."

"Nothing," Elvis said.

"What?"

"I said, 'nothing,'" Elvis stretched himself out a little, like he was trying to convince Jesse he was telling the truth.

"You're lying."

"Am not."

"Are too."

"Not."

"Too."`

"Not," Elvis flipped over and stared at Jesse. "I am not," he hissed through clenched teeth. "Nothing happened. You understand me?" Elvis' voice grew louder with each word. "Nothing. Nothing. Nothing."

They held each other's gaze, blue-gray locked into blue-gray. Finally, quietly, something dawned on Jesse. "You found him, didn't you."

There was a flicker in Elvis' eyes, a pause, then finally his face crumpled up like Mom had slapped him good. Elvis knotted up into his tight ball and cried.

Jesse felt paralyzed, like *rigor mortis* had set in. The light from the garage door opener flicked off and he was buried in darkness. Panic rose in his throat. He took a swig from the whiskey bottle, fumbled for the cap in his lap, screwed it on the bottle, then tossed the bottle to the backseat. The questions bounded in his head. Had Elvis ever said anything about this to anyone? Had someone else seen the body? Over and over and over again, the questions from then, from now, spun.

That night, back then, he'd decided to bury the man. He'd done it the next day. Now, staring into the darkness of the garage, Jesse Tieter could again feel the shovel in his hands and the look of horror locked forever in his father's eyes. There was so much stuff he hadn't thought about. So much he'd never anticipated. He'd been so young, so very, very young. Now, he was still trying to make up for that, wasn't he? The eyes, he could still see them, staring up from the grave. He should've brought quarters. He should've waited until he had the body in the ground, then covered the eyes with the coins. Then he wouldn't have that stare burned into his stupid brain. Yes. But he'd been so damn young. Too young to think of it all. And now? Now he was feeling it, wasn't he? Oh how it ached, the burden of it pressing against his heart like a prickly, pineapple-sized growth. Open the door, he thought. Go in the house. Get away from it, maybe, with the stupid dope in the drawer. But no. No, wait. The ache in his head turned the garage from dark to red. Oh. No. Impossible. But yes. Yes. Yes. Go. Now. He saw again, in his mind, his brother in a ball, the note from Lavern. Now, before it was too late. He had a job to do. Just like before.

Jesse pushed the car door open. At the wall, he found the light switch. He kicked off his shoes and pulled on the new workboots he'd left by the door. He picked up a blue plastic tarp, still folded in its wrapper. One high-powered light, a rechargeable with a snake-like neck, was on the floor next to the shovel. The other light, a halogen that also had a battery pack and a collapsible stand, was in the corner. In seconds he collected all the gear and was stumbling across the wet grass of the backyard.

It began to rain, but he didn't notice. He'd seen himself doing this, had worked out, gotten in physical shape for it, for months. The snakelight found the site easily; it helped that he'd had the landscaper mow a clearing out here for him. He'd told the guy, "Don't move a thing. I want it mowed; that's it." He'd paid the idiot enough to do what he said.

As Jesse rigged the lights near the oak at the edge of the clearing, he was struck again by the clarity of his memory. He'd met many adults who couldn't recall the traumas of their childhoods, but lately he'd been able to remember every sliver of detail of this thing. It didn't seem fair.

He aimed the snake light at the oak and found what was left of the old spike. It was a stroke of luck that it had been so big; the years of weather had eaten away at it, but it was still plainly visible. He wiped the rain from his eyes, sniffed, then stepped off the distance, altering his stride to accommodate the difference between his adult height and his child height. The first time, he found nothing. The second and third and fourth tries, he found nothing. Frustrated, he went back again to the spiked oak and tried a slightly different angle and stride. Two feet beyond the mowed area, in the high grass, he kicked something hard. Trembling, Jesse fell to his knees, swept the grass aside and directed the light at the two rocks arranged in a T. He smiled despite himself. As if on cue, the rain abated.

Jesse rearranged the lights, grabbed the shovel and jabbed it in a spot near the rock. He stepped back, heaved a sigh and closed his eyes—a mistake. The past, his father's eyes, the wound in his chest, the feel of the stiffened armpits; it came tumbling back to him down the long dark tunnel of memory.

There was a noise. Jesse cried out. He looked to the woods, his confidence trickling away. A breeze whistled through the trees. There was the rush of something—someone—through the underbrush.

Jesse scratched a knuckle, then another, dropped the shovel and rubbed the backs of both hands frantically against his pants legs.

Screw it. Go. Go on. Get out of here. Drink. Smoke. Anything else. But this? No. Not. Now. Yes. Yes. Now. Now, or what? Now or never.

Jesse set his jaw, picked up the blue tarp, removed it from its wrapper, and tossed both the wrapper and the folded tarp to the ground. He picked up the shovel, arranged his lights, and paced around the clearing, looking at it, golden and glowing. He'd come back. To solve this. To tie up the loose ends. He'd had to do it then, and he had to do it now. Her voice was in his head. "You're the responsible one," she always said. "You're the one I count on."

He began to dig. The sweat soaked his back, bitter bile surged in his throat. His breathing grew ragged. He could see her, smiling now, smiling that he'd been smart enough to do this. His ears burned with satisfaction and embarrassment. How could it still please him so to please her? But it did. Yes. She was smiling and that made him feel good. Dig it. Your mother will be glad with what you've done. Yes. Ignore the dark. Ignore that someone might see the lights and come back here. Dig it. You stupid Phi Beta Kappa. Make your mother proud. Be the good son. Dig it. Even though you want to hurt her, even though you want to tell her what she's done to you. Dig it. And you can make her happy. Just like before, back then, back when you were her best boy.

Dig. It.

He did. And she came to him, proudly, bringing him a drink because he was thirsty. "I'm P-R-O-U-D of you," she said. Not many boys would've done what you done," she said, handing him the iced tea.

"It really wasn't that hard," he said, his voice a wrecked half-whisper. "Just found the right spot and started digging."

She smiled and took him back, back in time, leading him through the creaking front door and back to the porch. They sat next to each other in the wicker chairs Dad had bought from a pawn shop. The chairs weren't white anymore, more a faded gray, and they leaned; when you sat in one you had the uneasy feeling you were going to tip over if you weren't careful. But she'd never let him sit in the chairs before. She never treated him like this. Jesse thought it was cool. Dig it, he thought. Dig it.

Jesse took a long hard gulp of the iced tea and looked at Mom. She was sitting, tipped toward him in her chair, arms folded. Dressed in a light blue dress, a sleeveless one, she was barefoot. He realized she'd been barefoot a lot lately. Her feet were bright pink the same way his skin was.

"What you think about moving away?" she said, pointing the question toward the road, her chin up.

Jesse choked on the last swallow of the tea, sat up in the chair, coughed hard then put the glass down on the uneven wood floor. It tipped over. "M... moving?" He bent down and fumbled with the glass, trying to save some of the ice. The cubes slithered away and turned black with dirt.

"Yeah, you know, getting away to somewheres," she said, focusing on him now. "Going where nobody knows us real good or, you know, knows him."

"Like where?" Jesse stammered. "What do you mean? Where'd we go, Mom?"

Mom smiled and looked at her lap. "I was thinking a nice place might be Iowa."

Jesse jumped to his feet and started pacing.

"Your Aunt Barb and Uncle Ed's out there."

He couldn't breathe. This was so like her. One minute everything was fine; he'd had everything worked out in his mind, then, Iowa. It hadn't been part of the picture. Jesse opened his mouth to say something, to shout or scream or something. But no sound came out, only his white breath against the cool night.

"It's a nice place to live, where they're at," he heard her say. "They got nice people. It's a real friendly, good town. There's no trouble, hardly any crime or, like, gangs or nothing."

"Uncle Barb's and Aunt Ed's." He gasped the names with disgust, not hearing how he'd switched the names. "You... we'd... you talked to them... I mean, about moving there?"

"Oh, yeah, sure—a little."

Jesse pictured his aunt and uncle. She had fake teeth she stuck in a glass on a table by her bed. Uncle Ed, he wore a funny little straw hat sometimes and was skinny and always nervous. He was a big shot for a company that made water heaters. Jesse remembered Uncle Ed giving him a Dutch rub the last time they'd gotten together. He'd talked on and on about water heaters and the Chicago Cubs. "How 'bout them Cubbies?" he'd kept saying.

"They're not against taking people in," she said. "Barb's my sister, you know. Families do that for each other. Someone falls on hard times, they pitch in, help out."

Jesse paused. Breathing hard, now soaked with sweat, his need for another bath was becoming desperate.

"Does it matter what I think?" he asked, already knowing the answer.

"'Course it does, baby." She took another deep breath and fumbled in the pocket of her dress for her lighter and a cigarette. She made a big production of lighting up and took a long, hard drag, then clenched her teeth and hissed the smoke out with another sigh. "Your opinion matters, baby," she whispered, her eyes turning again to him. The eyes were a little glazed now, and the smile was gone. "'Cuz you're the one that's going."

"What?" He hadn't heard it.

"I said you're the one that's going. I didn't stutter, boy. Clean out them ears."

Jesse couldn't move or speak. She held the cigarette in the air in front of her mouth, and smoke drifted up from it in a lazy, white curl. "You got no choice, considering what happened with your brother," she said, then took another drag on the Kool.

"Mom, I'm taking care of it. I am. You said yourself I done a good job, just a second ago."

"I'm not talking about the body or what you're gonna do. I'm talking about the boy who seen the whole dang thing and now he's seen the man dead and you still haven't taken no steps to make sure he keeps his stupid, addle-brained mouth shut."

She smoked quietly for several seconds, then pulled the cigarette from her mouth and looked up at him. She gave him a sick little smile and huffed a smoke ring in his face.

Jesse blinked. "He's not saying anything to anybody," he said in a voice that was cracking and weak. "I know he's not."

"You do not know that for sure."

"Well, yeah, okay, not for sure. But I know sort of. Yes. Yes. I know. I do, Mom. He'll keep quiet."

"Sure he will." She nodded, and stared off again.

Jesse turned and walked to the edge of the porch. He picked out a birch tree across the road and focused on it. When he spoke, his voice was almost a whisper. "So this is about Elvis?"

A car, an old Buick, rolled by slowly. It was people from Illinois gawking at the countryside.

"'Course it's about Elvis. Way I see it, you can't keep control over him, so I'll have to do it myself. I'll raise him here on my own, and I'll make sure he don't remember nothing that happened. I can do it. I got a way with the boy. Meanwhile, you can just go on and live your little life. You can be somebody. It's your reward, if you want to think of it that way—your reward for what you done." Her voice hung in the dark of the woods as though the foggy night had preserved them there. Jesse Tieter stopped digging and rested on the shovel. He could smell her breath, could taste the cigarette smoke. A shiver of a thought: Was he losing his mind? Then, a colder one: Did it matter?

He turned back to the digging, in earnest, hoping Mom

would leave him alone. But the air was suddenly, again, warm and heavy. A couple of blackbirds landed in a lower limb of the birch tree. They sat there, clucking. Standing on the porch, Jesse imagined shooting them the way he and Elvis used to shoot birds with the BB gun.

"What you told him the other night, is that what you want? You want me to kill Elvis, too?" he heard his kid-voice say. "You know, I could do it, if that's what you want." He said it, even though he didn't mean it. He didn't think he could kill, not again, not after doing it once. Even the thought of shooting birds with a BB gun made him a little queasy.

"Listen to you, talking all big and strong, like you're something else. You, the big man killer."

Jesse felt the tears coming. He clenched the shovel and began digging in earnest. He heard the blackbirds bolt, cackling.

"You're not man enough. You're not strong enough in your guts."

"I am. I am too."

The porch floor squeaked as mom stood, walked around Jesse and down one step, then she turned and looked up at him. Smoke curled from the cigarette, which now dangled from the corner of her mouth; a long, crooked finger of ash hung from it. He choked. "If you can do it, you're going to have to show me," she said, the cigarette dancing, the ash clinging on for dear life. "'Cuz I just don't know if you got it in you—not anymore." The ash fell.

Jesse looked away. What she was asking him to do he could not even attempt. "I can do it, Mom. I can." He couldn't believe the words were coming out of his mouth. "Really, don't you worry." He looked at her. "I'll show you."

Her eyes seemed to glitter through the smoke. "Let me make a deal with you."

"What?"

"You take care of your brother. I mean, really take care of him. But remember, you need a alibi. So you take care of him then come up with a story to where he's gone off to and why."

Jesse blinked and swallowed. This was too much to ask, way too much.

"If you do it, fine. I'll keep you right here, and when I get me a good job I'll buy you that record you been wanting." She climbed the step and went into the house.

Jesse's throat felt like it was swelling; swallowing was getting very difficult. He didn't want to kill his brother. That had never been part of the plan, had it? No. It hadn't been. That part was Mom's idea. No, wait, all of it had been Mom's idea. Yes, the deal with the Beatles' record had pushed him over the edge that day—made him extra mad at Dad. But it was Mom that made him think it was time to just kill the man, right? It hadn't been his idea. No. No way. He was just a kid, practically a little boy, and Mom had gotten his thinking all screwed up. Mom had convinced him to be a killer, an awful, vicious killer. And he'd gone right along with it. And now she wanted the same thing with Elvis. She wanted him dead. And here he was, part of him saying, "No mom, no way," the other part saying, "Sure, duh-huh, I'll do it." Such thoughts had brought him all the way back to Michigan and were driving him to dig and dig and dig in the middle of the night. What more would she drive him to do?

The shovel caught something. At first he tried to drive the tip through it. But something, the feel of it—not a root!—told him to stop. He dropped the shovel, fell to his knees and felt in the soil. His fingers grasped the thing and sent the message of recognition to his brain. The world began to spin again. His memory had been accurate. A dozen new worries and recollections, shards of thoughts from the past and today, collided. With them, unwanted, came the song "Strawberry Fields Forever" into his head.

Please no. Please no. Jesse couldn't straighten, he couldn't shut off the music and he couldn't shut out the truth that came with it: he'd killed this man—the man in this hole—over the price of a song. Mom, she'd made him think it was okay. She'd told him to kill his brother. And now was she leading him back here to finish the job? Had he ever stood up to her? No. No he hadn't. His hands dug deep and clutched the remains, and he clenched his eyes, fighting back the contents of his stomach. In his mind, he felt the porch tilt and spin, and he fell. His knees slammed into the wood floor, the rest of him crumbling after them. He lay there, dazed. From inside the house, Mom's voice: "You just remember, this part's up to you. I ain't bailing you out on this like I done... like I done on other things," she said. "If I got to take care of everything, you go to your aunt's house and stay there.

"Oh, and pick up that ice-tea glass before you come in for supper. I ain't running no pig sty here."

He heard her. And he heard the music, too. It was so clear. But there was something about it all, something in what she said or the way she'd said it that made his head spin even harder.

Chapter Twelve

He drove aimlessly, losing track of time, finally stopping at the river. He eased the Cordoba into a grove of trees near the water's edge and parked. The engine throbbed. The eight-track tape player made a soft swish-whir that told him the tape was recycling and couldn't find a track. He'd have to shut off the car to make the player stop running. He didn't want to shut off the car, and if he didn't want to, he didn't have to. It was up to him. Darn straight it was up to him.

He studied the rain now falling full force on the windshield. Droplets swelled on the glass till they burst and ran together, forming tiny rivers.

Elvis blinked and tried to pick up the motion of the real river out in the darkness. His mom had always told him he had quite the imagination, that he was good at making up things—seeing things—in his head. She'd been right. As he sat at the river's edge, he thought about the bridge that ran across it. He imagined he could walk over there, climb the bank to the sidewalk, hoist himself up on the railing, balance there for a breath, then just fall. The river would carry him away like a leaf. He'd be a leaf in a river, rushing nowhere. Elvis could see himself from above, his naked skin nothing more than a white stain gliding through the black of the water. The wind would whistle over him. The trees would rock and sway, waving good-bye as he floated past. Maybe a car would cross the bridge overhead, the people inside would laugh at something. He'd look up through the water and see them, their faces blurred and lit by the glow from the dashboard, their mouths open and heads thrown back, laughing at some dumb joke. He imagined it like a scene from that black and white movie, the Jimmy Stewart one they always show at Christmas.

Man sees no reason to live.

Man finds bridge.

Man jumps.

In his movie, in the Elvis version, there was no guardian angel to yank him out of the water. He just floated downstream and away, leaving no trace of himself except for a car he'd bought for next to nothing.

Elvis cocked the rear-view mirror so he could look at himself. His face was lit from below by the dashboard lights, his eyes were hollowed into his skull by shadows, and his nostrils looked like twin hairy caves. It's not true, is it? It's not. No. Yes. No. Stop it. Admit it. No. I said admit it. She's gone. She isn't. Yes. She is. Yes. She's gone. The only one, the only one that understood, the only one you could... and him, he...

He pounded the steering wheel with his fist, then thudded his head sideways against the window, eyes clenched. Suddenly he straightened, fury in his eyes—in the fiery eyes of the guy in the mirror. They cheated on you. Yes, they did. Yes. Probably. Maybe they didn't. They did. And, if they did? Well, then you can't trust anyone? No. No you can't, can you? No you can't. You can't because people, all people, lie. Not all. Yes. Yes. Absolutely. They do. Even the ones that, the ones that say they love you? Yes. Especially them. They do. Darn straight they do. They lie like dogs. Right. And you know what else? You know what? Say it. No. It's not true. Yes it is. Say it. They die. No. Yes.. That's it. They DIE. Yes. They lie. And they die. Yes. You get it now. Yes. All of them. All the ones that matter? Yes. Yes. They fucking lie then they die.

Elvis flopped back in the seat and shoved the mirror away, then sat up, eyes wild. Jimmy Stewart fell from a bridge on the edge of his mind. He slammed his naked shoulder against the car door. It wouldn't move. He tried again. Nothing. Suddenly aware of the cold, he flicked on the dome light, twisted around and rummaged through the junk in the backseat. He found a dirty towel, wrapped himself in it, then curled against the door. He closed his eyes and saw his mother's face. Whoa. He opened his eyes and stared out the window.

He was dead tired.

He stayed there, suspended, not moving, not thinking, not awake but not asleep.

Finally, deep in the night, Elvis stretched and groaned and threw the towel aside. He looked out at the night for several minutes, then leaned forward and pulled his wallet out of his back pocket. Fumbling with the flashlight, he managed to retrieve the scrap of paper.

M-43 East to Dormill. About 6/10 mi. down, left on M-140. Three miles out 140 to Fire lane 32b. Turn right.

He sat up slowly, pulled down the mirror, and looked from the note to his reflection. Slowly, he nodded, agreeing with himself.

❖❖❖❖

There was a convenience store that sold cardboard-like pizza twenty-four hours a day. He'd bought a large with extra pepperoni: The Big Meaty, according to the sign next to the cash register. As Elvis turned on to M-43, the open pizza box slid away and almost off the Cordoba's seat. He clamped onto the half-eaten slice already in his mouth. Gripping the steering wheel with his left hand, keeping his eyes locked straight ahead, he reached out with his right hand and caught the cardboard runaway.

A car roared past, cutting him short. Elvis didn't react. He was strangely calm and, despite being naked from the waist up, unaware of the cold. He imagined finding a little cottage nestled in the woods. He'd break in and find Donnel's socks on the bedroom floor, his shaving stuff in the bathroom, and that would be that. His fears would be confirmed, but heck, at least he'd know.

He tried to focus on the road, but his brain kept drifting. He was plenty pissed at Lavern, but the ache of losing her was wrecking the anger. Their marriage had been a lot like this car, he thought. This old car didn't run quite right, but the seat fit his butt, and that crease on the rear end was bad, but they'd gotten it in that fender-bender the day Donnel fell off the ladder. That funny smell, well, that was from when they were on vacation and the jar of olives busted in the back seat. Yeah, Elvis told himself, things weren't all that bad, not when you thought about them.

There was a guy standing in the middle of his lane, waving him down.

"Holy..." Elvis hit the brakes and reached for the pizza box. The car skidded on the slippery pavement. The guy jumped back. The Cordoba's nose stopped inches from his thighs.

He was short, fat and balding—about thirty, maybe thirty-five, Elvis figured. He'd fastened the kinky strands of his wet hair into a baby ponytail, so what was left of his hair was pulled tightly to his head. Red-faced and soaked by the rain, with his flannel shirt half-out of his jeans, he looked beaten and tired. His car, an old gray Camaro, was parked on the shoulder of the road.

Elvis rolled down the window and stuck his head out into the cold drizzle. "Car trouble?"

"Well, yeah. And ahh... that's not all, not exactly." The guy took a couple, half-scared steps toward Elvis' side of the car. "Look, man, I'm in some trouble... hey," the guy caught himself. "You got pizza?" He walked to the open window and gawked at the box on the seat.

Elvis followed his eyes toward the open box. "Uh-huh, with all the pepperoni in the world on it."

"Have some?"

Elvis looked at him. "You make a habit of stopping people on the road in the middle of the night and asking for food?"

"No. I'm just hungry's all."

Elvis hesitated. "You like lots of pepperoni on it?"

"Yeah," the guy smiled, sniffed, and wiped his wide flat nose with the butt of his palm. "Like everything 'cept anchovies. Had a uncle and a aunt once died from them—allergic."

"Well here," Elvis reached over and took a slice with two hands. He handed it through the window and glanced over his shoulder. There was nobody coming. "What kind of trouble you in?"

The guy started stuffing the pizza in his mouth. "I'm with this organization. It's sort of a brotherhood, you know." He leaned down and put his face just inches from Elvis'. His mouth was full of pizza and he was talking around it. A glob of red sauce on his cheek looked like thick blood. Elvis moved back a little, avoiding the pizza breath. "You know Jubal Brown?"

Elvis gulped. "You a friend of his?"

The guy swallowed. "Why you ask? Know him?"

"Sort of. Know people that know him."

"Cool, very cool."

"Well, not necessarily."

"What you mean by that?"

"Never mind."

The guy frowned. "Well, you probably heard Jubal got in some trouble today and…"

"Let me guess. You with him?"

"Yeah, how'd you know?" The guy squinted at him.

Elvis wasn't sure how he knew. "Good guess, I guess."

"Well, if you know Jubal, you know there's one thing he can't stand, and that's uppity niggers. Know what I'm saying?" He laughed.

Elvis didn't answer.

The guy started smiling and wiped the pizza sauce off the corner of his mouth with the back of his hand. He sniffed. "Well today, we come out of this store, see, me and Jubal…"

"Got the shinola beat out of him good, didn't he?"

The way Elvis said it—like Jubal getting the shinola beat out of him good was good—stopped the guy cold.

"You saw it happen then you ran away and now your car broke down and you're afraid the same thing's going to happen to you, that it?" Elvis suddenly felt awful about giving the guy pizza. He pictured Jubal in the hospital and Abe Lincoln's head puckered forever.

"Well, yeah," the guy stuttered, suddenly uncertain. "Yes I am. It's not that I'm afraid of those boys that got him. They just always gang up, that's all. They always come in groups. They don't fight fair's all."

"So you been waiting here for one of your buddies to come cruising along, or someone like me. Is that it?"

The guy smiled and nodded. "That's right. See, I lost my phone today and I figured I'd get someone that would understand, someone like you. I thought we'd go back into town and..."

Elvis couldn't stomach any more. He hit the gas and the car lunged forward, the outside mirror catching the guy in the gut. Elvis glanced in the rear-view mirror. The guy was on his knees in the middle of the lane.

❖❖❖❖

Elvis didn't slow the Cordoba until he hit a curve. His eyes searched for the fire lane in Donnel's directions. The car's headlights, diluted by dirt and loose connections he'd never bothered to fix, washed the brown roadside grass with a shaky, half-hearted glow.

Something gripped his heart. The countryside, with no street lights or landmarks or homes, was so achingly familiar. He'd grown up out here. For the first time in a good long time, Elvis could feel his childhood. Shadows of thoughts and fears seemed to flit by the car in the night.

He put his face out the window and let the damp wind slap his face, trying to forget the guy back on the road. About a mile from where he'd left the guy, he saw the sign.

Elvis slammed his foot on the brake and the Cordoba fishtailed on the asphalt, then slid to a stop. He punched the wheel with the side of his fist, yanked the car into reverse and jabbed the gas. The wheels spun as the near-bald tires looked for traction. They caught. The car jerked back; Elvis twisted his neck around and angled the wheel to the right. There, he thought, there. He hit the brake hard.

The pizza was now on the passenger's-side floor in a messy heap. Elvis squinted at the small sign. It was bright and official-looking, white letters on a red background. Fire lane 32b was a muddy track split by a knee-high Mohawk of weeds stretching off into the woods. The rain had stopped; the rubber wipers squealed across the dry glass. The pizza, which he'd eaten too fast, sent random cramps through his gut. The guy he'd knocked down suddenly worried him again, and the cloud of something dark and old hung in the car. Elvis gritted his teeth. "Let's get it in gear, boy." He slipped the Cordoba back into drive, gave it a shot of gas and flipped off the wipers. The car jounced down off the road and onto the track.

The car whimpered and groaned. The headlights jumped, throwing jagged, exaggerated shadows on the woods that surrounded him. Branches reached out and whined across the side of the car, asking him to reconsider what he was about to do. The weeds in the middle of the track played a tune on the Cordoba's undercarriage.

At a break in the trees, he stopped. Go home, he thought. Get out. No. Go on. Yes. Find out. Go see. Ahead, the fire lane disappeared into the dark. To his right was a hard packed, one-lane gravel drive that disappeared into the trees. Elvis nosed the Cordoba onto the gravel. He could always find the end of the gravel drive, find a place to turn around and get out of there. Yes. Yes. He could always do that.

The driveway carried the Cordoba through the woods for several hundred yards before emptying into somebody's backyard. Three old-fashioned street lamps illuminated a huge section of the well-manicured lawn. The house was new and, to Elvis, like something out of a magazine: two stories of brick with white trim and an attached garage. The yard was landscaped and wide; to his left, at the edge of the light, he could see a walking path cut into the woods.

Elvis figured it was a rich out-of-towner's house—probably

someone from Chicago. These places were usually empty this time of year, although Elvis wasn't sure; it was late at night and the people inside could be asleep.

He drove to the garage and parked. Two more lights, mounted under the eves, came on. Motion detectors. Elvis looked at the directions scrawled on the scrap of paper. Donnel knew a lot of people in town, just like Lavern did. Donnel had a way of making friends, even with the tourists. Maybe he and Lavern were house-sitting the place. Maybe, maybe not. He didn't know. Suddenly, he didn't want to know. Then again, maybe he did. Maybe. He wasn't sure what he wanted. Elvis backed the car up, wheeled off the gravel, dropped the car into drive and drove quickly back through the woods. At the intersection of the fire lane, he stopped, put the car in park and got out. Hands in pockets, hunched over, he paced in the dark. The night suddenly seemed endless. There were no turns out of it. Go one way, and you had the dead faceless man and the job he didn't have. Go another, Lavern and Donnel. Go another, and there was this weird guy in the road. Now he was here. In the woods, the old stomping grounds. At a house that wasn't his, owned by people he didn't know.

He couldn't go home. Not with all this stuff, all this bad hanging over him, turning in the breeze.

His hands shaking and suddenly damp, he opened the car door, got in, and drove till he found the driveway again. He stopped the car and closed his eyes. Elvis pictured Lavern scrubbing the fingernail polish from the carpet, Donnel shaking his head "no" and the faceless man on the floor dying. He thought about the hand of God. Ever since Lavern had gotten him to go to her church regularly a couple years back, he'd been half-aware of that hand. Elvis wondered if maybe all this stuff happening was God's hand working. It helped to think that way, especially when nothing else made a lick of sense. God's hand directed your life, took you places even when you didn't know it. Maybe God's hand was taking him here. Maybe it was for a reason.

If it was, God had one weird hand.

He drove to the house, parked at the garage, shut off the engine and sat for several minutes, looking at the directions written on the crumpled paper. Lavern had been here, at this house, hadn't she? Yeah, at least he thought so. Donnel too? The pain of both thoughts, of them being gone and being together, ripped through his chest.

For a minute, again, the temptation to leave—to just bag it—was almost too strong to fight. But the thought of God's hand, strong but old and gnarled, clenching his head, fixed him in his seat. That hand had brought him this far. Maybe, he thought, the rest was up to him.

Elvis set his jaw, grabbed his flashlight and shoved the door until it opened. He got out of the car and walked tentatively past the garage and along the back of the house until he reached the back door. He peered inside. The room was dark, but it looked like the kitchen.

Heart pounding, Elvis pushed the doorbell. A smooth, rich chiming responded from deep inside the house. Again, he hesitated, not breathing. There was no answer. He pushed the doorbell again, waited. He knocked.

"Hello?" he said loudly, then, even louder, "Helllllooo." There was nothing. No lights came on. No one rattled around in the house.

Elvis hung his head and watched the mist of his breath float away. Do it. No. Do it. Yes. Do it. He smashed the window in the door with the butt of his flashlight. The crash skittered through the woods.

With his left hand, he reached through the jagged hole in the glass, turned the lock, and twisted the knob. Once inside, he stopped and kicked some of the glass outside, then pushed the door slowly till it clicked shut.

The house was cool. If the heat was on, it wasn't turned up very high. A bluish-green digital clock gazed across the kitchen at him from a microwave that hung under a cupboard. It was 2:17 a.m. He'd been at the river longer than he'd thought.

The numbers warmed him the way the glow of a TV does when you see it inside someone's house as you walk by on a cold night, or the way a kitchen with steam in the windows warms you when you're driving past. Elvis let out his breath then fumbled for the light switch and flicked it on.

He was standing in a small entry area, a mud room. He half-expected to see a sweatshirt or something of Lavern's, but the brass coat tree was bare. A pair of muddy boots was on the floor by the door; they didn't look like anything Donnel would ever wear.

Deep in the house something squeaked or groaned or thumped; his tired brain only registered "noise." Elvis stopped and waited. Eyes closed, he half-expected a light to come on or the door on the other side of the kitchen to open. Go. Leave. No. Now. Yes. No. No. Run. Leave.

His mother wouldn't have approved of this, would she? Not on your life. This was one of those crazy things he did on the spur of the moment and if she'd caught him at it, she'd have busted his chops good.

Elvis could barely breathe. An echo of her voice: "What were you thinking? That you'd get away with this? You're in someone's house in the middle of the night? Does that seem something a smart boy would do?"

His voice, small and frail, would answer: "No."

"What do you mean, 'No'?"

"I meant no, no."

"Sounds like you meant 'yes.' Sounds like you thought you could do or think whatever you pleased."

"No. No, Mom."

"No, what?"

"I can't."

"You're so stupid; you're like an old stump or maybe a turd. That's it. You get pooped out of the dog like a turd?"

The words. So silly. But how they hurt. And he wanted to defy her. Secretly, just as he had when he was a boy, he wanted to show her he wasn't stupid. Not at all.

Why hadn't he stood up to her ever? Why?

Why did it matter?

Slowly, carefully, he shuffled through the open mud room door into the kitchen. It was a dream kitchen, the kind Lavern had always loved. She'd cut pictures out of magazines and showed them to him. There was an island, topped with a shiny, gray countertop. Above it, copper-bottomed pots and pans and serious black-iron skillets hung from a wide-wood rectangle, suspended by chains from the ceiling. The cupboards wrapped all the way around to the opposite wall. All of them were dark wood with that shiny, gray countertop. There was a stainless steel oven and range and a matching refrigerator with a see-through door. To his left, overlooking it all, was a bay window over a stainless steel sink.

Elvis walked to the island and put down the flashlight. He sauntered to the window and rested his palms, far apart, on the counter in front of the sink. The sink was empty and dry. A towel, folded, was on the counter next to it.

From the back door, there was a crunch that sounded like feet on gravel. Elvis whirled and eyed one of the skillets over the island. His gaze darted to the drawers. Which one had the knives?

Another crunch, the slow squeak of the doorknob then the door creaked opened. Slowly, a flannel-shirted arm and half a blue-jeaned leg inched around the edge of the door. It was the guy from the road, Jubal's buddy. It had to be.

"Hey, Donnel, get your big Negro butt out of that 'frigerator," Elvis yelled. "Get that fried chicken over here so we can cut it up with one of these butcher knives."

There was a loud laugh from the guy as he stepped into full view. "That Donnel buddy of yours is gone man, and you know it."

Elvis turned. His eyes searched wildly for a skillet, for a butcher knife.

"Relax dude," the guy said, hands up, palm out. "I come in peace." He shuffled around the island, crossed his arms across his belly, and gave the kitchen a once over. "You sure found yourself a nice hideout here, par'ner."

"This is my house. And I'd suggest you turn and get out of it."

"Listen to you, 'I'd suggest...' You standing there looking like something a cat gagged up. Sorry, man. This ain't your space."

"How do you know? How did you get here? How do you know..." Elvis struggled with the thought. "...about Donnel?"

The guy sniffed and wiped at his red nose. "Don't you squeeze your brain about that, man. I know enough about stuff, let's just leave it at that. You got yourself caught in a tit grinder and I'm gonna help you out."

Elvis frowned. "What makes you think you can help me? What makes you think I want your help?"

"You best keep your voice down."

"There's nobody here. I...this is my buddy's place. He's out of town."

The guy laughed again. "Listen, Elvis, calm your little pitty patty heart down. And keep that voice low. You and I both know you haven't had time to check and see if anyone's home. With all the racket of breaking in, you mighta rousted someone out of the sack. Could be they're upstairs calling nine double daggers right now."

"Nobody's around. I rang the bell."

The guy shrugged. "Suit yourself."

"Darn straight I'll suit myself," Elvis said, lowering his voice to a gruff whisper. He frowned again. "How do you know I'm Elvis?"

The guy took a step forward and lowered his voice a notch too. "I don't know what you got going on here. Maybe you're going to pick up a few things—a flat screen TV or a laptop or some such. I don't know." He sniffed, looked at the room again and smiled. "If I wasn't in such a hurry, I might be looking to do a little grabbing myself."

"I'm not here to steal anything. I'm not like that."

"Relax," the guy said with a laugh. "I was just yanking your chain, man." He surveyed the room again then turned to Elvis. "Look, Elvis. I'll make this quick."

"How do you know…"

"Someone tossed me a couple of bucks to follow you."

"Follow?"

"That whole deal on the road just now? That was me play-acting. I was just trying to get in the car with you."

"Who? Huh?"

"I ain't no friend of no Jubal, but I heard the deal of what happened and that you might've knowed him. My mom always said I had a real playacting talent. Said I could've been an actor, only I'm so ugly." The guy laughed, wiped his nose again.

"Listen to me." Elvis took a step toward the guy. "Who sent you?"

"Like I said, just this dude, some guy. He hired me to, like, watch you."

"You don't know the guy?"

"No, no, no. This was, like, a blind deal. I got a call someone was interested in a little help."

"You make a habit of that, going around doing favors—following guys—for strangers?"

"You make a habit out of breaking into houses?"

"I told you, I… that's not why I'm here. Breaking in, stealing stuff, isn't."

"Right."

Elvis ran his hand through his hair and sighed. "None of this makes sense."

"I know. You've had a heckuva day from what I understand. That's kind of why I'm here."

Elvis frowned. "I thought you were here to follow me."

"I am. I am. And I tried the tricky approach, but you ditched me on the road. I was hoping you would let me in the car and I could cruise with you maybe for awhile, just to see what you were going to do. Now I'm working the ol' face-forward." The guy held his palm up again. "I don't mean you no harm. Fact is, I'm looking out for your best interests."

Elvis sighed. He felt tired, more tired than if he'd worked a triple shift. He was almost drowning in sadness and thought again of the river, of him sliding into the water and away in the darkness. "You like that angel in that old Christmas movie, go around pulling guys out of the river?"

The guy thought for a second, then smiled. "Clarence?"

"Yeah. Yeah, that's the guy. Clarence."

It's a Wonderful Life. Jimmy Stewart." He shook his head. "The guy rocked. I'm big on 'Harvey' myself." He screwed up his face and wagged his finger at Elvis. "'S...s...say Harvey, y...y...you you see here...'"

"You're some kind of freak."

"No. No. Swear to God. Funny you asked about Jimmy Stewart, man. Dude was awesome."

"You saying that back there on the road you wanted to get in the car with me..."

"Trying to, you know, talk to you. Get a feel for what you got going on."

Elvis made a face. "That's just weird."

"Swear to Jesus. I got hired to follow you around, only now I, like, met you, you offering me pizza; I see you're maybe an okay guy—I see you're under stress and all, so I'm willing to let it go, you almost hitting me back there on the road. But now I'm thinking maybe you're interested in flipping the playing field here."

"Flipping."

"Yeah, turning, like, the tables."

"To help me out."

"Yeah."

"And if I don't believe you."

"Well, way I see it, and I don't mean to piss you off or nothing, but—again, way I see it—you got no choice."

"'Course I got a choice. I got all the choice I want."

The guy looked around the kitchen, then turned back

to Elvis and lowered his voice, "The hand you're playing ain't exactly the best."

Elvis looked down at his hand. "How do you know about my hand?"

"Trust me," the guy said.

Elvis closed his eyes. When he opened them, they were slits. "I pretty much dumped you back there on the road."

"That you did, but like I say, water under the bridge, far as I'm concerned."

"That's not what I'm getting at. What I'm getting at is you couldn't have followed me here. How'd you find this place?"

The guy just smiled and shrugged.

Elvis tried to breathe. Another image, a black bat of a thought: Donnel and Lavern coming here, playing grab-ass in this kitchen, hot dogs warming in the microwave, guys like this hanging out in the backyard, drinking beers. Elvis waved the image away. He thought for a moment. "Who hired you?"

"Guy who was working for someone else. I'm, like, a sub-contractor. Can't tell you much beyond that."

"So what exactly can you tell me, 'cept that you're ugly and not a freak or an angel?"

"And the thing about *Harvey.*"

"*Harvey?*"

"Yeah, I told you that too, that thing about Jimmy Stewart and *Harvey.* The one thing I didn't tell you was I drove my Camaro. It's parked back by the woods."

Elvis' head had begun to throb. He looked at the floor.

"Elvis, dude, listen. Here's the deal." The guy took a deep breath and let it out slowly. "The deal is that maybe you didn't have nothing to do with killing the dude at Bonner. The deal is maybe it wasn't the kind of accident or bad-heart thing that it looked like. Oh, and the deal is maybe there's other things that aren't what they appear to be either; like there's something going on that's about something else. I'm not sure what it's about but I can maybe, like, help you, if you're interested in what you call a reciprocal investment."

Elvis' knees buckled. He steadied himself on the kitchen counter, looked at the guy, and brushed the hair out of his eyes. "What are you saying?" he said, his voice a whisper.

"I'm saying what about scoring two ways on the same play? I give you some information, you maybe come back with a little back-scratch of your own."

"The guy at work? He? Him? And—other things? Donnel? Lavern? What?"

The guy smiled. "Things aren't always the way they look is what I'm saying, brother. And if you want to maybe…"

"What kind of back-scratch? Money? You trying to squeeze money out of me?" Elvis took a step toward the guy, suddenly angry. "What do you know? About… about the… about everything. That guy at work? It wasn't me, right? It wasn't. What do you… how… know?"

The guy took a step back and held up a hand. "Whoa. Cool down, partner. I can fill you in. But I got to have your help, you know—two way street—so I can maybe make a play the other way, too."

"Information? About what? I don't know anything about anything," Elvis was shouting. "What do you know? Who are you?" He lunged toward the guy. The guy, both hands in the air, spun away—like a dancer. Elvis stumbled and caught himself. One hand on the counter, he felt the kitchen twirl. The guy put a hand on Elvis' bare shoulder. The warmth of the hand, the gentleness of the touch, was surprising.

"Elvis. I know stuff," the guy said, talking fast, the voice, pushed by smelly breath, in Elvis' ear. "This stuff would turn your hair, like, albino white. And if I'm right, if I got my head on straight on this, you know some stuff already, too. You got it stuffed away in that bony head of yours, only you're not sharing it for some reason. At least if I'm right."

"Right about what?" Elvis said, his eyes meeting the guy's.

"Well, that's the part I'm not sure I'm right about. At least it's part of it."

"You're not sure you're right about something you're not

sure about?"

"Right, partly."

Elvis straightened, brushing the guy's hand away. "You're really starting to piss me off."

The guy sighed, took a couple of steps back, looked at the floor for a moment, tapping his muddy workboot on the clean, gray ceramic tile. Finally, he looked up and smiled. "Elvis, why don't you start at the very beginning?"

Elvis' eyes came up, cool and gray and weary. "What beginning?"

"Start at the very beginning," he continued, singing the words, half-dancing, like Julie-fucking-Andrews. "That's the very best place to start. When you read, you begin with A-B-C. When you sing, you begin with do, re, mi."

"You are a freak. Or you're stoned out of your mind." Elvis squinted at him, tilting his head. "You stoned?"

"Nope. Just trying to lighten the mood, my friend. Blame Sister Luckenberry."

"Sister Luck…"

"Fourth grade, Sacred Heart of the Bleeding Virgin Elementary, Chicago, Illinois. Always big on the positive, on laughing through tears. A spoon full of sugar shit, you know?"

Elvis shook his head. "What is your deal?"

"You already asked me that. I'm asking you what your deal is."

Elvis scowled. "Some dude's dead at work. My freaking wife is gone. My buddy's gone. My job is gone. And you're walking in here telling me you know stuff, like maybe…"

"Maybe what?"

"Maybe, I don't know," Elvis gulped at the thought. "Maybe all this, this stuff that's happened has to do with one another."

"I didn't say that."

"What?"

"I didn't say it all had to do with one another. You said it."

"Whatever. Whatever. Still, that's pretty stupid, you think

163

about it."

"Maybe it is. Maybe it isn't. Maybe it's stupider to think it's separate. Maybe it makes more sense that it's all related, like all for the same—all because of the same thing."

Elvis felt an icicle of pain in his skull. This was too much, way way too much.

"Look, Elvis, relax that brain. Start back a square or two. And trust me. Really. Trust me that I'm with you, not against you." The guy extended his hand and nodded at it. Wary, Elvis took it. The guy smiled and shook.

"Name's Harvey. Harvey Monahan. Mom named me for that damn rabbit, honest to Moses she did." He fumbled in his right pocket for moment, pulled out a wallet, held it up for Elvis. It was shiny, looked like alligator; not the kind Elvis figured a Harvey Monahan would own.

"I can help you man, but I can't without your help. Don't know how else to put it. Sounds cruel, I know." He threw the wallet on the counter. Then he reached in his other pocket and pulled out a business card. This he handed to Elvis. "Call me when you're ready."

Elvis, frozen now, card in hand, stared at the wallet. "You left. Your wallet."

At the door, Harvey Monahan turned. "Better keep your voice down, ace. And start at the beginning. Do, re, mi." He left.

✽✽✽✽

Elvis gawked at the blue lettering, looked away from the card and stared at the pans hanging over the island, then stared at the card again. He frowned and shoved it into a front pocket, picked up the wallet and flapped it open. A gold MasterCard peeked through a plastic window. The name on it was Jesse Tieter, M.D.

He rifled through the cards. There was a gold MasterCard and a gold VISA, a Discover, a card for an automatic banking machine, and a bunch of cards for stores Elvis'd never heard of.

The Redeeming Power of Brain Surgery

He found the driver's license and glanced at the picture. Something damp and cool wrapped itself around his chest. Trying to ignore the tremble in his hands, he slipped the license out of the wallet. Jesse Tieter, M.D.'s address was in Evanston, Illinois. Elvis glanced at the photo again then dropped the license to the counter. With sweaty palms, he opened the money compartment and pulled out a sheaf of bills. A piece of yellow paper slid out with them and fell to the countertop.

Elvis unfolded the paper carefully, pressing it down on the countertop, smoothing out the wrinkles.

"Do you always do what your momma says?" Someone had scribbled the message on the paper in red pen, making big, exaggerated letters. To Elvis, it looked like whoever'd written it had been in a hurry and had been trying to write funny. He studied the handwriting. His throat tightened.

The bills were all fifties; there were fifteen of them.

His head felt light, pumped full of air. Elvis returned the shred of paper and the money to the wallet and held the thing up. He stared at the shiny alligator hide and pictured a skinned gator lying on the bank of a swamp in Florida, pictured something—someone?—else, something he couldn't see clearly. Again, a sliver of ice, this time it knifed through his breastbone.

He dropped the wallet on the counter and scuffed around the kitchen, examining the stuff in his brain, seeing the pictures of the memories but not acknowledging them, feeling the jolts of pain and understanding, hearing the voices of life as it was, but not sensing, not accepting, not translating anything at all. He stopped at the window over the sink and studied his faint reflection. The license. Jesse. Jesse Tieter? No. Don't go there. Why not? Just. Just what? Just. Jesse. Just don't. Ohhhh. Oh what? It. Oh it hurts. Leave the bad thoughts alone. Can't. Can. Yes. Stop it. You idiot. You maggot. You nothing. Please. Please, what? Please. Don't. Fight. No. The note. The handwriting. Not that. Why not? Just not now. Then, Harvey? Could he be? The card said. Sure. Maybe it's a lie. Maybe.

But what about the wallet? That's your start right there. Yes. And the house. But wait. Could she be? Alive? Why do you think that? Don't know. Well don't. He said go all the way back. Wait? What was that? A noise? Maybe. Are you alone? Sure. Are you sure? Yes. No. Yes, well, no. Find out. Yes. Just go. Go easy. He turned slowly and walked like a drunk to the door leading to the next room, pushed it open, found the light switch and flicked it on.

Elvis leaped back into the kitchen and tripped over the trash can. It made a crash that could have woken the dead, which was appropriate because in the next room there was a man slumped in a chair at the head of a table. And the man appeared to be dead.

Chapter Thirteen

Jesse struggled to chin himself on reality, tried valiantly to get up to it, finally managing to open his eyes wide enough to see his surroundings. In a second of panic, he straightened in the chair and tried to place the room. Then, oh, wait. Yes. He was in Michigan, in the present, in his new house.

Elvis felt a rock in his throat. This was turning out all wrong. It was so out of control; all of it was out of control. He thought again about the day, about the man at work and Lavern and Donnel. Harvey Monahan. Again, a spasm of a memory of his mother's eyes, black marbles in her face, rattled through his brain. Why Mom? He wasn't sure. Lavern would know. Lavern would help. He ached for her.

Elvis turned again to face the door to the dining room. With a foot, he nudged the kitchen trash can back into place. He took a deep breath and closed his eyes, one hand resting against the door.

Jesse's stomach turned. The door was edging open. Someone was in the house. He pictured the grisly job he'd left unfinished—the remains wrapped in a blue plastic tarp in the garage. He scratched a hand. This whole thing was becoming a mess. He closed his eyes and saw his mother's face. Had she made him do this, this harebrained scheme? And what about all of it? Was there something he'd missed before? After he was done in the woods, he'd come home and gotten stoned and drunk, then what had he done? He'd called her; that much he remembered. He'd wanted to tell her off. But, in his gut, he had a suspicion that he'd failed to do it. He couldn't remember what he'd said. This worried him.

Elvis pushed the door. A hinge squeaked. He froze.

Jesse's mouth went dry.

Do it, Elvis thought, do it. Go. Into the room. See who. Go. Now.

The door edged open. Jesse grabbed the edge of the dining room table, trying to will himself to stand. His brain felt huge and useless: a slab of cold and lifeless meat. Who was this? Police? Maybe. Or who? Who knew? Had Mom done this, too? Had she called someone?

Elvis stepped into the room. Jesse stood, frozen.

Oh.

Lightning. Flies. Millions of them hummed through his brain.

His brain.

His. Brain.

Move. Get out. Get out. Now. Now. Move. Go.

Elvis stumbled backwards out of the room and fell to the kitchen floor.

This isn't right. No. Stop. Please. Wait. No. Know. Yes. Know.

Jesse bolted past him through the kitchen, the back door, and ran outside.

Wait, he thought. The key fob for the Mercedes. Was it in the house or in the car? He couldn't think.

He stumbled to the beater of a car parked in the driveway. Elvis' car. His. Yes. His. Jesse looked through the dirty driver's-side window. Keys, in the ignition. You found him, he heard his mother's voice saying. You found him. You found him. He heard the cadence of the voice as he wrestled the door of the wreck open—the engine caught, the transmission engaged and the wheels spun him back, away, away, away.

"You found him, didn't you."

"Yes. Yes, he did," Jesse heard his boy-voice say, as the trees of the woods approached with the smell of macaroni and cheese and the past rushing at him from the night.

"Found who?" Elvis said and looked up at her from his plate, his spoon frozen in air over the steamy yellow glob.

"You found him."

Elvis shook his head. "I didn't find nobody." He spooned up a helping of mac and cheese and opened his mouth.

Mom's hand was a blur; she sent the spoon flying, clattering into the wall of the kitchen. Mac and cheese splattered across the room, some sticking to the sleeve of Elvis' t-shirt. Elvis jumped to his feet.

"You don't get it, do you?" Mom said, her black-marble eyes telling Jesse to take charge. "Tell him. Remind him," Mom said to Jesse.

"You found him, and you are going to forget him," Jesse said, now looking toward the rear-view mirror of the battered old car. "You hear me? You have to forget. You have to."

Elvis stumbled to his feet, staggered across the kitchen and fell against the counter. He looked out the window over the sink. Elvis could see things in his memory—long buried things—things he wanted to forget. He wanted to run from the house. Now, as then, he wanted to find the other boy, the reflected boy, in the greenish surface of that scummy pond. He'd found him that day, right when he needed him. What he'd talked to that boy about had hurt a lot, but the other boy had understood. He'd said the same things Elvis had said. He'd nodded when Elvis nodded. He'd cried too—just like Elvis. Oh, he'd known it was a little silly. But he'd found something, something worse than horrible. And he'd needed to talk about it. The reflected boy had listened.

"You know he's going to talk about it. To someone, he will, unless you tell him more," Mom said. "Unless you tell him again what he needs to know."

Jesse opened his mouth, but the words congealed in his throat with the taste of macaroni. He gagged. He wheeled the Cordoba off the fire lane and onto the road toward town, her voice hissing now in his head. "Don't you make me do the dirty work." Her face, wild-eyed and wrinkled and real, rose like a fog on the windshield. "Don't make me take care of everything." He knew that she saw the weakness in him; she'd always seen it. It was the weakness she saw in his dad and brother, what made them failures in her eyes. "You trying to muck this up, boy?" she said, her voice now a near scream. "You want to muck this whole dang thing to hell just like you did the other?"

"But I didn't," he said, his boy voice a high tenor, shrill and wobbly. "I didn't muck anything up. I didn't."

"Don't you sass me. Are you sassing me?" She backhanded his plate of food, sending it into his lap.

Jesse leaped to his feet. The plate clattered to the floor. Macaroni clung to his cheek and chin and chest; a wet mess of it dripped down the front of his jeans. "What is wrong with you?" he said to his mother. He plopped back in the chair, brushing at the mess on his face and shirt.

"With me?" she said, laughing now.

"I've done everything you wanted me to do. Everything," Jesse said, tears in his eyes. He lost his grip on the wheel of the Cordoba and it snaked off the road, rumbled and rattled, slewing gravel. He seized it and muscled it under control, skidding to a stop on the shoulder. He felt a brick in his throat and a flame of anger in his chest. Smack. Mom hit the side of his face and his ear with the hand holding the cigarette. The brick broke loose; the flames in his chest blossomed. "I've done everything you asked," the words poured out of him. "Every stupid thing. And it's not enough, is it? It's still not enough."

The sobs were bobbing in his throat, making it hard to talk and think. He gripped the steering wheel and the wheel became her shoulders and he was shaking her. Her shoulders were thin and bony. Her head was bobbing wildly like a doll's head and her mouth was hanging open, forming a crooked "o" outlined in pink. Her eyes were wild with fear and something else, something stronger. Jesse realized he better stop; he was stronger than he thought he was. Besides, whatever was in her eyes didn't look good.

Elvis began to sob. He was suddenly cold and exhausted.

He knew it didn't make sense, that he should try to solve this, this mess he was in. But he'd had enough. For now, he had. He was overwhelmed by the need to sleep until things maybe made sense. He turned and tried to shuffle from the kitchen.

"Stop right now, you idiot." Mom's voice slapped them both.

Elvis froze. Jesse released her and fell back, tripped over his feet, and fell hard to the floor. Mom pounced on Jesse and grabbed him by the ear. Jesse's ear was on fire, little burn spots pulsing on his head from the cigarette ashes. She pulled his face into hers. With tears in her eyes, her head tilted to one side, she stroked the side of his face with the hand that held the cigarette. "You think you been a good boy," she said, speaking not to him but to the hand that was being gentle. "You think you been a man, really, don't you?" She flicked a glance into his eyes, tightened her hold on his ear, then turned her attention back to the caressing. "Well, you're right. What you did was a man's work. You mucked it up some but you did it—you. You remember that. It was you that done it."

Jesse tried to struggle free. Elvis walked in a circle, wobbling in wild anxiety, around and around the kitchen, like a dog chasing his tail, until he was dizzy. Then he stopped and swayed, his hands over his ears and his mind stumbling. The tears were coming again, and it seemed there was no way he could stop them.

She tightened her hold on Jesse's ear, all the while caressing, caressing, caressing. "I tell you what, baby," she said to the good hand. "One day, you're going to get your reward for all this, that I promise you. Just do this one last thing, then there ain't going to be no going away, no one having to leave. We're going to live in a nice house with shiny things, pretty dish-washing machines and those oak cupboards in the kitchen. We'll have lots of that wall-to-wall carpeting, too, baby." Her hold on his ear relaxed ever so slightly. She stared at the hand stroking his face, continuing the litany Jesse had heard over and over; it was the dream she'd rocked him to sleep with when he was younger.

"We'll have a nice place, baby—just you and me. We'll have one of them big houses in the woods, know what I mean?" Her gaze drifted to his eyes. Yes, Mom, Jesse nodded obediently, tears rolling down his cheeks.

"But first you got to look inside yourself and find a way to be a man one more time. You got to do it, you hear me?" she said, now staring into him, her words going stronger as she made a final effort to change him. "You got to take care of the one last thing that stands in our way. Know what I mean? Know who I mean?"

Yes, Mom, sure, Jesse thought as he nodded and the tears flowed. He pictured his father's face; heard that voice say, *"Please, no."* The face became his brother's.

"Please, no," Elvis repeated. He turned from the horror and ran from the kitchen, through the dining room, barely noticing the elegant living room as he floundered up the stairs, found a bedroom and fell onto the bed. It seemed stupid, being there in someone else's bed, but his brain was racing and he was so, so, so tired. He lay, eyes open, begging for the will to get up and for the past to retreat. Elvis could see the dresser, a chair, and a picture on the wall. His eyes stopped on the picture. It was of Jesse and someone else.

"Not now."

"Not. Now." Jesse whispered the words. And he knew by the look in Mom's eyes that she didn't like what he was saying. She could see his weakness, Mom could. She knew he'd maybe try to kill his brother, for sure he would. But he would fail, because when it came to murdering people, he was basically a one-trick pony.

"If you don't do it, you know what you're going to do, right?" Mom continued, gripping his ear harder still, the caressing all but forgotten. "You know where you're going to go live and be nice and mind your aunt and keep your mouth shut while I stay here and take care of this mess, just like I took care of the other? You know that?"

He nodded, the tears flowing now unchecked. "Yeah, Mom. I know," he murmured. With that, finally, she released his ear.

Jesse stared out the windshield of the Cordoba.

Elvis stared at the ceiling.

He missed his life and his wife; he hoped he'd turn and she'd be there next to him, but he didn't turn because he knew she wouldn't be.

He reached out, feeling her body although it wasn't there.

A truth was missing, and his brain knew it but stubbornly refused to see it. It was something about his mom, about the way she'd talked, something funky in what she'd said.

He closed his eyes and could hear the flies. He told himself to stay awake, but the flies beckoned him to stay. And he slept.

❊❊❊❊

She came to Elvis as he was sleeping. She reached down, took his hand, and held it. In the strange way of dreamers, he hoped she was his wife and thought she was his wife, but at first she was not.

Someone, another boy, was with her. He could see the other boy's hand also holding Mom's hand, but Elvis kept his head down, looking at the body, avoiding looking at Mom or the boy.

"You don't get it, do you?" his mom said, standing there beside him on the dewy, coppery-lighted grass.

Head still down, he shook his head. The dead body at their feet looked ugly. This made him sad. He tried to focus on the grass instead.

"Well, if you keep on acting this way, if you keep trying to muck things up, I'm going to have to do something about it, aren't I?" He felt Mom's eyes glaring now at the top of his head.

"Everything's going to be okay," the boy on the other side of Mom said. He could see the boy's shoes, PF Flyers, and his bare, mosquito-scarred legs. "No one's going to do anything

173

now. No one's gonna know anything."

"Darn straight no one's going to. No one better know nothing or do nothing." Mom's body turned slightly as she shifted her attention to the boy on the other side of her.

"You're hurting my hand," the other boy said, his voice soft and weak. His mom's grip tightened and the other boy gasped. Elvis gasped too. Elvis finally looked up at her, wanting to tell her, "Hey, cut it out, that really does hurt," but when Mom looked down at him again, almost daring him to say it, she had no hair, and he couldn't speak. Hair was something she'd never not had before, and he didn't know what to say about her not having it. He was just a boy, after all. When you're a boy there are a lot of things you can't do anything about. Hadn't she told him that?

He held his free hand out in front of his face, trying to block his view of her.

"Being blind to something can't keep you from getting hurt," she said quietly.

He stood like stone, trying to understand what she meant by that.

"Put your hand down," she said.

Slowly, he did as she demanded. She was no longer Mom. She was his wife and she was sad but smiling. She opened her mouth and he knew she was going to explain it all. He was afraid of what she'd say, but he wanted her to say it. It was an awful, tortured feeling. But as she opened her mouth to speak, the other boy jerked free from her, forcing her to turn away. The boy was running off down the street, his tennis shoes kicking up behind him.

His wife whipped her head around, shooting him a quick glance just to keep him in his place. She was Mom again, with hair. "He's a good boy, but you make him feel bad. All the time, you do," she said. She let go of his hand, flicked her red hair away from her face, then turned and walked briskly toward a car that was parked at the curb.

"I better go catch up to him and see what he's up to." She

was his wife again, and she was getting away—going to the other boy—leaving him alone. He watched, feeling helpless, as she stepped down off the curb and around the back of the car, the side of her face framed by a wave of that dyed-red hair.

"Hey." His voice squeaked.

She acted like she didn't hear, just reached for the handle of the driver's side door and pulled, frowned, pulled again, looked over the roof of the car, gave him that sad smile, then ducked down and in and swung the door shut. The engine of the Cordoba started and she drove off down the street.

He was left alone and reaching, wanting her back.

Chapter Fourteen

Elvis awoke smelling Lavern and realized it was morning. The sun was up; there was light in the room, although it was the grayish light of a cloudy day. The sheets and blankets were knotted around him.

He reached out. The fact that the other side of the bed was empty surprised him. It made him think about a guy he'd met once at a bar. The guy'd been in the first Gulf War and told him that when you lose a leg, you wake up in the hospital and forget that it's gone. You reach down to scratch your thigh, the guy'd said, only to remember that the thigh and the rest of your leg were cut off. It was tough, he said, imagining your leg wrapped in a black plastic bag and dumped in a big Rubbermaid trash can, when it's still itching.

Elvis sat up in the bed. It was a big bed—a king, like the ones you got in hotels, not like the double bed he and Lavern had. The bedroom was large, as big as his and Lavern's living room. It was nicer than any hotel room he'd slept in: gauzy curtains at the windows and thick, deep-green carpet. Elvis suddenly felt a little creepy. This wasn't his place. The bed hadn't been made when he'd fallen into it the night before, had it?

He got up and stumbled past the open suitcase on the floor and into a bathroom. He tried to ignore the shaving kit on the vanity, the toothbrush in the shiny gold holder, the glassed-in shower with the twin shower heads and all the reminders that this wasn't his, wasn't his, wasn't his. Elvis relieved himself, showered under one of the shower heads, found a towel in a cupboard then toweled off. From his jeans pocket, he pulled a comb and ran it quickly through his hair, taking just a few anxious minutes at the mirror. Then he dressed in his dirty underwear and jeans and returned to the bedroom.

For several minutes he sat on the edge of the bed, trying to distract himself, trying to decide what to do for a shirt. He glanced at the picture on the wall. It was a photo of what had to be a teenaged Jesse Tieter with some old gal who hardly had any teeth. Jesse and the old gal were standing in front of a shrub on a summer day. If you looked closely, you could see Jesse was holding two fingers up behind the lady's head, giving her horns. The lady was grinning a big toothless grin like she had no idea what the guy was up to.

Weak-kneed, Elvis stood and walked to a long dresser that hugged the wall opposite the picture. He opened and closed each drawer, pausing to stare stupidly at the contents. It dawned on him that this was a man's room—no women's clothes. Finally, he settled on a sweatshirt—a "fleece" was what Jesse probably called it—pale blue and expensive. He put it on, then sat again on the edge of the bed.

Slowly the fog from the night before was lifting. This was wrong, he thought. Being here. Was. Wrong. Is. Wrong. Wearing this. Wrong. Someone could come back. Any minute, someone—he—could walk through the door.

Elvis gawked at the wound on his hand, the one he'd gotten when he'd punched the mirror; when had it been—yesterday?

The scab had hardened. The knuckle was red; you could barely see the feathery outline of the old scar beneath it.

The smoke of a memory billowed through the room.

Elvis covered his eyes. He felt pain, real pain, from a place he hadn't touched in years.

"He ain't coming back, you just remember that," Mom said. "And don't start no crying. There's no use crying over spilled milk, anyhow."

He could see her. She was standing in the kitchen, peeling potatoes, staring out the window at the station wagon turning out of the driveway. Her hands were working really fast on the potatoes, faster than he'd ever seen them work. A gallon of milk was next to her, right on the kitchen counter. Elvis wanted to dump it over. He wanted to see what she'd do about the spilled milk.

The other boy had been all dressed and ready to leave when Elvis came in for supper that summer night. Standing there in the kitchen just inside the door, the other boy looked pale and uncomfortable, like he and Mom had just argued or something. It took Elvis a second to realize he was dressed in his best blue jeans and a shirt he usually wore to school. Then Elvis saw the dirty old suitcase and the beat up cardboard box overflowing with books and airplane models and stuff.

Elvis stared again at the picture on the wall.

"Where you going?" Elvis asked the other boy.

"Away."

"Your books? Your books going, too?"

Mom, behind Elvis, laughed.

"Yeah, they're going too."

"But why? Where? What's going on?"

"Just a change of living arrangements is all," Mom growled. She danced slowly into his vision, clicking her lighter casually to the beat of the song on the radio.

"Living... what?" Elvis took an uncertain step past the other boy and caught a whiff of something. His head swam and his knees went weak. He stopped and faced him. "Y... You're wearing aftershave?"

The other boy looked at the floor and coughed. "I took a bath."

"He took a bath and got all slicked up for his aunt and uncle," Mom said. "Like how he smells all pretty?"

"But..." Suddenly Elvis felt like he'd been slugged in the stomach. The aftershave was Old Spice and the idea of the other boy taking the Old Spice bottle down from the shelf in the bathroom—the idea of him splashing on that smell— well, it wasn't right. "Y... you used the aftershave," was all Elvis could say.

"He can use what I tell him he can use," Mom said.

Anger welled in Elvis' throat. "That's not right," he shouted before he could stop himself.

Mom was on him in a heartbeat. Smack. The back of her hand caught him on the right ear.

"You hush that bad thought right now, you hear me? There's going to be no more of that from you. If I have to smack you every day, there's going to be no more of that."

Through the rush of tears Elvis saw the station wagon pulling into the driveway, the other woman and that man with the hat—the toothless woman with the dumbnuts grin on her face and the hat-man nervous and joking—and the suitcase and box being picked up from the floor. Mom, for some stupid reason, not asking them to stay; she walked to the sink and started peeling the potatoes, fast. Elvis wandered away, out of the room, his addled brain struggling to understand what it all meant.

He couldn't get it. He didn't want to get it. Maybe.

The phone rang.

Somehow he had walked downstairs to the living room. The clock on the mantle over the living room fireplace read quarter to eight. Who'd be calling Jesse Tieter, M.D. this early? The phone, phones, rang again. From the bedroom, from the kitchen, from the living room, too.

He couldn't decide what to do. Do I answer it? No. Yes. What do I say? Hello, Jesse's house? No. Just hello. Yeah. Maybe. Maybe not. No. Just pick it up. Pick it up and see what happens. Say nothing. That maybe would work. Or just hi. Maybe just that. Hi.

Another ring.

Elvis walked to the far end of the living room and found the phone on a table against the wall. The table was nearly hidden by a tropical plant that hung over it. The plant reminded him of one Mom had always kept in the house. Elvis had hated that plant, and he hated this one, too. It blocked the phone so you couldn't see it right away.

Elvis pushed the plant back with his one hand and picked

up the receiver with the other, cutting off another ring.

❉❉❉❉

"Jesse Tieter." He groaned and unraveled himself, the cell phone to his ear. His neck ached. His head throbbed. He blanched at the pizza on the floor of the car. "Hello?" Jesse rolled down the window with his free hand, trying to get some air.

"Yes, Mister," the voice on the phone said. "Ah, hold on—sorry—it's *Doctor*, Doctor Tieter, this is Detective Harvey Monahan calling, Michigan State Police. How are you this morning?"

Jesse sat up. "What the f…?"

"I said this is Detective Harvey…"

"Oh, no, ummm, sorry, sorry, Officer…"

"Detective."

"Huh?"

"Detective. Not Officer. We detectives take offense."

"Oh, ah, fine, Officer—I mean *detective*. Um. What I meant was, what can I do for you?" With his free hand, Jesse tilted the rear-view mirror down and frowned at his image. He ran a hand through his hair.

"Well, Dr. Tieter, it appears we have a friend of yours in custody, and we were just wondering how we could maybe have you amble in for a chit chat. He's been singing your virtues to some buddies of mine here for half the night and gave them this cell number, but I figured you'd want your beauty sleep; I know I need mine, otherwise the ladies, well, they just don't respond like normal, know what I mean? You like the ladies, doc, or you one of them homosexuals? Listen to me, talking about a man's sexual orientation at the crack of dawn. There's a joke there somewhere, but I'll skip that. Anyways, I don't give a blind dog's right eye about which side of the plate you whack it from, doc, but I sure could use your help here. This friend of yours is all giddy about seeing you."

"What? What friend? What friend? I don't have any around

here, not really." Jesse was fully upright now. "Where are you? You're here. Michigan? Right? Right. You said 'Michigan.'" He stuck his head out the window and sucked in some air. Jesse was cold but suddenly he was sweating. He glanced at himself in the rear-view again. He looked like crap; his eyes were wide, his mouth was open like an idiot's. "What are you, what is this all about?"

"You feel friendless, Dr. Tieter? Well sit me up behind the anchor desk and call me Tom Brokaw, I got great news for you. This young man we've been talking to says you and him have been awfully close lately. Says you and him had a business proposition. And now there's a man over at Bonner Wire—check that, isn't at Bonner Wire anymore because he isn't at all. He's not among us any longer, this guy isn't."

"No. This can't... I... he can't be," Jesse stammered. The pizza on the floor of the nasty old car, the smells from the upholstery, the hangover. Had he really called Mom? Then had he showed up—had he been in the house? Now, he was in his car? Suddenly, he felt the urge to vomit. He wrestled with the door. Open. Open, please.

"You okay doc? Need a doctor? I know a dandy in town, you need one."

The door yawned, Jesse held the phone well away from his head, leaned out the door and puked.

The siren, distant and mourning, didn't register. He felt better now. His head was clearer. With the back of a quivering hand, he wiped his mouth, then rubbed his hand on his pant leg. Get control now, he ordered himself. Get control.

"Breaker, breaker one-nine," the cop said. "Hello. Knock-knock. You hearing me? Roger wilco, you got your ears on doc?" This guy was a real comedian.

"I'm here."

"Doc, this man who isn't among us? That would mean he's dead. And there's this deal, this state statute we got here in the wolverine state, against the taking of life? Well, let's just say we need to clear some things up. To make this easy, mind if we just send a patrol car your way? Where you at right now? We'll just put the Michigan taxpayer dollar to work for you."

Jesse turned the key in the ignition, glanced again at himself in the mirror and remembered. The house. Last night. Him. He'd found him. Yes. No. Yes. With a palsied hand, he adjusted the mirror to its original position. "Shit," he said.

"What's that, doc?"

Of the thoughts scrambling like hermit crabs across his tired brain, one was leading the pack: get out of the area for a little while, get some time to think about this. "I said, um, no... no problem. You just tell me where the state police post is. I'll come on over." He steered the car onto the road, heard the siren approaching but still didn't think anything of it.

"Now doc, now don't you put yourself out, buddy. We'll send someone to you."

"No. No, that's fine. That's just fine." Jesse pushed the gas to the floor and the car ca-chugged its way to a top speed of maybe 45. Stupid car. Now there was a flashing light in his rear-view. A cop. Wait a second. A cop. The cop hit the siren again. He was pulling him over.

Jesse braked and brought the car to an uneasy stop on the shoulder. He gawked at the rear-view mirror. There were two guys in the front seat, one in uniform, driving, the other on a phone, smiling. And talking. "Hey doc, you still there? Doc? You ever hear of that global positioning, doc? That G-P-S? Why, you got it right on your cell phone. Did you know that? Around here, your cell phones send out a GPS signal so emergency personnel can find you when you're in trouble. Ain't that good doc? Ain't that so very good?"

Jesse closed his eyes. This was going so wrong. So very, very wrong.

❖❖❖❖

"Jess?" A voice from far away hummed through the phone line. "Jess, honey. It's me. That you?" The voice was old and familiar and, at first, it didn't register.

"Ah... ah... Hullo?"

"I'm just calling to see if mister smarty pants doctor is going to get me soon," she said, "or you gonna let me rot."

Something twanged in Elvis' stomach, something he'd swallowed long ago.

"I been sitting here at the bus station for half the dang morning. Like to starve or die of loneliness, 'less you come and get me soon. Or you forget that you sent for your mommy? That it? You forget that you called last night and asked after all these years for her to come see you so's we could talk?"

A dream. Yes. Definitely. After all, she was dead.

"Are you there?" The voice was shrill now. "Are you listening to me? You ain't listening to me now, are you?"

Elvis saw the circuit breaker go. Inside his head, he saw sparks shower—they were beautiful, really, like Roman candles—and he heard a snap, then blackness.

****

The line between sane and crazy is thin. Some people say it's not really a line at all, and they're probably right. It's more membrane than line; a milky, translucent membrane. You can see through it. You can know what's over on the other side. You can push against it and stretch it to get an idea of what you're in for over there, if you've a mind to know. He was doing that. He'd dropped the phone and had closed his eyes and fallen. Yet, inside his mind, he was standing and leaning, arms outstretched, feet apart and palms against the membrane. He was trying to see what was on the other side of sane, thinking maybe, just maybe, it was safer over there.

He could still hear the voice coming from the phone. And he could hear all the other voices behind that voice. It was like they were all lined up behind him, all in the sane world, and they were talking to him, laughing at him. All he wanted was to get away from them. The crazy side, he could almost see, was definitely possibly beautiful, like maybe a nice, cool pine grove on a hot day. From the sane side it looked peaceful, safe and good. The only problem, as far as he could tell, was this humming, this buzzing coming from the crazy side. As he stretched and pushed and strained, the membrane thinned. Then it weakened and tore just a little—it opened a hole about the size of a quarter—and he realized that something had gone bad over there. It smelled like something sweet, but way, way too sweet. He could hear the hum, too. It was rising and moving, undulating like a quivering, living thing.

He squinted, looked through the hole and saw the other boy. The other boy was all alone, just standing there on the other side. Around him, on him—everywhere—were flies, black and mean, buzzing, darting, jabbing at his head, crawling up his shirt and over his face. But the other boy just stood there and stared at him with a calm, quiet look in his blue-gray eyes.

He jerked away from the wall and the membrane snapped back, first against his face, then against his whole body, blowing a little of the smell back at him through the hole. With it came a single buzzing, darting, annoying demon fly. This fly dove at him, jabbing into his ears, on his neck, into his open mouth and out again. The smell was leaking through the hole, blowing back at him, a slow leak from the crazy side to the sane. He wanted to kill the fly and shut off the smell because now he wanted to stay here. He could cope with the voices, but he knew he couldn't cope with that smell, that odor, and whatever had made it.

"Honey, you okay?" One voice behind him spoke loudly and clearly above the others. "You stay right where you are. You'll get it. Just reach out and let us help you. You'll get it."

He turned slowly from the membrane-wall and looked. It was her.

"Don't you worry, baby. Just stay with it," she said. "Just stay with it, baby."

She was right behind him, on the sane side of the leaking membrane. She was holding her hands out like she wanted to caress him. He felt like a little boy. He wanted her to kill the fly with a swatter, touch his forehead and make all the bad go away. Please, please, please. Hold me. Oh baby. He felt his lip tremble. And he started toward her with one heavy, weighted-down step, then another. The bad smell from the other side faded and the fly disappeared.

Her hands moved slowly toward his face. Yes, oh yes, she touched him. She cupped his face in her hands.

Her eyes were looking into his, telling him something. She was telling his brain that now it had to remember. Now, she said, he could no longer live a lie; he had to tell the truth. And next to her, leaning in and gawking at him with bug eyes was Harvey Monahan. Only Harvey wasn't laughing at him; he was saying softly, "Yes. Yes." And she was nodding and crying just enough to show him she still cared. This, she was saying, would soon be over.

He wanted to hold her and say, "Hey, let's go make an omelet or something." Instead, he let her take his face into her hands. She leaned to him and kissed him, lightly, on his forehead. Then she was gone. He could hear her footsteps, the closing of a far-off door. He was cold and slipping back into this world, still sane but once again feeling the ache of her leaving.

Chapter Fifteen

Elvis awoke and sat up, confused. He looked at the phone, which was next to him on the living room floor, and remembered the voice. His bowels clenched.

Stay with it, he told himself. Stay. Calm. Calm down. Elvis let his breath out slowly, got to his feet and picked up the phone. "Hello?"

There was nothing at first, then music and a voice, sounded like they were coming from a radio. Elvis strained to hear. "Mrrlmald riruffta degrees for a high," a muffled announcer was saying. "Trealdnad a dalldd back to the music."

It came up weakly, some old country song, distant and soft, more like a memory than a song. It was the twangy kind of thing Mom had always listened to while she was cooking and fussing around in the kitchen. Waylon or Willie or someone—music from the white plastic radio that sat next to the stove and propped up the Betty Crocker cookbook. Sometimes, Mom would turn it up good and loud when a favorite came on. She'd sing to it and sway. That was the only time Elvis thought she seemed young and happy. Then the phone would ring, and she'd say something really quick under her breath, a little swear word or something. She'd take three hard steps to the radio and turn it down, not all the way down, just so it was murmuring. And she'd answer the phone.

"Hello?" Her voice jerked Elvis from past to present. "Hello? Jess Icabone, you talk to me. You don't dare leave me hanging here like that—ever. You understand?"

"Jess… Icabone?" he said.

"Well, that's your God-given name ain't it? Or are you going back to that, back to how you're so hoity-toity Jesse

Tieter's in your blood forever now and oh don't call me nothing different? I gave you that name to call you Jess, not Jesse and the Icabone's unfortunate-as-can-toodley-be but it's there, too, on your birth certificate. I don't care no never-which-way who raised you. I named you for the King's dead twin brother—my idea. I told your daddy that. We got us Elvis and we got us his dead twin brother, Jesse, I said to him only I wanted to call you Jess, and I still will, 'cuz I can."

It was her. Alive? Gripping tightly to the cordless phone, Elvis walked to the couch and sat. "I ... a ... there was... a pot boiling over on the stove. I had to run and get it."

"Well, you could have said something. You could have said the pot was boiling." Her voice made Elvis choke. "You didn't have to just leave me here, hanging in the wind. You ever think to bring that wife and that kid of yours when you come to that big spanking new house? She'd take care of your boiling pot. She sure would, if she was half the wife she should be, she would."

Elvis was still trying to wake up, to understand, trying to catch up to her.

"You still there or you got another pot?"

"Yeah. I'm um... here."

"Speak up boy. Speak."

"I said, I'm here. I'm here. I think."

"You getting addle-brained now? Only knew one addle-brained boy in my whole dang life, and it wasn't you." The words rammed him. He squeezed the phone and held his other hand to his chest. "You know the addle-brained boy, now don't you? We talked about him just last night, didn't we? Leastwise, I think we did. My brain's half gone these days and I got thoughts running like runny eggs all together now. Where was I off to? Oh, yes, your brother. Addle-brained boys is trouble. They stumble around and bumble around until one day, boop!, they got something in their brain from a long time ago, something all bad that they shouldn't never even remember, and then alls the sudden they's causing me grief.

The Redeeming Power of Brain Surgery

Know anyone like that, do you?"

She hated him. She always had. It was all there in her voice. Every word was a dart, he was the bull's-eye, and she was hitting home. She was like a drunk at a party who's nailing the middle of the board and everybody's laughing because they can't believe it. Bull's-eye. Geeze, how'd she do that? Elvis felt his confidence ebbing again, the past creeping across his misty mental field.

"My money's almost up here. You got me talking on a dang pay phone. You know that? 'Course I got no fancy phone like you got. Got your poor mother down here on the bus— couldn't get in any of those fancy cars of yours and drive up and get her—got me drove down on the dang bus. Now you forgot me at the bus station. Couldn't even call me a cab or nothing. Nice young man here offered. Said he'd call me a cab, but no, not my boy, not my uptown brain doctor boy."

"You're here… in… in town?"

"'Course I am. You asked me last night to come on down. You made the dang arrangements. You sure you ain't that other boy of mine?"

Think. Think. How? How? Oh Lord, help. Help me. "Ummm. Um, you say there's a guy there that can call a cab?" Elvis felt like his heart had slid up into his mouth. "Um, why don't you have him, um, do that and, um, send you here?"

"You can't come and get me? You too lazy for that? What's a matter, too many pots?" She cackled.

"Yeah, yeah, that's it, M…" he couldn't say the word "mom"; it wouldn't come out. "Yeah, too many pots."

"So I'm s'pose to get my own dang cab and get myself hauled out there?"

"If you wouldn't mind. I mean, if that's okay. I mean, I'll pay the dude, the fare I mean, when you get here."

"What am I s'pose to say to him? Take me to the brain doctor's house? That what you want?"

"No, um, just have him bring you out here."

"I don't know where dang 'here' is. Where is 'here?'"

Elvis closed his eyes and pictured the directions on the paper. He recited them to her.

"I'm supposed to remember that? You expect me to…"

"Listen, um, let me, let me come and get you."

"'Bout time. 'Bout time you did something for me instead of expecting me to take care of everything all the time."

"Just hold on," Elvis clenched his eyes again. Stay. With. It. He let out a sigh. "I'll be there. I'll take care of it."

"Darn straight you will. For darn sure straight. If it's the only thing you ever took care of. Never could take care of this or that. Always having to have me clean up the mess. Listen to me babble on like an old woman. You getting over here soon? I'm about to catch my death here in this drafty place."

"I'll be there." Elvis' voice sound like a boy's.

"What?"

"I said I'll be there, M…Mom."

✳✳✳✳

Elvis ended the call and then wandered upstairs to Jesse's bedroom. He sat on the edge of the bed. The circuit breaker in his brain was humming. Too much was happening here. Way too much.

He thought maybe he should leave. Get out. Get some time. Think things through.

The local cops said don't leave.

Monahan, that guy, he'd said go back to the beginning.

Mom was here to see him. She was dead.

Then there was this other deal. With him. Who? Jess. Jesse.

Jesse.

His brother? Had invited his dead mom? To his brother's house?

It was too much.

Something moved behind him, in the doorway. Elvis turned. No. Not this. Not this too. Couldn't be. It was. No. Yes. It was. Hey buddy, we got to talk, man.

Donnel, big as life, tears on his face.

Elvis could see Donnel's mouth making words, but the words were hard to hear; the electrical hum rose in Elvis' head. This was too much, too, too much. Donnel, cheeks shining, a fat porky hand reaching out to him. Elvis sucked his chin to his chest as the hum became a voice.

"Get out of the way," the voice inside his skull screamed. "GET OUT OF THE WAY. DON'T LET HIM TOUCH YOU!"

The voice was Donnel's. Elvis shook his head, trying to clear his brain, trying to take in the fact that Donnel was here now and alive. But shaking his head only made things worse. Again, he was falling, falling, getting sucked back to the black hole of when he was a kid. No. Please. Please. Don't.

"GET OUT OF THE WAY. DON'T LET HIM TOUCH YOU!" The memory roared in, overtaking the hum and the adult Donnel that stood in front of him.

They were boys, two buddies, standing in the woods; Donnel daring him to poke his head into the burrow—to see what kind of wild animal had dug it. Elvis laughed and stuck his face down in the cool darkness of that hole, then fell back in alarm. A fox came up fast, cutting a swath into the heat and the blinding gold-white of the day.

Elvis screamed then scrambled backwards like a crab, hands palms-down in the dust. He fell, righted himself momentarily, then fell again.

The animal danced, yipped, snarled around him, over him, its slobber flicking on his face, its breath hot and smelly. Elvis was crying and rolling, crying and rolling as the animal danced and lunged.

"GET OUT OF THE WAY. DON'T LET HIM TOUCH YOU!" Donnel screamed.

The fox lunged at Elvis' sweating kid-hand in the dust. Elvis tried to pull it back, doing his best to avoid the teeth. But his best wasn't enough. "Ahhhhhagggggghhhhhh!" The fox clamped on the hand—his right one—grrrring as it did.

191

Like a dog clamped on an old sock, it jerked its head, sending red-hot forks of pain up into his arm, his shoulder—his heart.

"Ahhhhhaggggghhhhhh!" Elvis remembered it all. The pain, the heat, were from the place where the devil lived, from hell. The animal's eyes were fire.

Donnel. Help. Please. Help.

The fox wouldn't let go.

Donnel, tears running down his fat expressive cheeks, reached out with that big porky hand. Elvis could see the rock in it. It was a huge rock for a kid, but not for a Donnel-sized kid. Donnel swung it up through the white-gold sunlight and screamed, "NOOOOOOOO"—Elvis thought, just for a flash, that maybe that wasn't such a good idea. He thought maybe the fox didn't understand "no"—but Donnel cracked the rock up under the jaw of the fox. And the fox let go.

Then it clamped again, harder, and Elvis screamed again. The scream sent Donnel back on his butt. Elvis could see him through the haze of the dust, bawling on his butt. The fox was shaking Elvis' hand and snarling. Grrrrr. Grrrrrrr. The pain—oh man, the pain—it was suffocating. The scene was a horror movie in his head. The fox's eyes were blazing and Elvis' blood was flecking on its red hair, dying it redder. A blue-hot ache gripped the bones of his hand.

BWAAM.

Elvis remembered the explosion as more of a smell than a sound. It was gun, dust and wild animal. And it was none of those things. Elvis couldn't tell exactly what happened. Someone just sneaked up and, BWAAM, turned everything into that smell. But when the BWAAM was gone, well, the fox was twitching in the dust. Most of its hind-end was gone, and it looked like half the fox it had been before. It made Elvis sick just looking at it. His hand made him sicker: it was all mangled and bloody at the end of his arm. The blood was everywhere.

The BWAAM had stolen his hearing. Elvis, crying and bleeding, turned to Donnel. Chubby, dirty, baby-faced and husky-sized Donnel was still on his butt, and he was crying. But Elvis couldn't hear him. And despite everything, despite the dying animal, the mangled hand and the heat and dust and tears, that's what bothered him right then: the silence. So deep and empty that the nothing became something—a ringing hum in his ears.

Later, he'd spent the hot evening on the couch in the living room, his hand wrapped and throbbing and his mom kept throwing him ugly glances, mad at him for the cost of the doctor bill and for the tantrum he'd thrown over the possibility of rabies shots in his stomach, if the fox turned out to have had rabies. Elvis, he kept worrying over that ringing and how it kept him from hearing, from understanding what was going on around him.

"I said we got to talk, bud," Donnel was saying.

"Huh?"

"We got to talk." The voice, Donnel's, thank God, finally was breaking through the hum.

"What?"

"Talk. You and me." Donnel's voice was clear now.

"I ain't your bud. You're dead," Elvis said without tasting the words. "You're dead," he said again, getting a little taste this time.

Donnel eased himself down on the mattress and moved in close, like he had something private to say. "Man, I know this has been a real tough couple of days for you."

Elvis let out a slow breath through his teeth.

"Lookie hear, first off, I'm alive. See?" Donnel pushed back the cuff of the sleeve of his flannel shirt and rolled the arm over to expose the coffee-with-cream-colored underbelly of his wrist. He pinched himself and winced. "See? Now and 'nother thing, see, I talked to this cop dude, see, he's been like, working on this thing."

"Thing."

"This thing with, like, you and… your mom and your… your brother."

Elvis swiveled his head slowly to Donnel. His heart started pounding funny, like it was missing every other beat.

"I've knowed about your brother for a good while, see." Donnel said. "He's your twin brother, you know. Not like identical. Fraternal, they call it. See, you don't look exactly alike. Close, though."

Elvis couldn't breathe.

"And... and she knows. She knows him, too."

"Who?"

"Him, your brother. She knows your brother."

"Lavern knows?"

"Yeah, bud."

"She *knows*... she's alive?" In a corner of his brain, Elvis thought he heard the fox panting.

"Yeah. She is, bud," Donnel said softly, like oh—oops—he'd forgotten to mention that. Donnel's face contorted. "She's alive, buddy. We both are. And we've knowed, knew, about this brother of yours for a little while now. I don't know if you remember him or what. But you got this brother, see, this patern... fraternal twin."

"I know." Elvis said it without meaning to.

"Seriously? You? You remember?"

"Sort of," Elvis sighed. "Yeah. I guess. It's. It's weird."

"We tricked you with that accident, bud; she was hoping you'd remember. They got this special neurogonist... this brain study program thing that pays big-time docs to come to small towns like this and study and teach and, you know, do their stuff on patients. He built this house here. He was going to have her move in eventually; way I see it, he was. I... I hate to say it but, well, seems like they maybe had somethin' cookin' between 'em. Least that's what I told the cop."

"You called a cop?"

"Yeah, like I said, I been working with him. Called him right after your brother showed up. Only Lavern don't know it. I guess I sort of don't, like, trust her right now; like I said, he built the house for her I think."

"Who?"

"Your brother."

"For who?"

"Lavern, bud. Lavern."

"You don't trust her?"

"Not right now."

Elvis squinted against a sharp pain in his head. He peered up at the picture on the wall. He heard the fox snarling, felt the breath from it on his hand.

"Elvis, I don't know that I'm right," Donnel said. "I don't know diddly squat about what's going on for sure. Alls I know is I couldn't take not coming here and talking to you about it. I was s'pose to wait and see how things went. This police dude I hooked up with, see, I talked to him again last night on my cell, right after Lavern got me doing that fake accident. We got banged up a little more than I 'spected, but we was okay. Afterwards, see, Lavern was telling the deal to the guys that drive the ambulance and I got a second to call the cop and he told me to just, you know, sit tight like I have been ever since I first called the cops a few months ago. But I can't sit tight, not no more. That's why I borrowed a car off Shaqua."

"Shaqua."

"Yeah."

"Shaqua your sister? Or Shaqua your aunt?"

"Sister. Called her and asked her to, you know, pick me up. Anyways, she and Darnella Cole, her friend that works with her? They come and brought me a car, at the hospital. That's how come I could kind of follow you."

"You tricked me."

"Lavern's idea, dude. She worked it all out, see, with the ambulance guys—one was Jaz Tomkin. And with this chick that works with your brother at the hospital; she helped Lavern on this. But once we got to the hospital I, like, just checked right out on their plan. Once you got there and, you know, just left? I got in Shaqua's car and I followed you. Man, like I say, I'm sorry. See, Lavern, she says we had to wait for you to figure this all out. She's saying she did it for your own good, man, but I'm not sure no more. This cop I was telling you about, I think he's on the same kind of track, wanting to…"

"Harvey Monahan."

"Huh?"

"The cop."

"Yeah, that's the dude. He's the one. He's, I think anyways, that he's like Lavern, wanting you to kind of figure this thing out and maybe lead the rest of us to whatever happened—to the truth of, like, whatever happened with your…" Donnel caught himself. "He caught up with you, didn't he? Monahan? He talked to you?"

"Yeah."

"That's good. That's real good. What was it he said to you? I'd just like to know. I mean, we don't have to hold back nothing, far as I'm concerned. It's all up to you. I can definitely tell you what's up. I can fill you in. If you want. I don't have to. But I can. That's why I'm here."

Elvis flopped back on the bed. He shut his eyes and saw the membrane again: the wall between crazy and not crazy. He wanted to go to the other side, where it was safe. He opened his eyes. The fox growled nearby, maybe from under the bed. The ceiling was turning slowly, like a huge ceiling fan.

"Hear about Jubal Brown?" Elvis muttered. "Shinola kicked right out of him." He smiled. The ceiling still didn't respond, but the fox growled softly. Elvis thought he could hear it scratching at the floor.

"Never mind that right now," Donnel said. "Look bud, I got a lot of things planned here to help you. You know, we got to straighten all this out, but first you got to pull yourself together. You're not going to do me or nobody no good acting spaced out like this."

Elvis lay there, a day's worth of anger and worry and frustration melting, mixing with a lifetime of, of what? Of, of, of swallowing his thoughts and hurts and questions. Of thinking but never saying. Of wondering but knowing not to ask. All of this, all of it, long-simmering inside him, began to boil—the whole mess rising, steam releasing, becoming red mist in his head. When he spoke, Elvis' voice seemed to come from some place dark and far away. "Tell me this, my black-ass friend," he said. "Tell me. How long do you think I'm gonna lie around and take this from you?"

"Hold on there, bud. Whoa."

"Whoa? You f-ing whoa." Now there was a vibe in Elvis' voice; a crazy, lazy, creepy vibe. "You want me to just lie here like some whore and take whatever you shovel at me and say, 'Oh that's cool'?" It was him, Elvis, talking to the ceiling of his brother's house. But the tone, the voice, seemed to not be Elvis at all. "You're all like, 'She's alive,' like it's some big birthday surprise you two worked out. You're telling me you faked all this and that—ha ha and tweedly dee—I'm s'posed to just be the idiot that accepts it, that it?" The room hummed; the air had gone cold. Donnel shivered. A thought dangled. Elvis, this Elvis, could kill a man. No. That was stupid. But yeah. Maybe. Yeah he could.

Elvis abruptly rolled to face Donnel. When he looked up, the eyes had gone empty, like the blue-gray had drained away. "Here's the deal, Donnel. You're trying to steal my wife. After all these years, you figure, 'Oh that Elvis, he got his nose on the grindstone and his brain mushed off and he don't see nothin.' So you and her decide to get it going, get it on. And know what? That's cool. 'Cuz I been asleep at the wheelhouse. You snooze? Well you, you get no booby prize, am I right? I mean, hey, you're a man and a man's gotta get it when he can, right? But you shouldn't lie now, my brother. No. That's way bad, lying is. You saying all this and that about her and… and… him. But all the time it's been you? That's shameful."

"Dude. Wait. No. Not like *goin' on,* not like that. We got something working, see, to *help* you, see…"

Elvis could see the fox now, eyes blazing. Stop, a voice in his head said, stop that talk right now. Elvis ignored it and sat up. "You fat ugly scumshit. You… Least you can do is come clean."

Elvis was on his feet, had two fists worth of Donnel's t-shirt, and was propelling him back, back, back, until he slammed him against the wall. The big man's eyes went wide as the wind blew out of him—oomp. Elvis heard the fox grrring. This was wrong, very wrong, dangerous and wrong. His mother wagged a finger in his face. Elvis shook his head.

"All my life, Donnel, all my shitty life, I got people walking on me, busting my ass, acting like I'm the dumbest piece of shit that ever dribbled down the pike. Like I don't know what they're up to. Like I never noticed anything." His hook nose was within a hair's width of Donnel's nose. Their eyes were locked, Donnel's brown and worried, Elvis' now vibrantly blue-gray and cold as death. "I'm s'pose to keep it all under control, you know? I'm s'pose to take your crap and everyone else's and just ease along with the flow, man. But..." Elvis frowned. His face suddenly went slack. He looked at his fists, confused—how did they get here? Elvis let go of Donnel, looked in his friend's eyes, searching, the blue-gray swimming.

"Maybe what you're telling me is the truth. And maybe, yeah, sure, maybe a lot of it is. But maybe. Maybe."

He walked to the door, turned and looked at Donnel; a look of sadness and something else, something scary. Then, before Donnel could stop him, Elvis was out the door and gone.

Chapter Sixteen

From the front seat of the squad car, Harvey Monahan angled around to shoot a look at Jesse Tieter and allowed himself a quiet smile. "You don't look so good, doc. Look like you had the shinola beat out of you or somethin'."

The neurosurgeon turned to gaze out the window, his face a stone. One cool character.

Harvey gave his driver a look of smug satisfaction, but got no response. Behind the wheel, Trooper Clayton Diebold was right out of the State Trooper training manual, buckling up, checking his mirrors, doing a full turnaround to check the prisoner then the road. Perfect. A young cop, mouth shut, ready to haul ass back to the post, no small talk.

Harvey looked out at the drab day and the smile turned to a ghoulish grin. This couldn't be better. For the first time in a long, long time, life felt crisp around the edges. The world was in balance. Granted, there was no atoning for past sins. The shrink had said what happened would always be with him. Heck, if he closed his eyes right now—he wouldn't—Trooper Diebold's peach-blossom skin would become the blushed cheeks of Sandy Tandy, age seventeen. If Harvey allowed it— he couldn't—the passing scenery would become a stretch of Lake Michigan glittering in the sun of Chicago, late summer. If he let his eyes linger on the passing scenery—he shouldn't— a flash of something in the roadside weeds would become the girl splashing along, her head buried in the chop from the offshore breeze, that one arm a flash of warning against the blue green water.

If Harvey Monahan let his guard down—never— Diebold's hands would become his, gripping the wheel, turning hard, hard, hard, one hand leaving the wheel to cut the throttle, to reduce the *excessive speed* as his brain tried to work its clumsy fingers around the thump, the awful thump. If Harvey Monahan steeled himself—impossible—he could imagine Diebold's razor sharp and attentive brain becoming his, muddy and mushy from working too late and the beer and the sun and shocked! that he'd been unable to react, or to explain why he'd steered the damn boat so close to shore.

She hadn't died, thank God. But he'd been finished in his home city before the story had hit the *Trib* or *The Sun Times*. The psychologist, Dr. Bernie Cook, had helped him hold it together through the civil trial, the loss of his badge—the hardest part—and the civil settlement. Getting started again, well, that had been rocky but it helped that he was single, smart, and well-connected. In Chicago, you don't work fifteen years as a street cop and detective and *not* have some useful information tucked away on the powerjockeys and brokers downtown. His City Hall connections had earned him the deal that sponged his record of any criminal wrongdoing. An administrator in the Police Department with a history of fidelity gymnastics had gotten him the interview with the Michigan State Police. The rest had been up to Harvey Monahan and his solid record as a cop.

Half the reason the Michigan State Police had hired Harvey Monahan at the backwater post on the lakeshore was that he was unknown; he could poke around places more-familiar faces couldn't. The low profile suited him. So did being in a hick town on this side of the big lake. In his new-found Michigan haven, Harvey had few friends other than Jake Vanderzee, a local charter boat captain and an equally happily embittered recluse, and that was fine. Harvey had bought a turn-of-the-(20th)century bungalow near Lake Michigan. He had a new boat (although it had taken a year of therapy to muscle himself back on deck), a yellow Labrador named Rabbit and a reasonable Internet/cable TV package. The Cubs and Wrigley Field were just a two-hour Sunday drive away.

The Redeeming Power of Brain Surgery

Beer was five minutes to the Quick Stop. Harvey Monahan had come half way back to being a happy man.

Now he was nearing euphoria. Harvey had been working on an unrelated case, trying to nail the local whacked-out white supremacist's cell on a weapons charge, when he'd gotten the voicemail from Lavern Icabone, the cute-faced chubby chick that took his check for the water bill at city hall, about her husband's father, who'd been missing since the 1960s. A couple of days later, Lavern Icabone's husband's buddy had showed up at the post, asking to talk to a detective about the same forty-year-old case. The local cops had budget-cut their detective staff, so it had been relatively easy for Harvey to convince the post commander, Nabors Jefferies, that crew-cutted-by-the-book-bastard, that he could handle both the white supremacists and the missing person's deal.

He was glad he had. Over the last week or so, the dead-file case had uncoupled as easily as a bra off a hooker's back; the answers, like a lot of cop work, coming by pure-as-snow dumb luck. Actually, you could work a lifetime in this business and never have it come so easy. When the white power creep, Plannenberg, had come to undercover Harvey, asking him to help follow this Elvis Icabone, Harvey'd wanted to raise his eyes to heaven and thank Sister Mary or whoever upstairs could still see through the cigar smoke of his life and bless him with such luck. Two cases, wound up together in a neat little bow—the guys back in the precinct would never have believed this.

Truth be told, Harvey was suspicious. His inner-cop divining rod was twinging, jerking toward some bad water he thought had to be here. Nothing had ever been this simple. He tried to reassure himself that nothing was wrong; that because he was in a small town now the puzzle pieces were just easy to find. No one had ever looked very hard; that was obvious. Heck, the puzzle pieces were not just close together, they were as big as his ex-wife's ass.

He had no body or weapon, which was a problem. Maybe.

But at the very least, Harvey Monahan figured he had the outlines of a couple of solid circumstantial cases.

The brain surgeon, he thought, had offed the old man—when the surgeon was a kid, a twisted, half-stupid kid. Later, sometime, he'd probably killed the mother. Guilt and worry had driven him home to frame-up the brother. Harvey chuckled, picturing the looney old Iowa couple who'd raised the boy-killer. Clueless, they were, but the three hours he'd spent with them in Davenport had given him a good picture of this brain doctor part-son of theirs. How the mother fit into this or how she'd died Harvey Monahan wasn't sure. Everybody he'd asked was damn short on details about her. No funeral? No grieving? He hadn't had time to get up to Traverse City to badger the folks at the home where she'd supposedly died. He probably should track down the coroner up north and have the body exhumed. He hated the thought of what he'd find. Lord help us, Harvey Monahan thought, gazing at the muddy fields and woods alongside the road. What a sick world.

The young State Trooper accelerated the car along the shoulder, hit the turn signal and made one last check over his left shoulder for oncoming traffic, then edged the car onto the roadway. The sound of the rear door opening and the sudden change in air pressure flashed Monahan back to his days in the Army, to the sucking of a Huey's rotors against his eardrums.

Harvey Monahan whirled. Jesse Tieter had popped the door, was pushing it, arms locked, shaggy hair ripping in the wind as he groped for the release button on his shoulder harness. Harvey's eyes flicked to the green-horn Trooper, his baby-soft face bloodless, mouth unhinged, eyes gawking at the rear-view mirror. He hadn't secured the door? Before Harvey could stop him, the fool braked the car. No. No. Not that. He was pulling over, a natural reaction, but the wrong one. And his revolver, the Trooper had managed to pull his revolver? There it was ugly, pointed awkwardly, crazily toward the ceiling as the car jiggled to a stop.

*****

The jolt of his shoulder striking the road was lightning that cracked through him, yellow-white and blinding. Then nothing happened and everything did. Jesse was tumbling, tumbling, face skidding through gravel. There was mud, exhaust, heat, then the cool of the wet grass and the darkness inviting him, his mother's face, and those eyes, blue and gray and pleading, no, please, no, buck up, come on, be a man, stay with it, please. Finally, he was on his feet, limping and stumbling, running in the opposite direction, first toward the woods then angling back up the road, remembering the Cordoba, his phone, freedom.

A car door opened. A voice was shouting. "Hold up, doc. Stop now. Stop, doc. Stop."

"Detective, I have this."

"No. No you don't. Put. The gun. Down."

Jesse waved wildly at a fly with a hand that seemed to float away from him. He stumbled and fell again. His shoulder screamed. Jesse rolled to his back, sat up, and the fly was on him, darting at his face, in his ear. He closed his eyes and everything wavered, nausea rising in his throat.

"Remain on the ground, sir. Stay in the car, detective."

Bright, stainless needles of pain probed across his chest from his shoulder, sending sharp minions marching to his brain. Through the pain, Jesse tried to stand, wavering between now and then, here and there. He could hear the car's door slam, the rush of feet in gravel. He could see the road's shoulder, slewing away from him and, down the gun's barrel, the fat black kid with the rock; Donnel, his dumb brother's buddy, the tears running down those fat, expressive cheeks.

"GET OUT OF THE WAY. DON'T LET HIM TOUCH YOU."

It was a huge rock, for a kid, but not for a Donnel-sized kid. Donnel swung the rock up, up through the blinding light of the sun, screaming "NOOOOOOOO." The fox let go of

Elvis' hand. But then the fox clamped again. Elvis screamed. Donnel fell back on his butt.

Jesse got to his feet and floundered down the road. His brain was spinning. His shoulder throbbed. Someone was yelling. He could see the fat, comical boy-Donnel through the dust, bawling on his butt, the fox shaking Elvis' hand and snarling. Jesse could hear Mom's voice, teasing and taunting him.

"What do you think you're doing with the gun?" she'd said, laughing. "What do you think you're doing with that?"

Mom knew he couldn't do it; he couldn't kill anybody else. She was laughing and the footsteps were coming, there was this commotion behind him and now Donnel was sobbing harder because the fox wouldn't let go and Jesse was running away. Then Jesse was going back, feeling his fingers on the double triggers as he tried to draw a bead; Elvis' image lined up with the sight for an instant, the next it was gone, obliterated by dust and sun and fox.

He could see the Cordoba. His chest ached, sweat stung his eyes and the boy-Elvis was a blur. Come on, Jesse thought, stay with it. Stay with it, baby. Then, just when he was ready to give up, it came: a breath of a breeze for his lungs and head. Elvis' back was there, in line with the sight, clear. The handle of the car was cold against his hand. Jesse held his breath, tightened his fingers and closed his eyes.

"PLEASE. NO."

Show her. Show her what kind of man you are.

"No. Please no." The voice echoed in his head and rolled into his chest, colliding with the ache and making it impossible to breathe. Jesse saw the eyes, the blue-gray eyes, of his father and his brother. Please no, the eyes said.

No! Someone shouted?

"NOO!"

BWAAM.

Chapter Seventeen

Whirrrrr.

The phone again.

Elvis was paralyzed with indecision. He was in the kitchen, on his way out of Jesse Tieter, M.D.'s house, away from Donnel. He had to get going. He absolutely had to. But. Yes. The phone. Could be Mom. Mom? Maybe. Maybe he had to pick her up. Bus station. Yes. He took three quick, clumsy steps and grabbed the cordless, then turned and rushed toward the door.

"Hello?" Elvis said as he turned the knob.

"It's me."

Elvis opened the door. From the phone, there was noise, like a crowd, and music. The caller was in a restaurant or a bar or someplace. "Hello?" He said it loudly.

"I said, 'It's me.'" The voice was familiar.

"Who's me?" Elvis took a step.

"You know, the guy that took care of your friend. At the plant."

The world tipped a little. Elvis' knees turned to Jello. Jerry. Plannenberg.

"You there?" the voice said. Yes, it was. Had to be.

Jerry. Jesse. The faceless man. Oh.

"You best be there," Jerry said. 'Cuz, tell the truth, dude, you got me in some kind of mess here."

The truth, a glimmering, quartz-encrusted shaft of it, sliced through his head. With a silent gasp, Elvis eased to one knee, his hand still on the doorknob. "What, what do you mean…" He took a breath, steadied his voice, "What do you mean m… mess?"

"Look man," Jerry said. "I don't know what the deal is, but someone tipped off the cops or something. They got me charged for this thing. Me."

"Really?" Elvis slowly stood. "Really?"

"Yeah, really. Me."

"H… how?" Elvis couldn't pull it all together. Jerry. The ponytail and the Dr Pepper, and the cops and don't leave town, and Donnel and Lavern and, and, and Monahan The Cop. Start at the very beginning, the cop had said. Which brought him to his mom. But now, Jerry was—the police had him? Elvis' overtaxed brain judged that Jerry being involved with the Mr. Faceless thing was good, that maybe his luck was turning, but he couldn't pull the puzzle pieces together; they were too far apart. "How?" he repeated.

"How what?"

"How?" *How?* That was the best he could do? The only word that would dribble out of his mouth? Elvis stopped. Be Jesse Tieter. Come on. Be a man. Buck up. He gulped a lungful of air and let it out. "How did they get… apprehend you?"

Jerry groaned. "I don't know, man. Well. Yeah. Yeah I do. I mean I don't know how it happened, but I got double-crossed. There was this cop, see, that was double-crossing me, only I didn't know it; same guy I got to follow the dude turned out to be a cop. Can you believe this shit?"

Elvis couldn't believe it. His mouth felt frozen.

"Now, don't you start pulling the pussy quiet stuff on me." Jerry's voice was low and angry, speech slurred like he'd had a couple drinks, even though it was too early for drinks. But Elvis could feel panic too—Jerry Plannenberg was scared. "See, you're in this, man. This is you. All you. They questioned me half the night. I got a jerk-off lawyer; he made 'em let me go for now. But I wasn't expecting to get into it like this. It was all gonna be nice and easy. Now it's… you're in this, man. You are most definitely in this."

This thing was coming at Elvis from all directions. There were too many angles. Mom. He had to get her. Lavern. He wanted to find her. But. Maybe not. And Jerry. Jerry was. Jerry had. He'd done this? The police had him. But not. Not now. From inside the house, there was the dull clunking of heavy footsteps coming down the stairs from the second floor. Donnel. Not now. Too much. So much to think about. Hurry. Hurry up.

Elvis spoke but couldn't feel the words.

There was a crash from Jerry's side of the conversation, a pause, then a crowd laughing. "What?"

"I said, where are you?" Elvis shouted.

"You don't worry about that. Your worry is what I'm gonna do to you. I'm bailed out for now," Jerry was getting hysterical. "But they're gonna pull it all together and when they do, I'm... I had the guy... I killed the... Man, you had me do this. You did."

"Elvis, you still in here somewhere?" Donnel was in the dining room.

"They said they turned up something in the autopsy, traces of the stuff I slipped the guy. Guy I got it from must've lied, man. He said that shit showed no traces."

"You poisoned him?"

"What you think I did? You wanted violent."

"I did." Elvis said it like a statement but meant it as a question.

"Damn straight you did. And know what? I did everything you asked, even got that guy to follow him around. How'd I know he was a cop?"

Elvis tried to regroup. Harvey. Harvey Monahan.

"Now they're talking to people. And I am in no way, shape, or form going to stand here and take this deal alone, I tell you that."

To Elvis, that part didn't figure. How could Jerry have gotten in touch with Harvey Monahan?

"Elvis, wait up, man." Donnel's voice was suddenly clear. He was in the kitchen.

"This is on you," Jerry's voice said in his ear. "This is all yours. There's no way you can, like, avoid it. No where you can run to."

Donnel was walking toward him, his eyes wide and sad. His face had a hound dog look. "Elvis, man. Don't leave. I'm trying to help you's all."

Elvis closed his eyes. This was too much. A cloud, mean, menacing and thundering, rumbled in his head. He pictured Jesse and Lavern in this kitchen. Or maybe it was Donnel and Lavern. He imagined Lavern peeling potatoes and humming to a tune on the radio. Maybe there was milk on the counter just begging to be spilled. Jesse-Donnel, leaning against the counter, was reading the paper and mumbling about excise taxes and mutual funds and the Dow Jones industrial average and stuff she didn't know diddly about. Then he saw his mother at the bus station with an ashtray cocked by her ear; she was waiting to sling it at him. The fox growled. Elvis swallowed and opened his eyes. He flung the phone at Donnel.

"It's for you."

✻✻✻✻

His car was gone. Jesse had taken it.

The only option was Jesse's car. Elvis walked toward the garage, praying silently that the car was in there and that it had keys.

The garage had the scent of exhaust and something else; it was an odor that was soft and sweet but, in a funny way, overwhelming. Elvis tried to identify it but it seemed to drift away into the shadows.

The guy's car was gorgeous—a silver Mercedes. Gorgeous. It was the kind of car that looked like it was moving when it was sitting in the middle of the garage. The garage itself was awfully clean, and the smell seemed out of place; it hung, strong, smoky sweet and sickening in the air. There was none of the usual garage stuff—no tools, no peg board or anything— just some cardboard boxes stacked next to the door and on the far side, in the back corner, a black, new-looking wood stove.

The Redeeming Power of Brain Surgery

The stove door was closed. A shining metal pipe connected it to the roof, and there was a mess of what looked like leaves and dirt on a tarp on the cement floor in front of it.

Elvis walked around the back of the car. On the clean, gray concrete next to the Mercedes—in the second stall of the garage—was a muddy shovel, some wood kindling stacked in a painstakingly neat pile, one of those adjustable, goose-necked work lights, and what looked like another work light on some kind of collapsible tripod.

Something in his gut slithered. The longer he stood there, the more smell he absorbed.

Get out of here. Go. Now. Yes. The Mercedes. Maybe. No. Yes. Keys. Maybe. Elvis took two wobbly steps toward the car then turned back toward the tarp. He thought he heard something outside. He stopped and looked out into the yard, holding his breath.

Nothing.

Go. Now. Go.

He moved quickly back around the car, running a finger along the finish, then grabbed the door handle and pulled. Ca-click, it opened on the first try. The scent of leather and cigars rolled out at him, partly masking the other thing. He also sensed another vague, familiar scent.

Whoa. Hold on. Elvis swayed a little, then steadied himself. No, no way, he thought, even though he wanted to believe what he smelled was real. Oh, please, yes, he did. He took a deep breath, got in the car and closed the door.

The Mercedes had a—"whatchacallit?" Elvis thought—a key fob. And the thing was in the ignition. Elvis imagined the hand of God, Mercedes Benz fob clenched between the fingers, coming down through the moonroof and sliding the thing into the ignition then pulling back up, up, up into the sky. He bowed his head and closed his eyes. His mother's eyes stared back. No. Please. He opened his eyes and his gaze wandered from the dash to the seat next to him. A piece of yellow paper, folded, stood out against the burgundy leather.

The way his name was written was the way she wrote. Mrs. Feely had always given her high marks for her penmanship, all the teachers had. "Elvis," the note said, in her penmanship.

Slowly, the car grew warm and Elvis could feel his heart trying to crack through his ribs. The paper was turned just so he could he read it. Watermelon perfume, Zest soap and Butterfinger candy bars; he smelled them again. He tasted the other thing, the smoky, sick thing, and swallowed.

The paper was in his shaking hand. He sat, staring at it, blood pounding in his ears. Once again, he wanted her to explain it all. He'd need a couple beers to get through it, he knew that. But he wanted her to explain. One Lavern please, he ordered to an invisible waitress, with a beer chaser.

He unfolded the paper slowly, laying it open on the steering wheel like a surgeon opening a patient.

The letters were firm, perfectly looped, cursive letters in red pen, maybe red-orange:

Elvis:

I love you baby. I always did. I always will.

I'm here. I've been here. And I know you might be mad at me but I hope you're not! I'd hate to have you mad at me! I'll explain everything as soon as I can. To everything there is a season and a reason, right? Really, I hope you're not mad because I did what I did for a reason. Donnel, too, he's a trooper, you know? And he loves you, really. I know that sounds funny, him being a guy, but it's not that kind of love, like queer or anything. He doubted you a while, to be honest, I think. And I'm sorry, so sorry to tell you so did I baby. I'm so so sorry. Please forgive us, me. We've been through a lot and I doubted but now we know we shouldn't have. And we been trying to help. And I think it worked. I think it helped! You're doing stuff you never would have done if I hadn't done what I did, what we did, you know? That's confusing, right? But it's kind of supposed to be. We was desperate. I thought a lot of it up last night when I had Donnel roll the truck. Then, after I found out you'd gone out here to the house, I was so proud of you! That was an answered prayer, you know that? But it told me we'd done the right thing, OK? I know it hurt some but I also knowed I had to keep pushing you, Elvis. I wanted to get you to remember, baby, 'cuz I knew something bad did happen back then; I just didn't know what. I wanted you to find out the truth on your own. With God's help. God led you back. God will. Do you BELIEVE that? Now I been thinking something and you think it's dumb just ignore it because maybe I'm going too far and I hope God don't mind and you neither but maybe you need to go back to where you used to live. You don't have to but maybe that might JAR something. It was just an idea. You don't have to. You're doing just great. Great!! But I want you to REMEMBER everything. I don't, I can't tell you everything because there are things I don't know, except I know you're not BAD. Stay with it baby. I love YOU. You're not BAD. But you got to remember what happened back then, you know, a long time ago.

Lavern.

Lavern. The way she formed the letters and capitalized some words—he could hear her in that. He breathed deeply and he could smell her. Watermelon perfume, Zest soap and Butterfinger candybars. Oh. Lavern. What had she done to him? Why? Why? Donnel didn't trust her. Should he? No. Yes. He should. Yes. Lavern *cared*. Lavern was good. She was EVERYTHING, wasn't she? No. She'd lied. Lied and DIED. She'd cheated. With him. Maybe. Maybe not. Trust. Donnel. Of course. Yes. Trust them both. She's here. Him too. Here. For a reason. And you know. You know why? Yes. No. The hand. God. Help me. Please. Mom. Oh. Mom.

Elvis fumbled for the latch and, out of habit, pushed hard against the car door. He flung himself onto the garage floor, his face skidding on the concrete. He rolled to his back with a groan. Get out of the way. Don't let her. Don't let her. He turned and ran, away from them, away from this house, away.

Chapter Eighteen

He'd heard other cops talk about how it feels to be shot. Some dwelled on the cartoon-world impact, like taking the full hit of a Ford F-250 at 60 miles per hour in the (choose the body part being shot). Pretty much everyone mentioned the rush of adrenalin and tingling heat and everything around you going super slo-mo.

He felt all of these things and a few he didn't expect, including the nearly irresistible urge to release his bowels and bladder.

And after the worst of it, shuddering in the cool grass of the ditch, Harvey Monahan looked up at trooper Clayton Diebold and saw the panic-paralyzed face of a young man whose career was bleeding in front of him.

"Get on the radio. Get some help," Harvey Monahan heard himself say. "And put that sidearm away before you kill some damn raccoon or something."

Diebold fumbled for his holster and stuck the gun in it. "I'm...oh, I'm sorry... You jumped in my line of fire." He turned and leaned into the car, pulled out the mic to the radio, dropped it, bent over and fumbled for it, the gun sliding out of the holster and clattering to the pavement. "I didn't... you..."

"I was keeping you from shooting an unarmed brain surgeon, you wiseass," Harvey groaned as the kid recovered the gun and microphone; he heard him making the call for backup and an ambulance.

"Forget the ambulance. I'm fine. And relax." He groaned. "We'll find some way to explain this, baby boy."

Rising to his knees, Harvey tested the shoulder. It moved. He groaned and tried to stand. The ditch slid out from under him. He clawed his way to his knees and managed to stand. The world swayed. A hawk or something like it waved at him from a goofy angle in the slate sky. The shoulder hurt. It hurt. He pulled a trembling hand away from the hot hole in his shirt and looked at it. Surprising. Not too much blood. It dawned on him that it was on both sides; the bullet had gone through. He was going to be fine. But now the stupid doctor was on the run.

He'd been having a good day, a really good day. This couldn't be it. No. This day had been too good to end this way.

❊❊❊❊

Jesse Tieter reached the Cordoba, fought the stubborn latch, got in, and slammed the door. The cell phone was ringing. No. No time. Someone. A gun? Shot. Big trouble. Hurry. Now. Not the phone. Not now. He turned the key in the ignition. The car coughed. The phone rang. He had to go. Get out of here. Not now. But. Stupid car. He stomped the gas pedal and tried again. The phone rang. The engine tried to turn over, but nothing. What if. Go. How. Hurry. Who could call? Someone. Shot. A gun?

He answered the phone. "Hello," he said, trying to catch his breath. Jesse glanced out the windshield. Up the road the cop was down. Shot. The kid, the driver, he was on the radio. He'd done it? The driver?

"You coming to get me or not? I got to call every phone number or what?"

Mom?

"I'm down at the bus station like I said. Like you wanted me. You want me to get that dang cab?" The anger in her voice, the instability in it, snapped and crackled in the receiver. "I called every number I can get my hands on. One's busy. Another's got a dang answering machine with your kid on it. What you got, another pot boiling? You too busy cleaning house to answer the phone? You always were a neatnik. Neatnik beatnik. That's you. Had to keep all your shirts lined up in the drawer just so. Egg on right, bacon on left. Hup hup and chinnee chin chee, bossing momma's the life for me. That was you. Mr. Puckerbutt Neatboy. Liked everything tidy, clean, and perfect. Always."

Huh? No. Wait. Hold the phone. "You here?"

There was a quivering, ugly silence then her voice, low and vicious: "Like you wanted, I am. Like you said a million hours ago, 'Sit tight;' that's what you said, neatnik beatnick."

"Where? Where are you?"

"O'Goolys. The news stand. The bus stop. Where you think the bus has been stopping forever? O'Gooly's News…" For a minute, she was so angry she couldn't go on. "You sure you ain't that other boy now? You sure? You my messy boy, idiot boy or you the neat one?"

"No. Mom. Mom. I'm, no. Not Elvis. You're, you're here?" What had she meant, pot boiling?

"Like you wanted, I'm here. You coming or not?"

The cop, Monahan, was in the ditch, standing or trying to stand. His shoulder. Oh. Wow. Jesse clenched his jaw. "Mom, just hold on."

"I been holding on long enough, don't you think?"

"Mom. I can't… wait. Just hold on."

"What more holding you want?"

Monahan was mad. He started to yell something, looked toward the Cordoba, wobbled and fell down again. With a trembling hand, Jesse reached for the key. His shoulder throbbed. His hands itched. He clawed at the hand holding the phone. "Mom, I have to deal with some things right now."

"What now, you got doily arranging need to be done? I tell you what, you one of the fanciest little boys there ever was. Liked all that pretty stuff. Every time I ever showed you a picture of something pretty, you was all google-eyed over it. Liked your baths, too."

Jesse ground his teeth and turned the key. The car groaned, coughed and sputtered like an old man. "Shit."

"What you say? You swear at me young man? You swear?

I'll wash your mouth for sure. You'd like that, too. Whoa, couldn't get no dirt on you. And if you did, you had to wash, wash, wash. A regular pretty little angel. You're just what I needed to go 'long with my war hero and my half-retard other baby. That's the way I looked at him. Half-retard. No basis for it, you know. None. They call 'em, what, motorskills? The motorskills was just fine on him. I told the stupid doc there was something wrong with him, but the motorskills was fine and he was in his percentages, he said and so what, la-dee-dah that his brother's ahead of him, different kids is different. One real extra advanced baby doesn't mean the other one's abnormal, just not advanced is all. That's what the doctor said and he was asking about the stupid spot on Elvis where he fell on his back, like babies do that are learning to walk, just this spot, talking how that was maybe why he was crying so much, the spot, staring at me the whole time and looking at your arms and legs and checking out your belly and back and asking about did I ever get mad at you babies, asking me if I was okay and talking about dee-pression like there was something wrong with me or you and not your poor little dumb baby brother. Doctor needed suing. What he needed. Both of you, our fine little rewards from God your daddy'd say. God works in mysterious ways, he used to say. Used to come back from church and ask 'how you been,' and tell me one baby bawling all morning was a blessing and the other was a blessing and the way God works is mysteriousness, then he'd try to get me all in the mood. Used to come home all lovey-dovey like the preaching was a turn-on and me with you needing a change and that brother squalling, squalling, squalling all morning. No mysteriousness in either of you. That's God. Way I see it. Take this. And that. See how you like them kumquats. See what you get for getting all hot in the hay with your little cowpunk before you had the ring and the paper. Oh, but he was a fine one at first, Lord. Oh, he was. Lord, see him? Don't you see? How could I not? I was all shot up with vinegar and looking for trouble and there he was. When he was young, a stallion, all wild with that hair and those cowboy boots, standing all tall there. Something. Whacked in the head, though. That's how they sent him back from the war. They did. Sent him back, brain all jelly. Strawberry-jammed head. They done it. Sent him back half-baked. Wasn't his fault. The government. They could've fixed him, but they didn't. And that's way I remember him. All pretty and fine outside. All cooked up like bad meat inside. Was me that named the babies and raised them. Elvis Pelvis and his dead brother twin. Was me. He didn't know nothing about babies and didn't care and got those buddies of his coming over and got to so he thought it was fine and dandy to just laze around and drink and yell at me when the food wasn't hot enough or when his pants wasn't ironed just so and oh he was so good about wanting things perfect—wanting everything just so. His food all arranged right on the plate before he'd slop it down then head out to who knew where. I was scared, living out there in the sticks with just me and you boys half the time. Got so I learned how to shoot; him gone all the time I had to protect myself. Truth be told, I was worried about him too; used to wonder if maybe he'd go over the deep end and I'd need to be ready if he came after me or you. Used to practice with this old pearl-handled thing he'd traded off some buddy in the army. When he was gone and you was older and off at school. Wasn't wrong of me to do. Not wrong. Not at all. Come in handy, now that I think about it."

Blah blah blah. He didn't hear her. He couldn't. There was too much to take in. Jesse clenched his eyes and tried to form a plan. Lavern. Jerry. Monahan. That fat, stupid Donnel. Mom. And Elvis. How? He groaned again and twisted to see himself in the rear-view. The side of his face was scraped; his hair was wild. His lower lip was swollen. Sheeze. He needed to get out of here. Hotel. Indiana. Maybe. Yeah. Hide there. Get this shoulder set, then a bath. But this car. And now, the guy. Monahan. Was on his feet. The kid-cop was coming around. He was going to Monahan. Monahan was climbing the side of the ditch. Looking this way. Even from here you could see his face. It was red, blotchy. Holding his shoulder. He was coming. Trying. This way. Wait. Wait. The kid was yelling, his vapor-words punching the air: "Wait. No. Monahan. Come on." Sweat trickled down his spine. Monahan stopped and turned, annoyed at the kid-cop. Monahan's face was gray. He tottered. Jesse scratched the back of one hand, the other.

"You never could do nothing right, know that? Never." Mom's voice pattered in his ear. "I should've known better than to expect you to not muck this up like you mucked up the other thing."

He reached again for the key and groaned. "I'll come, Mom. I'll be right there," he whispered. This had to work. He thought a prayer, a small one. Please God. Make this work, mysterious though you are. "I'll be there."

"No."

"What?"

"No. Know what? I'm going to tell you something here. I'm calling me a cab and I'm going to tell him to take me home," she said, her voice warming.

"Home?"

"To my own house. And I'm sitting on the porch like the old days. We'll talk all about this then, like we always talked. Before you took me away, sent me off like a chicken in a cage."

"Wait. No. No. That's stupid."

Monahan had fallen again, this time to his knees, one arm slack at his side. Kid-cop, bent over, had a hand on the elbow of Monahan's good arm, helping him up. Monahan jerked the elbow free. Kid-cop slipped on the grass and went down on his belly.

"You don't call me stupid, 'cuz you know who the stupid one is. The stupid one is the one that was always going to be a man but wasn't. Should have known better than to send a boy to a do a man's job. I'm always best off doing stuff myself. Always. I come down here for you but now I'm doing what I should of done a long time ago. I'm going home because I want to, then I'm gonna get all this straightened out." The line went dead.

Monahan was standing again, one hand holding the opposite shoulder, face red, bellowing obscenities at the kid-cop, who was now on his knees like a sinner in church, alternating pleading for mercy and attempting to brush the mud from the front of his uniform. Mom's words echoed in Jesse's head, bumping into snatches of Monahan's tirade. Home. Going home. Why? Asshole. Boy. Man's job. Rookie. Should have done a long time ago. Bastard. Stupid. Doing stuff myself. Something Mom said, he'd missed. Jesse felt it crawling up his belly. Something big. For a long time, he'd sensed it. But. But what? What had he missed?

Jesse kicked the gas pedal and turned the key. The phone rang again. Jesse slammed his fist against the steering wheel. He answered. "What?"

"Jesse?"

"Of course. It's my phone number, isn't it?" Silence, then the voice registered. "Is that... Sorry, honey. Is that you?"

"Yes, it's me. Are you okay?"

"Yeah. Ah... yes. Yes. I'm fine." He wiped a hand across his face. Unexpected, tears chugged to his throat. "I'm okay," he croaked.

"You don't sound okay."

"No. No. They've just been working me hard here is all."

Monahan and kid-cop were now nose to nose.

"I've been so worried. We haven't heard a thing from you, and you took so many clothes and things and there's been a policeman calling here, and—"

"What did he say?"

"He was asking questions about you and where you were and about when you were younger. I don't get it. I don't know. I don't. You've been acting so weird lately, and I told him that and he started asking things that didn't make sense but did and now I'm just, I don't know. I'm here."

"You're where?"

"Here. In town."

"What?"

"I'm... don't get mad."

"Robbie? He okay? He with you? Where are you? Why are you here? Why? Why did you come here?"

"Robbie's fine. He's staying with the Spencers. He loves their dogs, you know. I was going to drive, but then the car wouldn't start. Jesse, you've been so, so strange. And I've been, I've been thinking a lot, and the policeman, and you cleaned out—I mean, cleaned out—the closet."

"Gretch... what were you thinking?" He groaned. He had to get the car started and get going. Up the road, Monahan was on his knees, bent over, retching. Kid-cop put his hand on Monahan's back. Monahan straightened up on his knees and swiped at the kid-cop's hand. Kid-cop held both hands out, palms out, in self defense. "Gretch, why? What's wrong with the car?"

"I don't know. It just wouldn't run and I got so frustrated and scared and, I took... I got a stupid bus ticket I was so mad and rode over here with these sweaty, smelly people. But," she paused. "I had to come, Jesse."

"You couldn't call a mechanic? Service comes with the lease; I told you that. Why did you... a bus? You don't ride a *bus*. Why didn't you rent a car? Or borrow a car? Why are you *here?*"

"I'm here because, I don't know, of you. I wasn't thinking at all. I just, I guess, panicked. Something's wrong, Jesse, and I didn't want to talk to anyone we know. I just wanted to come. Something's wrong. I know there is. Something's always been wrong, hasn't it?"

Jesse gritted his teeth. This could not be. He closed his eyes and imagined her. He felt her voice—*"Jesse? Are you there?"*—pressing against his heart. Comfort, surprising and cool as mist, whispered through his tired brain.

Gretchen. Oh. Man. Gretch. Wrong? Something wrong?

Let me tell you. He treated her like the enemy most of the time. He held her at arm's length. But she'd always been his salvation, hadn't she? Yes. He wanted her now, wanted just to talk, to reason things through. But he didn't need her here. Not yet. Jesse Tieter ran the trembling edge of a fingernail along the spine of his hand. He pictured her. On a bus. Staring out the window. Arriving. Here. With a bunch of flannel-shirted idiots. Wrong. Her. Here. On a bus. A bus? He sat up, his blue-gray eyes wide.

"Where are you?"

"The bus station."

"You mean right downtown."

"Yes, the one—there's this tiny bookstore here. Why, is there another bus station?"

The bus station. How could she? How could this happen?

"Jesse, listen. I'm... we... have to... to talk."

Jesse stared out the dirty, pitted windshield and thought he saw his mother's face. Wrong. All of this. What else? What else had he missed?

Monahan was coming his way. He was scuffing along, holding his shoulder, kid-cop behind him with a hand on his holstered side arm. No. Not this. Not now. Jesse reached for the key in the ignition. From far off, another siren yodeled to life. There was a blur in his peripheral. He turned. Elvis was standing there, chest heaving.

Elvis yanked on the door handle; the door wouldn't budge. He gritted his teeth. "Open the door." His breath blushed the window.

Jesse shut off the phone and clawed at a hand. No. No way.

"Open it."

Jesse turned the key in the ignition. Nothing.

The siren, mournful and still far off, was growing louder. Monahan's flushed face looked determined, his kid-cop partner anxious. Jesse turned back to his brother.

You.

You.

Mom.

Lavern. Gretchen.

Donnel.

The bus station.

Gretchen. Lavern.

He'd missed something.

Mom.

He'd missed. Something black.

The fox.

Their eyes met.

The past.

Remember.

Now.

No.

Yes. Something heavy and swinging in the shadows, in the sunlight and the shadows; both saw it. A black thing swinging through his field of vision. Both closed their eyes for a second—to fight it away or to see it more clearly?

The siren. Louder. Monahan just thirty yards away with the fresh-faced kid-cop.

The bus station. She's there. My wife.

This thing. Something in his eyes.

He gets it, Jesse thought. He freaking gets it. But do I? What did I miss?

Go. Move.

Hurry.

The car wouldn't start.

A silver Mercedes rocketed past, bucking the Cordoba. Elvis' hair seemed to explode then settle back into place.

No.

Wait. Not now. Not NOW.

The siren. The bus. Her. Him. Who? When?

Before Elvis could react, Jesse was out of the car, brushing past and running. Jesse stopped and threw a wild look back. Mistake. His shoulder screamed and he squeezed it in place with one hand. Elvis stood by the car, mouth open. Just a few feet to Elvis' right, Monahan and kid-cop froze, mouths open too. From up the road, there was a squeal of tires as the silver Mercedes ground to a stop. The thought hit Jesse then—my car? The backup lights blinked on and the car began careening wildly back toward him. Jesse, gripping his aching shoulder, half-ran, half-slid down the steep ditch, up a slight incline and into the woods.

For Elvis, the world tipped and teetered and the memory blipped above the cockeyed horizon. It was. Him. In his brother's eyes. He'd seen him. Elvis felt the tears and swallowed hard.

The siren whooped. The cruiser skidded to a stop behind the Cordoba. Harvey Monahan, just a few yards away, holding his shoulder, was bleeding. The driver, young and big, looked scared.

Elvis had no clear thought of what to do next. His head ached. His stomach churned. Wet with the cold, damp sweat of the memory, he trembled. He closed his eyes and saw Lavern, his brother's eyes. Those other eyes. Oh. It ached. His head. His heart.

You're letting him get away.

He ran after his brother.

❖❖❖❖

In the quiet, in the nothing that followed the BWAAM, the boy-Donnel sat there, spattered by blood, bawling and deafened. In the dust and the sunlight, inside himself, under the crushing weight of the BWAAM, he cried. Slowly, he heard sounds fading in. A whisper of wind in the trees, then Elvis' own sobbing, then the other things, the sounds that scared the bejeesus out of him. They came out of somewhere a long ways off, some things low and ugly turning to groans and an awful reeling eerie crying—great, big agghnnnnnns. These sounds were like something from outer space or a huge and ugly animal, something furry and wet and red-throated and angry. They were from him, from Donnel.

Donnel hadn't saved Elvis from the fox.

Now, driving the Mercedes, a block of hardened sadness floated in his chest. It was an old feeling, familiar and worn smooth by the years but heavy still, moored against his heart, leaning against it, heavy, so heavy. Heck, he could still hear that sound, the BWAAM, then the sounds from his chest, could still *feel* the way they sounded. He could see his husky-blue-jeaned legs, cuffed and shoved up above the socks and black tennis shoes, all the dust on the shoes and the jeans and brown powder on his chubby calves. The chubby boy-Donnel, unwadding, turning and following Elvis' eyes, staring away from the awful twitching fox body, and there she was: chubby-cheeked, dark-haired Lavern, that gun in her hands, lips pressed in a hard pink line, walking through the dust and stopping over what was left of the animal. The front half of it, the head and the shoulders, were there, looking like a fox-front taking a nap. The back half was a jumble of fur and blood and open, raw muscle and bone—naked, whitish bone. Donnel didn't want to look. It made him sick. As she bent down, Elvis yelled, "Don't touch it. Get away. Don't touch it.

"DON'T TOUCH IT. GET AWAY. DON'T TOUCH IT."

Don't worry. It's okay, her face said. And Donnel, the boy, had so felt that gush of relief and pain that he'd wet himself, and he'd done something worse: he let Lavern do what he should have been big and strong enough to do. But there she was, Lavern, looking at the two of them and smiling. He was so happy and so, so sad and jealous and guilty, yeah man, *guilty.*

Donnel could see her, the sweetest thing on God's sweet earth, and could still feel the thing against his heart. He shook his head and tried to focus on the road, but the memory came on stronger, accompanied now by a siren. The siren, he was vaguely aware, was here, behind him on the road. But in front of him, in the windshield or somewhere between him at the glass, was Lavern, the girl-Lavern. It was all he could do to keep the car pointed in the right direction. The girl-Lavern picked up the monster, the dead fox, the front half flopped over one arm, the snout and the closed eyes looking at the ground, the back half—the sick, awful half—draped over her other arm. The girl Lavern's back was arched against the weight of it, her face all bloated and red and strained as she took the fox back to its burrow. Her clothes, the shorts and shirt and those chubby legs were gooey with its blood. Donnel could see her, hear her, telling Elvis how she'd run the hundred yards or so to her house and got her dad's rifle so she could shoot the fox. Then she bent over and dumped the fox in the hole, shoved on it with her shoe. She was smiling and yes, yes, Lavern was crying too. The tears were sliding through the dust on her cheeks as she stomped, stomped, stomped, stomped on the fox, each stomp sending a shiver up her chubby, bloody body. It didn't make sense, what she was doing, and it made Donnel feel funny to see it—good and warm, safe but guilty. He watched Lavern stomp until the thing was pushed, squeezed back down inside. Part of his heart squeezed. He should've done that. He should've put the fox in its place.

Caught up in the daydream, Donnel was past the Cordoba before he recognized it. He hit the brake hard and slammed the Mercedes into reverse, then twisted around to face the rear as a police car roared over the hill and angled toward Elvis' beat-up car. Someone broke away from the Cordoba and started for the woods alongside the road. Elvis. It was Elvis.

Donnel wound the wheel to the right and parked the Mercedes at a wild angle on the shoulder. He threw open the door and struggled out of the car. A cop in uniform and another guy were stopped on the shoulder, frozen like statues, staring after Elvis. Yes. Yes. It was Monahan, holding his shoulder, his one arm limp, shouting something at the uniform cop, then stumbling off, almost falling, going after Elvis. Donnel watched Monahan make it to the trees and disappear into the woods.

Donnel ran after Monahan.

✽✽✽✽

There were no customers in the ancient book store. The girl working the counter—one of the Shanleys but Lavern didn't know which one; there were a slew of Shanleys—gave her a vacant nod. Lavern returned the greeting with a smile and tipped her head toward the rear of the store.

"Bus?" she said.

The girl nodded and managed to return a weak smile, ground herself into what was, apparently, a comfortable position on her rickety stool, then returned her gaze to a magazine she'd flattened open on the counter.

Lavern made her way through the cramped quarters, frowning at a rack of porno magazines; one called *Holsters* had a cowgirl on the cover that looked an awful lot like someone she'd gone to high school with, but Lavern couldn't place her. At the back wall, next to a long wooden table leaning under the weight of hundreds of VHS tapes, a narrow doorway opened to a tiny room. Lavern's legs were suddenly heavy. She stopped.

Inside, two women waited, each seated on a plastic chair. Between them was a coffee table with a cheap-looking Mr. Coffee coffee maker and a tired pile of—what else?—more magazines. One woman partially blocked Lavern's view of the other; both were staring through the room's big window at the bus belching smoke in the parking lot. The one closest to Lavern was middle-aged and classy: tall, thin and pretty. She was a red head in black slacks and a leather coat, with a suitcase on wheels on the floor next to her chair and a garment bag on top of the suitcase. The woman beyond her twisted away from Lavern and toward the window, to get a better look at the bus. She was old with messy reddish-gray hair; she looked cold in a blue sleeveless dress and was playing with the ratty handle of a big purse. Something about her seemed familiar. Before Lavern could consider what it was, the younger woman turned and smiled.

Gretchen?

"Lavern?" Miss Classy said, rising, looking relieved. Lavern felt the weight drop away. Smiling, she crossed to the woman and held out her hand. Gretchen ignored it and opened her arms, tears suddenly shining in her eyes.

Lavern accepted the embrace, momentarily overcome by tears of her own.

"There's a lot to do still," Lavern said, sniffing.

"I couldn't wait any longer. I couldn't."

"That's okay."

"I know but, it's just, I'm so sorry, me hauling over here like this, I couldn't…"

They released each other. Gretchen, eyes on the floor, fumbled for something in her coat pocket, pulled out a wadded up tissue and dabbed at her eyes and then her nose. Lavern watched the puffing bus in the parking lot, wiped her face with the palm of her hand and sniffed. There was a chill in the waiting room. She wondered if the heat was on.

"I talked to him on the phone just now. I told him. He knows I'm here." Gretchen said.

Their eyes met.

"You talked?"

"Yes, just a little bit ago. I'm sorry. I just…"

Lavern frowned.

"I told him everything you said, everything you told me, trying to, like, jar him, you know? But someone came, I think, I think it was Elvis."

"Elvis?" Beyond Gretchen, the elderly woman had turned and was staring, her eyes black marbles in a yellowed and wrinkled face. Something that felt like glass shattered in Lavern's chest.

"I got a boy, Elvis," she said. "He's named for the King. Got a twin brother Jesse, named for the King's dead brother. Get it?" She laughed and shook her head. "Used to live around here. Not far from here at all. Out in the country. My cab's coming right now to take me there. You know an Elvis, too?"

Chapter Nineteen

Having stumbled through the trees, fought his way back through the overgrowth and the years, he found himself, hands on knees, chest heaving, in the place where his journey had begun. Saplings and bushes and high weeds blurred the line that had defined woods versus yard. The house, scarred and wheezing in the wind, squatted in the overgrowth in front of him about twenty yards away. Off to the right, where the weed-choked driveway snaked around from the road, the old station wagon rusted, choking on weeds, stubbornly waiting. Jesse bent, sniffed, and tried to smooth his breathing, palms toward the ground, nervously stretching his hamstrings as though he'd finished a quick morning run along Lakeshore Drive. He tried to tell himself that coming here was merely an accident. But part of him felt the force of the place—he'd been drawn to it, had meant to come here all along. Lungs still burning, he straightened and turned toward the sound of his brother, still behind him, coming through the weeds. Suddenly he knew, he *understood,* it was time. Time to put an end to this.

❖❖❖❖

Elvis felt the house, too, before he saw it. A bleak, cold heaviness in his stomach told him it was ahead. Stumbling, floundering, arms flailing, he navigated through the last of the tall trees, guided by his gut and misty memory. He reached what had been the backyard and fell to his knees, then rolled to his back, his vision swimming. His heart thudded. Here. He was here? Yes. Why? How? Now what? He was here, with him. And the past was close; he could feel it. The gray sky was swollen and brewing, moody. There he was, Jesse, working his way through the weeds and grass toward him, walking slowly and holding his shoulder, that shaggy hair and the face pale, scary-weird familiar against the sky. Elvis rolled his head in the cold, wet weeds. He arched his neck and cocked his eyes toward the house. Two second-floor windows, menacing black eyes, gazed down on him. *Welcome home.*

Elvis closed his eyes. He was tired. So, so tired. He heard a rumble of long-forgotten thunder and the sound of chirping birds, smelled something that was strong and a little too sweet. He saw Lavern's note and Donnel's face. He heard Lavern whisper, "Stay with it baby."

He suddenly believed her, believed both of them—Lavern and Donnel. The thing between Donnel and Lavern had been the lie. He'd over-thought it and made it something it wasn't. And whatever had gone on between Lavern and Jesse, well, he figured that was all part of what she'd tried to do to help. Maybe.

Elvis ground his teeth and forced himself to sit up. Still holding his shoulder, Jesse had stopped and had dropped to one knee. He looked toward Elvis, gritted his teeth and struggled to get back to his feet.

Speak, Elvis' brain sent the signal. His mouth obeyed but not his voicebox. He closed his mouth, re-sent the signal, then opened it again. He coughed and looked nervously toward the road, suddenly wondering about his mom and his wife and the cops. He turned back and looked at his brother, who took another step toward him and stopped. His brother's pain-filled eyes stared at and through Elvis, through to the back of Elvis' brain, to where vision was controlled, skewering into the gray matter, and Elvis suddenly could see, blue-gray to blue-gray, he could see in a way he hadn't seen in years. No. Please. Don't. Not him.

Yes. He saw *him.* He was tall, all knobby boned and skinny with his shaggy brown hair. Yes. And he had that hook kind of nose, too, and a tattoo on his forearm that looked like a heart and had "Mom" in fancy writing across it. He could feel him, his aura—the good light that shone out of him on those days when he wasn't drinking and had worked and come home and showered and smiled at his boys in the yard. Those were days that ended with him sitting out front on the porch, in the blue-gray twilight of summer, fireflies winking from the edge of the woods across the way. Yes. Oh yes. Nights that were pure-honey summer, he, Dad, had you sit right next to him on the porch—on the steps. Sitting there—then, now?— he traced the blue-vein line of that tattoo and he not only could see, but he could hear the story, in a low and soothing voice stained sweet by a southern boyhood, of how he'd gotten the tattoo from a fat woman in Seoul during the war. The voice, soothing and deep and low and real, was a warm hand on his shoulder; it told him the world was at last, again, in balance. The woman in Seoul had been fat, ugly and stunk, that Tennessee-tinged voice said. She had a big gap in her teeth about the size of Ohio "if you don't include the part up by Lake Erie," he said. A little-boy giggle jiggled out of him and he felt the gritty warmth of his father's face, that warm and whiskered cheek against his silky boy cheek. He saw his father's eyes, content and glittering in the dying light. He smelled his scent; it was a gentle, pleasant aroma of man and SCORE hair cream and aftershave, Old Spice aftershave.

He had loved them, hadn't he? Oh yes, he'd loved them. Dad had loved both his boys, despite all the pain, the hate, that waited, scowling and smoking, in the shadows of the house behind them.

The meanness had been in Dad too. He'd been two people, hadn't he? Part of him had the love and the other part the mean.

Jesse was now just a few yards away, leaning with his good shoulder against a tree in the old yard, chest heaving. The brothers' eyes, cool and blue-gray and liquid, locked.

You remember, Jesse's eyes said. Yes. You do. We both do. And in the way of twins, their brains seemed to meet.

The thunder rolled through the gray shadows of entwined memory. The cool of the day evaporated. The humidity and heat rose. It was hot and the air had gone thick. The first drops came, fat and shocking—falling onto a ragged yard, a skinny man bent over a lawnmower—then the lightning ripped open the cloud of their shared lifetime of silence and the past, at last, hurtled in fully, fat belly high and bursting, coming down.

A gun. Not a .22. Bigger. Meaner. Why was he carrying that?

Show her.

You're aiming it at Dad? Wait.

Show her. Show her how strong you are.

No. No. Mistake.

Show her. You can.

Screen door open. Mom? In there, too. Watching.

Show her. Now.

No. Hold on. Don't. Don't do that. Don't.

Show her.

DAAADDD! Look out!

Yes. Now. Show.

STOP. HEY! WAIT!

Show her.

Say something! PLEASE! NO!

Show her who the man is.

NO!

BWAAM!

A siren howled, eerie as an animal. From the front of the house a car door slammed. Gravel crunched. Sitting, knees to chin, arms hugging his legs, Elvis rocked back and forth and heard none of it. Jesse couldn't move, couldn't breathe—he sensed something in his brother's eyes, in his own mind; it was the thing he'd missed until now. He tried to see it, but still couldn't.

Elvis looked through the wild overgrowth between himself and the past and saw the horror: smoke from his brother's gun, smoke from the back of the house, from the screen door. Elvis saw what Jesse couldn't see. In his mind, Elvis saw that his brother had gone flat on his back, the ugly canon-gun pointed up at a cockeyed angle. There was a limb shattered and falling, falling, falling from the old tree behind Dad, Dad, oh, Dad. Those boots were digging. Get up, Dad. Get up. Please, Dad. Why? Dad, why? The shaggy head was cocked up in the air and his face, gray and twisted away from him, looked toward the house. The blood, black-red, was leaking out from under him.

Another car crunched to a stop in the gravel at the front of the house. There was a pause, one door opened, another, then each door shut, bam. Bam. Still leaning against the tree, Jesse groaned against the hollow ache in his shoulder and tried to force the air back in his lungs. This was wrong. All wrong. For a few seconds everything was a jumble. The events of the morning shuffled through his brain in no predictable order, flashes of images overlapped and careened past one another. Nothing had gone the way he'd figured it would. Even after he'd done everything, everything he'd planned to do, it all seemed wrong. And now this, this certainty that he was really uncertain. That he'd missed something that day. Something important. He closed his eyes, but the world kiltered and swayed, so he opened them again. Come on, he told himself, buck up, you have a job to finish. Yes. Yes. Take care of this. He forced himself to walk toward his brother.

"WHHHHY? WHYYYYYYY?" The voice, half-whisper and half-scream, swirled around the yard on the dirty breeze. Jesse's legs nearly failed him. It sounded weird—*unreal*—a fake voice from a movie or something, and it quivered down his back like a wiggle of electricity. He took a step as though to get away, but stopped himself, eyes cloudy, frowning. Wait, he thought, wait. Get a grip.

Jesse took the final tortured steps to Elvis. He stood over his brother. Elvis' face, the pasty-gray face, was so twisted with pain that it punched his gut. Again, Jesse's knees wobbled and his breath squeezed to nothing.

"You…" Elvis said. "You got a gun. You. She… my… our… Why? Why? Later, she… you… You went away. You did. Left me here. She made you then you left. Why? My God why?"

Jesse tried to force a synapse around a word.

"You meant to kill him. You did." The words seethed out of Elvis as he stood. The twins were now just inches apart, facing each other, hook nose to hook nose. "You were just a kid, we was just kids. Just kids! How is that possible? How could you get a gun and walk out here and just—you pointed it and… and…? How is it possible? Then just, what?"

The full weight of it seemed to hit Elvis. His eyes widened. "You just disappeared? How could she? You? Go? It. I. You. I was so stupid. I didn't think. Forgot. I mean, it was there, but it wasn't. There. I didn't stop you, her. I didn't say anything. I could have. Oh. Dad. Shit. Dad. Why? Why did I not? How could I just stand there? How could I stand there and let her, you… How could we just have… then walked away. All these years?"

Jesse was trying to buck up, but the chemicals in his brain were sluicing free, torn wires were whipping like snakes, cracking and snapping. He floated above himself and—what was this?—he was sobbing and backing away from Elvis, stumbling in the grass. He tripped over a rotted tree limb, fell and landed, his back slamming against a tree. He cried out but made no sound. Now it was Elvis who stood over him. This was wrong, all so horribly wrong. He clawed at a hand. Buck up, he thought. Buck. Up.

"Give me something. Please," Elvis said. "Give me a reason. Just. Please. Answer."

But, for Jesse, the angels had returned, humming, humming, humming in a wild, rushing chorus that drowned out all else. It sounded like fire, musical fire, fire fanned by the wings of a million soaring doves. He heard something odd, too, that thing he'd missed before, a syncopation off. Beat. His tired, struggling brain could not pick it out and—oh, hold on, wait—what? There was a horrendous crack—lightning?—then thudding, something thudding to the ground. Jesse closed his eyes and saw it falling, falling, falling, the black-rotted wood behind Dad as he, boy-killer, clambered to his feet, scattering the doves and angels.

His adult-brother's face was twisted in agony, the lips dry-pink and talking without words. His boy-brother, young and skittering through the weeds, was seeing without being seen. Dad was at once dead, twisting in the shaft of dusty sunlight, and looking toward the back door, the familiar head kicking against the right front wheel of the Craftsman lawn-mower. The cowboy-booted feet cut muddy scars in the soft green of the yard. The man's skinny hands clawed the air like he was trying to pull up on some magic chin-up bar to get out of the dark, deep pit he was falling into. Jesse took it all in, gawking at his grown brother's tortured face, struggling to catch the one thing he'd missed, hearing the crack and watching his life slip away, wasted by a subconscious misery he had been too stupid to understand.

There was something, something here. It was so slippery, the logic and meaning of it, and Jesse couldn't hold on. The fall from the police car and the pressure, pressure, pressure of planning and having it all come unraveled and now Gretchen, she was here and Mom, Mom too, and why? He felt drugged and wished he was. He needed a drink and a bath. Definitely a bath, and maybe a drink to figure this out. This. This had not gone well. None of it had. And something was missing. He'd missed something. He'd missed. Jesse struggled to stand. He pushed past his brother and stumbled toward the thicket at the edge of the old property.

The screen door slammed. "You gonna let him get away?" The voice, phlegmy and familar, skimmed through the damp air like a forgotten boomerang. Jesse stopped. Elvis turned. No. Oh. It was her. Or maybe not, maybe she wasn't real. But no. Yes. Yes. She was coming out of the house, coming this way, hunched and baggy and ugly—a knot of bones and

Paul Flower

wrinkly skin in a wrinkled blue dress, carrying a battered black purse that hung, heavy, from her shoulder and was too big for her, a cigarette listing awkwardly from her mouth. She was looking at him, Elvis, floundering toward him, sniffing, her nose red from the cold, stopping to scratch a bare leg, the strap of the purse sliding off her shoulder, she pushing it back up, those eyes never leaving his, then coming on, relentless, until she was in front of him. It was her. She was shivering but didn't seem to notice, the eyes diamond-hard and certain. She reached for him and he recoiled. She snared his earlobe, clamped it hard, and yanked his face down into hers. She smelled like something out of the ground, something that had lived in the dark for too long. Elvis jerked free. She grabbed and clenched the ear even harder and shook it. "You're going to let him get away."

Elvis followed her gaze; by twisting his head just so he could see Jesse had reached what looked like the edge of the old woods. He was just standing there, one hand holding a shoulder, the arm limp at his side, just staring their way like an idiot.

Behind Jesse there was movement in the trees. Someone else was in the woods.

"You gonna stand there and cry and let him get away?" Mom's voice was high and nervous. She took the cigarette from her twitching lips and sent a shaft of smoke out the right side of her mouth. Elvis could feel her foot tapping the ground in front of him. His ear burned.

"I shot him, Mom."

The words, the voice, prickled the back of Elvis' neck.

"What did you say?" Mom snapped, shooting a withering look across the old yard at Jesse.

"I shot him, Mom." The voice was Jesse's, but Jesse didn't feel it. He was lost. Forlorn, he looked like a child, his face sagging with sadness. Tears brimmed in his eyes. "I k... killed him. No... nobody's... getting away. Elvis is stayin' here. I nailed the sucker to the ground. You saw. I can go away. It's

236

okay. I did it and now I can go."

From the back door, inside the house, there was a muffled cry. "Oh, Jesse, *no.*"

Mom frowned and slid the duct-taped handbag strap back on her shoulder. "Wait a second, there. This is my man-boy right here. This is the one that done his duty. Don't go tricking your old mother now." Holding the wayward strap in place, she reached up with the hand holding the cigarette and caressed Elvis' face. "This is my good boy now; you're my Jess, aren't you?"

Elvis opened his mouth. The back door creaked open.

There was a noise from the woods.

"I asked you a question, Jess." She jerked Elvis' ear. A tunnel of pain opened in his head, but Elvis barely noticed. Lavern was edging out of the house and behind her, there was another woman. The other woman was pretty, red-headed. She was crying, holding a handkerchief to her nose.

Donnel lumbered out of the woods, stopped, fell to his hands and knees, his breathing loud and ragged.

Elvis forced himself to breathe. Donnel was here. Lavern, Lavern The Freaking Ghost, was picking her way through the overgrowth toward him and Mom, giving him a small sad smile that reached across the yard. A surge of heat, of confidence, shot through him.

More noise, far off, then a few yards beyond Donnel, the cop, Harvey Monahan—his face white-gray and bloody hand to his shoulder—fell to one knee. Behind him the kid-cop, tall and straight-backed, stepped into view and reached down to help Monahan. Monahan growled something, brushed him away, and struggled to his feet.

"You're my good boy," Mom cooed.

"I'm Elvis."

She looked puzzled. "'Course you aren't."

"No, no, Mom. It's me. Elvis."

Mom's eyes clouded and she tightened her grip on his ear. "Stop that. You're not my dumb boy, you're my smart one."

He tried to get free. She yanked him down and the tone of her voice shifted. "You're the right boy. Don't I know my boys when I see them? You're him. Jesse, twin to the King. The King, he's all flash but not dash. You're the one smart enough to understand things and keep your yap shut, aren't you?" She grinned. "You ain't brother dumb-dumb over there. You at least know what you screwed up. He's got the motor skills but not the smarts, am I right?" She shot more smoke in Elvis' face and toyed with the strap of the giant purse. "I mean, heck, you know the truth about everything, but you can't seem to fix the parts that are broke is all. That's the dingaling thing of it with you. You got that fancy education but don't know you didn't do what you thought you done and what you had to come back for but you can't seem to get it all straightened out is all. You're a screw-up is all. Not dumb, a screw-up is all."

From Jesse's throat, there was a sound, half groan, half swallowed scream. His brain was suddenly clear, too clear. He covered the ground quickly and was at Elvis' elbow, his face red and in her face, eyes wide and wild. "You idiot. You sick old idiot. It was me. Me. Don't you remember? Me. I did everything and that's all you have to say? After all this, all these years, that's it? Everything you ever asked, everything, I did. You. I don't. Believe it. You made me, she made me," he was screaming, looking around the yard at the audience. "She made me do it. Then I had to leave. I had to just go on. Can't you believe it? She packed me away. To Iowa. Corn. Corn. Everywhere. And those simple-minded, those people." The words were coming, unchecked and illogical and red-hot—spitting sparks from the rusty metal mental drawer in which he'd locked them. "I did. The gun, the... I snuck up and... He talked." Jesse covered his eyes for a second and saw it, the back twisting, the shaggy-haired head coming around. He opened his eyes; they were wide and bloodshot and filled with tears. "He turned and talked to me. And still I did. I did it. Everything. I was a kid. Just a sick, stupid, screwed-up kid. And she twisted me all up inside until I couldn't think straight. I couldn't think. My God, I couldn't. And no, here. I came. I. Back. It wouldn't leave me. It wouldn't go away. Ever. I couldn't get away." Jesse looked toward his wife. He was sobbing. "God hates me, I know he does. You. Him. He knows. He knows everything. No matter what I did I couldn't come clean. I couldn't tell anyone. I just tried to make it. Right? I tried to make it right. But it was her, her. I did it. And I know you can't ever. Forgive me. I was just a kid, a *kid*. And. I'm so sorry. Dad. *Dad.* I just. He was my dad. My dad. I just. God knows, he's always known. And now this. I. I buried him. I *buried* him." Again, he stopped, his own heart unable to take in what his brain was sending it.

Gretchen walked to him and reached to caress his face, but Jesse shook his head violently. "You don't. Don't stay. Go on. Get away from this. Take Robbie. Oh how? How? Could never undo it. I. You. Go. Get away. Don't let it touch you. Any of it. You hear me? You hear me?" Gretchen, a sheen of tears on her face, stepped back, then stopped and held her ground.

Jesse, suddenly exhausted, clawed at an itching hand and fell silent, his eyes fixed on the ground.

Elvis looked in his mother's face and saw it, a smile, cool and liquid, curling on her lip. A new storm of memory, fierce and frightening, rumbled through his tired mind. He tried to brush it away but he saw Dad's eyes dancing, the smile on his face, early that Saturday morning. He remembered their final moment together: Elvis' hand, his boy-hand, trembled as he picked a penny from Dad's man-hand as Dad told him how Abe Lincoln was on the penny 'cuz Abe always knew the truth and stuck by it. Between sickles of lightning, Elvis could see past the walls he'd built, past the denial years and his dad's eyes. He saw the penny in his own hand, felt the fullness in his heart and his dad's knuckles Dutch-rubbing his butchcut boy head. He saw Dad bending over to work on the lawnmower, leaving Elvis to walk away light as a baby bird, penny clenched in sweaty fist. The world that morning was hot and muggy, but beautiful until he reached the edge of the woods and the gathering storm. Elvis saw himself turning at the sound of the door and Jesse walking into position with the gun, that ugly canon-gun. He saw the screen door opening, rusty gauze hiding Mom's face. The whole ugly scene played out again as Elvis twisted his head now, trying to break the burning grip she had on him; Jesse now yelling about what had he missed, what had he missed? Elvis heard the sound of death, then he saw again the limb falling, the back door easing shut and Dad. Oh. Dad. Then he knew what he'd always known. Through all the years of living with her, of pretending it wasn't true and finally acting like it had never happened, he'd known. He'd tried to forget. But he'd known.

"You killed him," he said to his mother, his eyes open at last.

Jesse frowned. It didn't register.

"She did it. She shot," his voice quivered as he tried to pull away from her, away from the smell of her. "She shot him. You missed. You missed him completely. And then, I lived with her. With it."

For a moment, nothing. The wind held its breath. The trees stopped their endless moaning.

Then Jesse heard the angels.

Elvis twisted free.

Mom slapped Elvis' face.

Lavern and Gretchen gasped.

Donnel stood.

Kid-cop unsnapped his holster.

Monahan grabbed kid-cop and growled "hold it."

"You stupid nothing idiot," Mom hissed. She looked at one son, then the other. "Both of you. The apples falling from the tree. Way it goes. I had to do everything. You," she jabbed a gnarled finger at Jesse. "Nothing in your brain at all." Then she jabbed at Elvis, "And you, you was gonna be a man," she said. "But you couldn't. You, Mr. Fancy Pants, all full of yourself. You got in over your head and you missed. Good thing I was ready. Good thing I was aiming and shooting, too. You stupid, stupid idiot. You missed. Darn straight, you missed. And now you come all the way back and look now how you mucked it up. You mucked it all up."

She snared the purse and fumbled to open it. The thing burst open and its contents, including a pearl-handled revolver, spewed to the grass. Mom snatched the gun and leveled it at Elvis.

Elvis grabbed her arm.

Jesse took two steps, stumbled.

Donnel ran and dove toward Mom.

Kid-cop drew his gun.

Jesse fell.

Lavern reached for Elvis.

Gretchen stumbled toward Jesse.

Monahan screamed, "Hold it."

BWAAM!

Chapter Twenty

Harvey Monahan spent three hours, one liter of Mountain Dew, and four trips to the bathroom on the report.

She'd aimed to shoot Elvis or Jesse or both. That's how he wrote it. But this Donnel, this buddy of Elvis, had come out of nowhere and body-slammed the old witch to the ground. Lucky he didn't kill her. Broke her wrist. Self-defensive move, Harvey noted. He wrote that the errant bullet had gone right through his, Detective Monahan's, shoulder; it was a clean shot, no ballistics fingerprinting available, unfortunately.

She'd shot her old man forty years ago when her poor kid had missed, but she was being charged for shooting a cop when she'd missed the kid. It was screwy.

Throw the Jerry Plannenberg thing into the mix and, well, this was a humdinger. He thought about a guy in Chicago, an agent, and made a mental note to call him. This would make a heckuva book.

Harvey chuckled as he re-read the last of the report and signed it. He loved irony. The young Trooper hadn't seen the beauty of it, but he'd gone along. Third generation cop, and he didn't want to explain to papa and grandpa how he'd nearly zipped his partner the first week on the job.

Harvey stood, checked his watch and slipped the report in a manila envelope. Twenty minutes, time enough to get home and feed the dog. He sighed. It wasn't that he minded meeting the Icabones for dinner. They were so grateful, how could he refuse? Harvey felt like he'd let them down. There was no way they could charge the old gal for the old murder. There was just nothing to work with; the pitiful brain doctor had reduced the remains to ashes. Fine tooth combs don't turn up bullets that aren't there. And as far as Jesse Icabone-Tieter was concerned, well he was going to have to answer to the conspiracy charge for the death of the guy at the factory. A good lawyer and sympathetic judge would see the guy hadn't been in his right mind. Talk about your extenuating circumstances. Who knew how that would end up?

Harvey Monahan sighed again, flicked off the lights in his cubicle, and closed the flapper door on the overhead cupboard. On the way out, he dropped the folder on the basket at the front desk and let himself smile. Darn, he had to admit, this one still felt good to solve.

❊❊❊❊

Gretchen picked her way through the clutter of Lavern's gloomy living room and fell into the overstuffed easy chair. She closed her eyes and swallowed a wave of tears. You can only cry so much, she thought. She'd begun to wonder how much that was.

"How was he today?" Lavern's voice was irritating and soothing; the question was expected and welcome, just difficult to answer.

"Oh, he's a little better. But he's so medicated, he sleeps a lot right now. Sleeps and dreams," she choked back a sob. "He cries in the dreams." She took a long shaky breath. "They say he needs time. Really. Space and therapy and time." She opened her eyes. "There's a lot ahead. Prison time, probably." She stared off, then turned to Lavern. "Listen, Lavern, I just want to thank you again. For finding me through the hospital, for making contact. For everything."

Lavern plopped on the couch opposite her and held up a hand. "No. Stop that."

"It's just that without you…"

"Stop."

The tears welled again. Gretchen looked away and sniffed. The weird-looking bird, a cockatiel, Lavern called it, cocked his head at her. Gretchen looked away. The cat darted across her feet and she jumped, then laughed. Gretchen let herself run from laughter to tears then back again. When she was done, she felt better. She felt as good as she had in weeks.

Lavern was looking at her, dabbing her own eyes. "You know, you're welcome to stay here. Really, if you want. And you could go get your boy and…"

Gretchen suddenly felt clear-headed. "No. Really, no." She looked around at the room and smiled. "I think I'm going to check out of the hotel and head home." She sat up. She stood.

Lavern was worried. "You sure you won't… What about…?"

Gretchen set her mouth in a determined line. She opened her purse and took out a tissue. "There are a lot of people who can help him, people he knows very well, and I'm going to make some arrangements, get things settled, then I'll be back this weekend."

Lavern stood. She opened her mouth. Gretchen held a finger to her lips, then to Lavern's. She smiled. "We did it, you know. What we had to do. 'The truth shall set you free.' I believe that."

Lavern smiled. "Yes. Yes. I do, too."

❉❉❉❉

Elvis threw the hand on the table. "Uno."

Donnel chugged his beer, groaned, and looked at his watch. "This two-handed crap is useless. 'Sides it's 'bout time for you to leave, anyways. You going to supper with that cop and all."

"I told you you could come along."

Donnel stood and started clearing the mess. "Some stuff I just feel like moving beyond, know what I'm sayin'?"

Elvis stared off. His mother's face, Lavern crying as she told him what she knew, tears in her eyes—it all flowed through him like a ribbon of water. And just beyond it flowed the trickle of memories of his dad. It was a lot to handle. The cop, Monahan, had given him a name of someone. Someone he could talk to about it. He'd offered to set it up, said he'd tell the guy everything if Elvis wanted him to.

"Sorry, bud. I know you been through hell here, and I'm complaining." Donnel's hand was on Elvis' shoulder. "You okay?"

Elvis snapped away. "Yeah. Yes. Yeah, I'm fine, dude. I'm fine."

"No you ain't."

Elvis felt a quiver in his head. His eyes burned. He pictured a penny. He saw his mother's face and Jerry Plannenberg's ponytail. He felt an ache in his heart for his brother. He opened his eyes. Suddenly, Monahan's offer seemed like a good idea. "You're right, I ain't." He looked at Donnel's sad, expressive face. "But I'm gonna be, Donnel. I'm gonna be."

Elvis set his jaw, picked a cigar butt out of the ashtray on the table and jammed it in his mouth. "Jesse, he's gonna be fine too. Way I see it, he's gonna be."

❋❋❋❋

The "Strawberry Fields Forever" lyrics were strangely clear and plaintive above the rumble of the thunder in the cloud. From his place in the bathtub on the floor of the garage, Jesse could almost see the musical notes through the steam. He could feel John Lennon's voice, washing him along with the soap he was using to scrub his skin. The only problem was the smell. The garage smelled of smoke and the thing in the tarp, and Jesse needed to get rid of that smell. He needed to cleanse the air of it. In his head, as the music played and the cloud rolled through the garage around him, he tried vainly to get the feel of it from his skin. The smell was coming off of him, but only in tiny, dry, blackened flakes, flakes that turned to flies as they hit the water of the tub.

As he washed, the flies fell, floating in the water, bobbing there, turning it black.

ABOUT THE AUTHOR

Photo: Lauren Flower Witt

For more than three decades, Paul Flower has been an award-winning copywriter, creative director and a journalist. He has spent much of his life and career in West Michigan's beach-resort country, where wealthy Chicago tourists cross paths with a rich cast of made-for-reality-TV locals—the ideal backdrop for this, his first published novel. Paul and his wife, Lori, have four grown children and a yellow lab named Barney.

ACKNOWLEDGEMENTS

This book is the culmination of far too many years, spent alternating between blood, sweat and procrastination, to recognize everyone who has played a role in its development and publication. But I would be remiss if I didn't thank Bob Young, Dave Kagan and my daughter Tracey for their thoughts and insight. Nor would I dare overlook my other children; Susan, Aaron, and Lauren; for supporting, inspiring and challenging me. Thanks, too, Jennifer Baum, for believing in this story. And finally, my wife: Thank you, Lori, for putting up with me and this silly dream.